MOVING FORWARD SIDEWAYS LIKE A CRAB

MOVING FORWARD SIDEWAYS LIKE A CRAB

A NOVEL

SHANI MOOTOO

DOUBLEDAY CANADA

Doubleday Canada and colophon are registered trademarks of Random House of Canada Limited

Library and Archives Canada Cataloguing in Publication

Mootoo, Shani, 1957-
Moving forward sideways, like a crab / Shani Mootoo.

Issued also in electronic format.
ISBN 978-0-385-67622-9

eBook ISBN

I. Title.

PS8576.0622M68 2013   C813'.54   C2012-906600-1

Cover and text design: Jennifer Lum
Cover image: Cindy Patrick Photography
Printed and bound in the USA

Published in Canada by Doubleday Canada,
a division of Random House of Canada Limited,
a Penguin Random House company

www.randomhouse.ca

10 9 8 7 6 5 4 3 2 1

For Deborah
who reminds me always that while time is an
unparalleled gift, time to think is the truest luxury.

For Indra Mootoo (1936–2010)

and

for Frankie (1999–2013)

"If you run away from a thing just because you don't like it, you don't like what you find either. Now, running *to* a thing, that's a different matter . . ."

—Uncle Axel to David, *The Chrysalids*, John Wyndham

CONTENTS

—

FROM SYDNEY'S NOTEBOOK

Surely it is a failure of our human design that it takes not an hour, not a day, but much, much longer to relay what flashes through the mind with the speed of a hummingbird's wing.

There is so little time left now, and what Jonathan wants to know and I to say are not the same.

I realize Jonathan is a grown man and can surely take whatever words I offer him, but what good would come of it if I were to tell him how, ten years into my relationship with his mother, India, she informed me that I was a disappointment? I would not want to encourage him to consider this, lest in doing so he concur.

Nor does he need to know that there was a time after his mother and I first met, in those months before he was born, when India would ask after our lovemaking, "How did you know to do that?" Does he need to know that she gripped my shoulders and trembled?

Or, should he know? I wonder if he would believe it.

He certainly doesn't need to know that after his

birth, India and I grew cool with each other. And yet, nearly ten years later when we broke apart, I hadn't stopped loving her. Should he know that? He would likely scoff at this pathetic admission. It might even appall him.

After India and I first met, in the months before I moved into her house I saw my physical upkeep as part of a daily drama between her and me, and I made a job of keeping my body trim and groomed, my clothing and sheets washed and pressed, my shoes polished, my kitchen and bathroom clean and tidy, wine in the fridge and chocolate on my bedside table.

Ten years later, the list of what, it turned out, I was inept at doing included: putting up shelving in her office; organizing and cleaning the parts of the house where Jonathan and I spent time; enjoying myself—or at least, giving the appearance of such—at parties thrown by her publisher and by various literary festivals. I didn't make well enough of myself as an artist to be recognized by her peers. I failed to take Jonathan away often enough or long enough that she could have time to write. I indulged Jonathan too much.

My rendition of our rupture is, of course, one-sided, perhaps a little flippant, the rewriting of cold facts encouraged by time and distance. I once asked her, "And you and me?" To which her response was a gesture of her hand towards and down the length of my body, a delicate non-verbalization of waning desire. After this, the relationship could not be sustained. It was India who spoke the words first, and a short time later, declaring the obvious was as good as insisting upon it. Over the course of a few months we became territorial, keeping our belongings, our agendas, our thoughts to ourselves.

Then one day, I came home to find Charlie Bream standing in the doorway between the dining room and the kitchen. I couldn't see India, but knew she was in the kitchen. Bream was almost as tall as the height of the doorway. He wore the whitest dress shirt I'd ever seen, long sleeves rolled just below his elbow, and grey wool trousers. He turned and, although I had never met him before, greeted me as if he and I were old buddies. I sat on the bench in the hallway taking much longer to remove my shoes than was necessary. Bream's trousers were thick and heavy, and a black leather belt hugged him just below his waist. His black cap-toe oxfords with their blond inserts were neatly placed on the shoe mat. They were made in Italy. Size 44. One notices everything in such an instant. From where I sat I could smell Bream's cologne. India, who in the ten years we had lived together would not boil an egg, was grilling croissants with ham and cheese. I was offered one, but declined and went upstairs to Jonathan's room. There, I waited for Bream to leave.

I lay on Jonathan's bed and looked down the length of my own body. I had indeed "let myself go." I could hear Bream's voice, and India's. They spoke evenly and at a normal volume, which seemed as brazen as if they had been whispering.

Charlie Bream didn't last, and he was not, it turned out, one of India's more memorable encounters. But whenever I think of that time, I see in my mind an image of Charlie Bream in the doorway of the kitchen, and his shoes, made in Italy, size 44, on the mat in the entrance.

I could not bear to say goodbye to Jonathan and so I did not. India warned me not to try to fight her for any rights to Jonathan. As an immigrant, as a non-wage-earning person and, most importantly, as a person without her connections, I would, she assured me, lose in every way. Yet for some time I did fight her, not to match her callousness nor for the principle of the thing, but for the love of the boy I had raised. His needs were the structure around which my days had been built. But that was a time when someone in my position had no legal recourse. India was right; I was outmatched. The irony is that it was Jonathan himself who was at the heart of our tug-of-war, and soon I was no longer willing to put him through our struggle.

After I left, I discovered that it was not only Jonathan I missed. India used to rub herself, after she'd showered, with rose oil. Its scent would waft into our bedroom. Even after I had returned to Trinidad I would be taken hostage by this scent rising up out of nowhere. Sometimes, I imagined I saw, in my peripheral vision, piles of folded laundry waiting to be put away: Jonathan's little shirts and trousers, his underwear and T-shirts, India's black V-neck Ts, her black skirts, her black underwear, her black jersey dresses, my blue jeans and black T-shirts, and the detergent scent of mountain air would fill my nostrils. I would turn my head quickly to find that I had been tricked by a pile of books, or simply by regret.

In the end, these are not the incidents and reflections I want to leave with Jonathan. And perhaps what he wants to know is something else, something more personal too.

I suppose I could explain to him that I came to realize that the imagining and dreaming, the wishing and the knowing that led bit by bit to the being I am today had actually started long before I left Trinidad and went to live in Canada. Long before I met his mother. Long before he came into my life. How I have tried in the past to tell him—to tell him about Zain, that is—but he can't seem to take it in. Now I must explain it to him one more time—how on that particular day in my childhood when I was in the classroom at the new secondary school to which I had transferred, a student I had just met, this Muslim girl named Zain, pinched my arm. How I grabbed her wrist and told her to stop. But it was too late. I had already felt the strange mix of power and fear that would haunt me forever. Perhaps that was why, upon finishing high school, I left Trinidad and immigrated to Toronto.

Granted, I never told him that on one of my visits back to Trinidad not long after I had parted with India, Zain and I were sitting on the sill of her swimming pool, eating codfish balls and drinking lime juice—she by then an adult married woman and mother of two in a yellow-and-white two-piece bathing suit; I, the same age but feeling like some undecided, half-formed thing in my T-shirt and shorts; both our pairs of feet swinging beneath the surface of the water—and I told her in a rush about how one had to undergo psychiatric reviews to transform one's self in the ways I'd just begun to think about, and that only if it were determined that one's mental health was compromised would the insurance pay for what was needed. Zain was quiet for a while. Then, as she slid into the water, she said, "That's a shame, because there isn't anything crazy about you." She swam off and dipped under the water. Up came her feet, toes pointed at the sky. She stayed like that for a good minute.

I could tell Jonathan how a couple years later, during another visit, Zain pressed into my hand an envelope bulging with American hundred-dollar bills that, ever since that conversation beside the pool, she had been saving.

And some time after that gesture, I could say, I arrived one cold and snowy morning at a building in Toronto, entered a room at an appointed time with a bag full of cash and changed my life forever. And I could leave it at that. Perhaps these are the stories that would satisfy Jonathan. But they are only a fraction of the truth, and I need to tell him the rest. I need to tell him how I have battled with the belief that had I only been a different person, Zain would be alive today. *Had I been a different person.* This, more than anything, is what needs to be said. Still, that would be only a fraction of the story.

In the end, I hope that Jonathan will understand why, after coming to Canada in search of some sort of authenticity, after living in Toronto for more than three decades, I returned home—I returned, that is, to live again in Trinidad. But how do I explain it so that he doesn't think I ran away, gave up, failed?

One more chance is all I ask for. But time is against me, and there is so much to tell.

MOVING FORWARD SIDEWAYS
LIKE A CRAB

A Memoir

By Jonathan Lewis-Adey

PART ONE

I

It amuses me how the instant the fasten-seatbelts sign is
turned off during the flight from Toronto to Port of Spain,
Trinidadians get up and strut about. They seem to know one
another; they congregate in the aisles unabashedly airing
their business, telling jokes, heckling each other or reminiscing. Their anticipation is palpable. Some begin the journey as strangers, but through conversations struck up in the
interminable lineups at the airport or during the five-hour
flight itself, they inevitably learn that they know someone in
common, or are even related. I have always envied their ease
and willing camaraderie, and having been to their island
numerous times over the past decade, have often wanted to
contribute my penny's worth; but discretion—on account of
being just a visitor to the island—has prevailed.

On the approach to Trinidad, as the plane comes in from
the Caribbean Sea towards the dense blue of the Northern
Range—where there is always the surprise of mountainside

villages comprising three or four houses glimpsed through the clouds—another sign of anticipation occurs: passengers lower their voices and withdraw into more private preoccupations. Once the mountains are achieved, there is silence on board. The hub of Port of Spain suddenly appears and I take pleasure in being able to spot the Queen's Park Savannah, the NETT Building and the Lapeyrouse Cemetery before the plane heads out over the sea again, over the Gulf of Paria, where it circles into position to glide in to the airport, first over the Caroni Swamp and then over the fertile belly of the Caroni Plains.

Is it already two months since that last flight down? Although I could not have imagined then the full extent of what lay in store for me, I sensed that my life was on the verge of another of its ruptures, and I feared that this was, perhaps, to be my final trip here. And so I did not merely observe the passengers, as had been my habit since my first trip here almost a decade ago (my first trip as an adult, that is; the very first happened some thirty years ago when I was a child), and neither did I merely watch the view from the plane window; this time I tried to ensnare in my mind every detail of all that went on around me and all that passed outside the window. As we headed over the plains to the airport, I savoured the sight of the bamboo-lined, snaking Caroni River and, on either side of it, the farmers' houses sitting amidst remnants of cane fields, and the pigeon pea plots and the black-water rice paddies our reflection sailed across.

The usual pleasure of a visit to the island was tainted this time by apprehension, and so naturally I recalled the first time I had come here looking for Sid. After years without a clue as to Sid's whereabouts, Internet technology had put at my fingertips the means to realize my dream of finding the parent who had deserted my mother and me when I was ten years old. Resentment at having been dropped so flatly had plagued me since that time. In junior high school I had attempted to register my unhappiness: I'd failed at every subject save for Art and English Literature and Composition, and had embarked on a path of delinquency that included smoking at home and on the school grounds, skipping school, not doing homework—to name the most benign of my transgressions. One might say that I had no imagination when, in order to escape being at home with my mother, I hid away in the reading booths at the Toronto Reference Library on Yonge Street. But there in the booths I lost myself in chronicling my longings and grievances in a notebook. The school psychologist, with whom I was now well acquainted, encouraged me to show him the notebook, and it was with his sustained provocation and encouragement that I began in earnest to turn the facts of my early life into short fictional narratives and poems.

For years, well past high school, I managed to keep from my mother any knowledge of this scribbling, or the fact that it had become a passion. I did not attend university, but found instead a job as a clerk in a health-food store on Bloor Street at Spadina. This seemed to both please and unsettle my mother, but still I kept from her what I thought of as my real work. When I eventually signed a contract for my first book with her publisher, it was without her knowledge. I will never be sure that the publisher was not simply doing *her* a favour when he took me on. Perhaps, too, he might have thought that investing in the work of the son of one of his most successful authors made good business sense. My mother received news of that first book's release with undisguised consternation. She read the novel in one sitting. I waited for her response, ostrich-like, hoping that she would ignore the autobiographical nature of the work and see only the craft. The instant I saw her face, I knew that there would be little conversation about the book. I was right. "Oh, Joji, get over it, will you? Please," was all she said. Nevertheless, over the course of some years, two more books followed. On reading the second, India said, "You're not at all a bad writer, but you're repeating yourself."

I can't deny that with each book's publication I hoped that hype about them would attract Sid's attention. If Sid were to read any of my works, my thoughts went, she would surely find in them reflections of our past life together and my present longing, and would contact me and our reconciliation would happen. But no such thing occurred, and to make matters more unbearable, my books were not much of a success. Nevertheless, my publisher—my mother's publisher, I remind myself—maintained an interest in me. Pressed to present a new manuscript for his consideration, I tried for years, in vain, to come up with stories and themes that veered away from my personal experiences. When I realized I couldn't write any more, or so it appeared, I sank into a long depression during which there were periods when I pointed squarely at Sid's cold-hearted departure for what I saw as my failures. I took to hiding out again at the Reference Library, my laptop computer, unused now for word processing, the gateway out of my morass. And it was in this way that my depression and bitterness were reshaped, at the computer, into the hope of reconciliation—if not between Sid and my mother, then at least between Sid and me—and my search became an obsession. I imagined daily what it would be like if and when Sid and I were reacquainted.

The reality was not quite so swift or easy. Over the course of several years I typed the name "Sid Mahale" into the Google search box and found that while there were quite a few Sid Mahales in the world, none jumped out as immediate possibilities. Images that appeared beside that name were interesting but useless: a book that did not have any clear relationship to the name; photos of parklands, flowers, dogs. There was one image of a pyramid-shaped bottle of perfume, one of a pile of burning car tires and a few of the banks of the River Ganges.

I managed to find e-mail addresses for every Sid Mahale whose profile glancingly resembled that of my Sid's, and over time I wrote letters of inquiry to them all and kept my fingers crossed. To my surprise, all my letters received responses, but invariably they ended with the hope that I would soon find their namesake.

My Sid Mahale was Trinidadian, had immigrated to Toronto more than forty years ago, and was a visual artist—a painter. I eventually found an announcement on the Internet for an exhibition of paintings by a Sid Mahale at a gallery in Queens in New York, and bought a plane ticket there. As I recall this now, I am impressed by my own recklessness and the utter hope contained in that impulsive gesture. On the night of the opening I arrived at the so-called gallery, a narrow and claustrophobic living room, to find that this Sid Mahale was a thin young woman in her second year at art school. Her family was Ugandan and she knew no Trinidadians with the same surname. I bought one of her smaller paintings for a hundred and seventy-five dollars.

At the time I had no idea if my Sid had remained in Toronto, was still working as an artist, had gone elsewhere in Canada or to some other part of the world or had returned to Trinidad. For some reason Trinidad was the last place I looked; it only occurred to me to do so when I didn't find her in Toronto, in New York or elsewhere. I certainly didn't rush here. Hindsight suggests that in spite of my obsession with my search, I must have chosen to spin my wheels. Perhaps I knew in the depths of my being that it would be difficult, and possibly more painful than it was worth, to reconnect with a parent who had left me without word and had never made any attempt to be in touch. And so, after a while, the search degenerated into the *idea* of the search, and for a time it was my romance.

Sometimes there are elaborate calculations that lead to action, and sometimes there is no cognition, just action impetuously taken. For me, it was as simple as awakening one morning nine years ago and knowing instantly that I would go to Trinidad. There is no point in attempting to find a deeper understanding; I was simply and truly ready.

Thirty years or so ago, my mother, Sid and I had visited Sid's parents' house in Trinidad. That was the true first visit to the island for me, and it had taken place one year before the dreadful split-up. On the morning nine years ago when I bolted awake with my new resolve, I remembered that the Mahale house was in a small town called San Fernando. In the Google search box I typed "Sid Mahale San Fernando, Trinidad," and a message came up asking if I meant "Sydney Mahale San Fernando, Trinidad." I decided to try again. Sid's father was a doctor, but I didn't remember his first name, so I typed in "Dr. Mahale" followed by "San Fernando" and "Trinidad," and up popped an obituary from a newspaper. And there in the obituary I found Sid's full name: *Siddhani*. My heart pounded in excitement. I wrote "Siddhani Mahale San Fernando Trinidad" and a message came up asking again, "Did you mean Sydney Mahale San Fernando Trinidad?" On the link for *Sydney Mahale San Fernando Trinidad* there was no image to search under, but knowing that Trinidad was a small country and remembering the joking between Sid and my mother that all Trinidadians were related or knew each other, I thought that this Sydney might know of my Sid. It crossed my mind that I might discover this Sydney Mahale was, like myself, one of Sid's sons. If so, he might be, I supposed, a real son. *The* real son. This caused some jealousy, I'll admit. But he'd be a brother of sorts, too, I reasoned. I had liked the island as a child and I was already consumed by the idea of a trip. Perhaps I would be lucky, but if not, the trip would not be wasted; I had always felt an affinity for the place, and I could spend a week in Trinidad doing a bit of writing, hiking in the Northern Range and looking for the places I'd visited during that long-ago childhood trip, and perhaps I could attach to this another week in Tobago snorkelling.

The telephone book in my San Fernando hotel room was not an inch thick, and included residential and business numbers. It could not have been easier; while there was no Sid Mahale, I did find Sydney Mahale. I picked up the receiver several times to make the phone call, but decided, instead, to take a taxi to the address in the phone book.

Sydney Mahale's house was not, as I had expected, in the south of the island, but in the northwest. A man I would later come to know as Lancelot met me at the gate and asked whom he might tell Mr. Sydney was there to see him. I gave him my name, Jonathan Lewis-Adey, but added that Mr. Mahale might very well not know of me. I waited for what seemed like an eternity before the same man, Lancelot, returned and unlocked the gate's three padlocks. He pulled open the gate and invited me in. Halfway up the yard an older gentleman with an unsteady gait approached. It dawned on me that this was Sydney Mahale, and I realized at once that a person of this age could not be a child of Sid. He and my Sid were very likely of the same age. The gentleman and I looked at each other and I made the gesture of offering my hand in greeting. But before I could understand what was happening, my heart heaved. The eyes. I knew them. The smile. It was not a *resemblance*. The smile was the *same*. I was overcome by a dreadful panic. I could hardly breathe. Sydney Mahale did not shake my extended hand, but pulled me to him. I went like a child, and although I was a great deal taller than I had been when I was ten, I pressed my head to the shoulder of this person, once a mother to me, and I cried, like a child.

That was nine years ago. On finding Sydney Mahale, I had encountered not the parent who had from the first day of my life loved and understood me better than anyone else, including my mother, but a stranger who confounded and challenged me. Still, I came every year from then on to be with him, sometimes more than once a year. I would often stare at Sydney, baffled that inside this unfamiliar being resided the fullest picture, the fullest comprehension of who I had been as a child. Sydney's voice—like that of a pubescent boy, incongruent in a person of his age—the angularity of his body, the thinned hair and receded hairline, the coarseness of a face whose skin I remembered from my childhood as being silky—there was stubble on it now from the shaving—and the pungency of his skin, were a wall between the person I remembered and once adored, and the relationship I had expected to reignite. It took time, desire and patience on both our parts before I could see that while the material, the physical form of the past as I had known it had changed utterly, the heart of it was steady and true.

———

Nine years later, all has changed.

It was reasonable, on this current visit, to expect that there would be no beach limes, no crab hunting on the east coast, no Scotch drinking in the thick and foamy surf late into the salty night, no evenings skimming the obsidian waters of the swamp, scarlet ibis drifting inkily against the slanted sky. As it turned out, lowering my expectations that this would be a visit without the glow of a vacation was the least that would be demanded of me.

Outside the airport's terminal building the humidity, the heat, the incessant percussive and tinny steel-drum music that welcomed visitors, the crowd of passengers and their waiting family and friends were suffocating. How I wished that time could be reversed, that this was my first trip looking for Sid.

Thankfully, I did not have to wait long for Sydney's chauffeur, Sankar. Out of the chaos he slid, taking the bag from my hand, ushering me through the drizzle towards the car. I knew the drive past the capital city to the northwestern arm of the island well, and was prepared for the near-hour's journey to the house in Scenery Hills; it would no doubt be riddled with drivers' abundant infractions and death-inviting manoeuvres, traffic jams and, fringing the entire route to the house, dangerously situated vendors' stands that offered everything from bundles of barely alive blue crabs to battery-run fly and mosquito swatters, to cellphone cases, to papayas and avocados the size of soccer balls. I was, by this time, no longer discombobulated by the constant chaos on the streets or the unfamiliar attitudes to time and to laws, by the unexpected politenesses and solicitations, the heat and the bugs, or the sugary, oily and fiery foods. I had, after all, travelled here close to twenty times in almost a decade.

By the time Sankar reached the residential area of Scenery Hills the rain had eased and the sun come out. Sankar gestured to the tropical phenomenon of falling rain and brilliant sun—different in quality of light and even texture of the rain itself from the sun showers we in Canada know—and he said, as if it were a question, "The devil and his wife?" I felt like a child, but I knew it would please him if I finished his sentence. "Are quarrelling," I said. We were both pleased that I had remembered the local saying.

Sydney was usually wheeled out into the garden by Lancelot at four thirty or so every afternoon, but this time he had waited for me to take him out. In the past, he would almost lift himself out of the chair, reaching his arms up around my neck in greeting, but today he remained sitting, his hands on his lap, turning them palms up for me to rest mine inside. He had indeed deteriorated.

I pushed the chair through the wet grass to the edge of the garden and positioned it to face the calming waters of the Gulf, grateful that Lancelot had telephoned me in Toronto to say that I should come down at once. I had been skeptical at first, given that I had rushed to Sydney's side on two previous occasions because "Sydney take in bad-bad and only calling your name," as Lancelot had explained. "If he come through is only because God so good he spare him, yes," and therefore I "should come quick-quick." So down I rushed. Of course, Sydney had pulled through both times. After the last trip, I had returned home to Toronto thinking irritably of Lancelot as the nursemaid who cried wolf. But when he'd telephoned this last time, something compelled me to drop everything and head to the airport. Perhaps it was Lancelot's unusual restraint, and his use of standard English. "Mr. Sydney isn't doing too well," he said. "He is weak. We are a little worried. If you don't mind us saying so, Mr. Jonathan, we think you should come. If he sees you, he might pick up."

The red-and-black plaid wool blanket I had foolishly brought Sydney the first time I visited was draped on his lap as if the air were as chilly as a late fall Toronto evening. I am still embarrassed and amused by my own prior ignorance; knowing more now, I think of stories I've heard about aid agencies battling the after-effects of disasters in tropical countries, appealing to well-meaning people from colder climes—like my old self, I suppose—not to make donations of duvets, wool blankets, fur coats and the like. But Sydney used the blanket right up until the end. I don't know if it was because it suited his actual needs or because it was I who gave it to him.

That evening, Sydney didn't hold my hand like he usually did. He wasn't able to. His remained in mine only because I gripped it firmly. His skin was cool. It had become thin. I tried, and I certainly hope I succeeded, not to show my utter terror at how he had weakened and aged since I was last here. The thick gold bangle I have always known him to wear, a *bayrah* it is called here, seemed too large and far too heavy for his slender wrist. The sea ahead shimmered gold and onyx, and the sky, shot across only minutes before with wispy tails of gold-dappled airplane exhaust, soon turned bloody brown. We sat watching the light play on the sea, both of us quiet. Everything seemed, at once, dire and ultimately of no consequence. What words dare be spoken, sentiments expressed, in such circumstances?

Save for the screeching of parrots as they lumbered like stones through the air, the rustling of billowy stands of bamboo in the hills behind us and the passage of the occasional car below, it was a quiet evening. Time seemed to collapse, and once again I found myself acutely aware of my surroundings. I stored in my memory details of the view, of the scents and sounds, and at the same time my mind leapt forward in place and time, imagining looking back on the moment we were in. Then, quite contrarily, I thought of Toronto, of how cold it had been when I left that morning, so cold that I wore my leather jacket to the airport and left it in Catherine's hands as we said goodbye on the sidewalk outside of Terminal 3. Such cold there, I thought, and here such suffocating humidity—the extremes available to a person in a single day. Poor Catherine, I thought, too, and immediately wondered if it was fair to pity her and yet hold on to her. She had come to know that whenever I visited Sydney I was leaving her in more ways than one. And then I realized that in thinking of Catherine I had squandered precious moments with Sydney. I focused my mind and squeezed his hand.

He cleared his throat. I found myself saying lightly that his skin was a bit dry and that next time I came down I would bring him a good hand cream. He nodded. Ahead of us, the iron bulk of oil tankers faded rust-orange rode high and leaned back as they awaited cargo from the oil refinery to the south. From the refinery's harbour—an iron and asphalt archipelago in the Gulf—danced tiny points of orange flame that intensified as darkness descended. Lights on the lower decks of the cruise ships had lit up as we sat. The staccato sound of a police siren floated upwards on a breeze, followed by the monotonous two-tone siren of an ambulance. Sydney pulled lightly at my hand. I stooped at his side. In a low voice he asked how I was getting along with my work. I told him that I'd written a few small pieces for magazines. He asked more directly, had I been able to make headway with the writing of short stories or a novel? He must have known that I was not telling the truth when I said, "Yes, yes, I'm working on something," and elaborated no more.

He merely nodded again. Then he advised me that he had spoken with the pundit who would officiate "at the end." I chastised him, gently of course, saying that there was no need for such thinking, no need for such talk, and that once we were back inside the house we should telephone his doctor and request a house call, and that I was sure that he would in no time feel better. He let me ramble, but when I finished he was firm. Whether we liked it or not, he said, the conversation had to happen, and what would make him feel better right then was to know that he had said what needed to be said, and that I'd heard him.

I felt suddenly weak, and my tongue seemed to swell inside my mouth, stifling my words. The chugging of fishermen's boats grew louder and voices drifted our way. In my mind waxed an image of the market at the wharf in Port of Spain, a vendor's stall there, and on the counter deep trays of shaved ice that cradled plastic bags of fish tails, bones and heads—eyes blank and lips parted to reveal rows of tiny teeth and hard, fat tongues. Sydney said something, but his voice seemed far away as in my mind I levitated. Like a dragonfly I darted off, and in an instant I was high above the King's Wharf in Port of Spain looking down at the fish market, at beached pirogues, a cruise ship and the St. Vincent Jetty Lighthouse and the traffic circling it. I took off inland, around the humming towers and the wires of the city's electricity plant and over the cemetery, and only when I arrived at the Savannah, above a bromeliad-laden, centuries-old samaan tree, did I come to a halt—truly in mid-air. I angled myself to make a nose-dive into a coconut vendor's stand.

Sydney must have seen that I'd gone far away, for in his typical manner he sharply yet gently squeezed and shook my hand to bring me back to attention. Listen, Jonathan, he said. You must listen, please. He wanted me to take the lead in the ceremony, he said. I bore up quickly, and had enough presence of mind to speak around the thickness in my mouth, the lightness in my head. What would taking the lead entail? I asked. He brushed the question away with a gesture of his fingers, and said that Pundit would guide me through everything. My dread must have been evident, for Sydney said that I shouldn't worry too much, that it was all quite straightforward. I was to take charge of his affairs, too, he said. He had left notes outlining it all. He said he wanted me to know that the house, this house here in Scenery Hills, would be mine.

This last was too much at once, too premature. I may have arrived expecting the worst, but now that I was here, in his presence, touching him and speaking with him, I was not prepared to let him go so soon. Sydney then asked if I would wear the *bayrah* that was on his wrist. I held both his hands in mine, and brought them to my lips. When I was a child, such displays of affection had been the norm between us, but during these last years we had not been physically close. During Sydney's final days, however, nothing was as usual. If a script exists for such a time I have never seen it, and all that I had learned about how to conduct myself in the world fell away and had to be reinvented. Time and habits and ways shifted forwards and backwards and sideways, without reason. Sydney slid the *bayrah* off his wrist and tried to put it on mine, without success. I put it back on his wrist and our mutual distress was relieved with more laughter than the situation merited.

We moved inside the house as the last light faded. Sydney insisted he did not want the doctor. He wanted time alone with me, he said. His frailness in the lamplight appalled me, and, looking back, I have asked myself how could I not have seen that he was so close to the end? Still, I console myself with the thought that nothing about him indicated that he was anything but compos mentis, and perhaps I erred on the side of respect for his autonomy. Perhaps I should simply have heeded my own judgement and called for a doctor the instant I had arrived at the house. But there were things on his mind, things he'd begun to tell me and hadn't finished, and he insisted he needed to tell me everything *now*, for who knew if there was to be another visit.

2

During my many previous visits to his home in Scenery Hills, Sydney would regale me with stories. He had once said— and I'm not entirely sure if he was joking—that if I ever ran out of stories to tell, the ones he was telling me would surely serve me well. Perhaps, I thought, but only if he told me what *I* wanted to hear. If he wasn't telling me tales about his high school friend Zain, who had never left Trinidad, then he would tell and retell the story of a walk he took one early and snowy morning from his apartment in Toronto's East End to a clinic in the downtown core. Over the years I had come to anticipate those moments when Sydney would squint at the mercurial sky and fix his questioning gaze on some site where was written, it seemed, these seemingly unrelated anecdotes. Sometimes, as one recounting went on, it would contradict previous ones. He would pluck out of the tome in the sky some memory of Zain or of that walk— the blizzard the night before, or the street worker who had tried to get his attention, or the overturned, snow-covered wheelchair in the neighbour's yard—and resume whichever version he fancied. He had an astonishing capacity for recall and for detail, and in his penchant for digression he would often follow to great depth seemingly tangential threads that would be suddenly dropped, left hanging loose and frayed.

I would always listen with half an ear cocked for reflections on our family, longing to hear mention of me, some indication that in all the years after he'd gone away I had remained in his thoughts. And I cannot deny that this last time I was, again, hopeful that what Sydney hadn't finished saying, and now needed so desperately to say, concerned his relationship with me. I expected, too, that he would tell me immediately what was on his mind, but instead he asked me to take him into the dining room as it was dinnertime and he had asked Rosita to welcome me back with her stewed pork and red beans. Although he himself had no appetite and would not eat, he sat at the table with me. I was too worried about his condition to appreciate the meal. I had the good sense, however, to make some noise about how good it was, how touched I was that it had been made for me. I kept hoping that he'd begin to tell me whatever it was that was so urgent, but perhaps Rosita hovering in the doorway between the kitchen and dining room—a sign of her anxiety about his health—inhibited him. I helped him into his bed shortly after, worried that perhaps the right time had passed, or perhaps it simply had not come at all, and never would. But at just that moment, thankfully, he asked me to sit on the edge of the bed and stay with him a while.

He began—to my immense disappointment—by saying: Jonathan, you know that morning I told you about, when I walked in the snowstorm to the Irene Samuel Health and Gender Centre in Toronto? My heart that day was so heavy. There was no one with me, you know. There was all this snow and ice on the road, and as I've told you, there was that dreadful-dreadful wind, but I insisted on walking there. There were cabs about, but I wouldn't hail any of them. He laughed then and said, I didn't even want the company of a taxi driver.

My heart sank. Sydney was repeating—yet again—the story of that walk. Surely, I thought, he did not have the energy to embark on such a story, and I worried that precious moments were passing. I interrupted him, doing my best to reassure him that while I was always keen to hear that particular story, perhaps he ought to first tell me whatever was most pressing. He sighed and said, Listen, Jonathan, *this is* what I want to tell you about. I have never told you how that walk ended. But this time I must tell you. I must tell you all of it.

In my head—trapped there, thankfully—growled a rather loud voice: *All right; then tell me again if you must, but, for the love of God, please also tell me why you left our family.*

Sydney and I stared at each other. Then, as if he knew my mind, he said, Perhaps, Jonathan, you've been looking for simple explanations. But there is hardly ever a single answer to anything. And isn't it so that the stories one most needs to know are the ones that are usually the least simple or straightforward?

Sydney spoke in a soft voice, calculating his words. Contradictions are inevitable, he continued. You listening to my story is yet another angle; my story is incomplete, you see, Jonathan, without your interpretation—over which I have little control. No matter my noblest intentions, and no matter how detailed my accounts, you may still only catch a fraction of what I say. You must trust that in the story I will tell you tonight—God willing—is contained all you've wanted to know.

The writer in me understood, in a flash. I was silent then, and I listened. And Sydney spoke slowly yet evenly into the early hours of the morning.

He insisted on beginning with the winter walk and carried on as if there had been no interruption, and as if it had been an account he had rehearsed: As I was saying, he said, there were cabs coming and going, but I did not avail myself of them. There I was, in the cold, wet whiteness of that snowy morning, struggling against everything. As I walked along Shuter Street, I would have liked to hear a monkey howl. That morning I would have liked to hear the chug of a pirogue, a steel pan being played, cricket commentary coming from another immigrant's transistor radio balanced on his or her shoulder. As I trudged on the ice in Regent Park that morning, I imagined the blue stillness of the Tucker Valley in the Chaguaramas foothills. I was transported for a moment, thinking I heard kiskadees calling out to one another. And this is how it has always been: over there I thought constantly of here; but now, look—I am lying here in this heat, in this house, the tepid, salty Gulf just yards away from us, sick as a dog, and of what do I speak? Of walking in the snow one dark, frigid morning a quarter century ago. But how it pleases me to do so. I am recalling the rumble of a faraway city, the frenetic howls of ambulances and police cars, of fire trucks roaring down the Don Valley Parkway and heard even in winter when the windows and the balcony door in my third-floor studio apartment on Bergamot Avenue were sealed against cold and wind and wet. In the tropical comfort of a bedroom in Scenery Hills, with the whistles of frogs and cicadas in the background, the sound of boats chugging through the night, how clearly I hear the sizzle and hum that came from the light of the street lamp outside the building on Bergamot Avenue. I can see, in the light's yellowish pink shaft, exotic downy feathers of snow.

Then, to my surprise, Sydney began to speak of his friend Zain.

If I could have asked someone to accompany me to the Irene Samuel, it would have been Zain, he said. But of course, that was impossible. So I did the next best thing, and in the knapsack I wore that day I placed all the letters she had ever written to me. It was as if she were with me.

My mind, confounded by this turn in his tale, drifted as he spoke, and I recalled the first time Sydney had told me of this friend years ago. The sounds of the sea were a constant backdrop whenever Sydney and I were in the garden or here inside the house, and my recollections of first learning of Zain were full of those kinds of sounds—a car gearing up or wheezing on the brake as it went down the hilly road, a lone steel drum tinkling in practice somewhere nearby, a dog, or a chorus of them, barking. But that day I did not hear Lancelot and Rosita's chatter and bickering coming from inside the house, and I noticed their absence. It was midmorning—perhaps the third or fourth visit I'd made to Trinidad. I knocked on Sydney's bedroom door. There was no answer so I knocked again, and then opened the door just a crack to make sure that he was all right.

The windows were wide open, the ends of the tied-back curtains whipping up in the breeze. Coming from the other side of the street was the erratic whirr of a weed trimmer. A cool pleasant light washed the sparse room. Sydney was lying on top of the made-up double bed in red boxer shorts and a teal tank top that hugged his heavy torso, which starkly contrasted with his frail legs. He was reading a letter. I called to him, and finally he acknowledged my presence. He gestured me into the room and folded the letter. A green knapsack lay off to the side. Scattered around Sydney were several greeting cards, letters on formal writing paper, an uneven stack of torn bits of paper held together by a paper clip. He had been shaved and his skin was a light powdery grey. He hadn't had his midmorning nap, it seemed. I asked how he was feeling, to which he replied, with a tone of futility, that he was as good as could be expected. I asked if he'd taken his medications, to which he merely nodded. I glanced at the correspondence, feeling awkward about my intrusion. Letters from a friend, he said, as if I'd asked.

He gathered the scraps. These are the first ones she wrote me, he said.

I was a grown man, but transparent as a child to Sydney. He had spotted the flicker of curiosity in me, and commented, No, no; it's not like that, Jonathan. There was never a romance between my friend—Zain is her name—and me. Zain and I were, however, the very best, the closest of friends.

I felt these words with a prickle of jealousy as acute as if I, and not my mother, had been his lover. Seconds later, he elaborated in a fashion that unsettled me again, as if I were a pebble caught in the push and pull of small quarrelsome waves at the water's edge. In a way, Sydney said, it was better than a romance.

The letters, now part of his legacy to me, were written with a fountain pen, in ink that had turned a purplish brown. None were dated. I remember his voice as he read snippets from them aloud, one after the other.

Dear Sid,

Where are you? Why aren't you at school today? I'm not saying you are missed, so don't get a fat head. It's just that there is nobody to provide me with my much-needed quota of comic relief. This note—which, stupidly, you will only get when you return—is just to let you know that I am doing the job Miss Augusta saddled me with—looking after rejects from other schools. I'm getting to like it. Gives me a glimpse of my potential.

Dear Sid,
It was Eid yesterday. I brought you seiwine from home—my mother's own. Bet your mother can't make seiwine, can she? Your loss. The other Hindus, Moonsie and Bhags, enjoyed it. Zain

Dear Sid,
If you'd like—and I do think you should like, even if only for the seiwine—to become a Muslim I can introduce you to our Imam. He won't hold the fact that you are still a Hindu against you. We know our ancestors were once too. Choice and power. You too have it.
Z

As I recalled the substance of those letters, I was brought back to the present by Sydney's voice saying that Zain had never experienced winter, and that he'd always wished she'd had the chance to live abroad, on her own. Sydney imitated Zain, "But, *you* are brave!" I was impressed that in his condition, even as his voice shook and the effort came with some hesitation, he had the energy to imitate the high-pitched soft and musical accent. "But, Sid, how you could *live* in a place like that?" he mimicked, and followed with an explanation for my benefit that "living in a place like that" meant a place where it snowed, and where for almost half the year you had to have your arms and legs and feet covered because it was too damn cold. "A place like that," he said, meant a country where one didn't have the kind of family connections common in Trinidad. In Trinidad, friends of your cousins' cousins' in-laws accorded you the same treatment as if you were related to them by blood, as if you were a brother or a sister—meaning that other concerns would immediately be put aside, without question, if you called in a moment of need. Whereas, he continued, in "a place like that," friends passing your home wouldn't dream of stopping in just to say hello because such a visit hadn't been pre-arranged. It was a place where you didn't know the names of your neighbours and couldn't ring them up and ask them to drive you here or there. To someone like Zain, being able to live in "a place like that" was a testament to Sid's mettle. I was pleased when Sydney added, But you have been here often enough, Jonathan. Surely you know these things by now.

He was on a roll, on a subject that interested me, for I had spent the first decade of my life with one parent who had little time for me, and another—this one—who'd dropped everything to attend to my slightest murmur. In my years of coming to Trinidad to visit Sydney, I had often wished people around me were not quite so attuned to my every need, while on returning to Canada I missed and longed for that same attentiveness.

I asked Sydney what he meant by the phrase "someone like Zain." He paused, then said: Someone who hadn't tried to make him into who he wasn't, but rather helped him to become who he already was.

That night, Sydney told me that throughout his thirty years in Canada the same thought had come to him every winter as the mercury plummeted and the snow descended, outlining the weathervane on the balcony. I would think, he said, how I wished that my dear friend Zain—and how I wished, too, that my dear mother, my dear father, my high school teachers and all of my classmates, my gynecologist in Trinidad, even my dentist, not to speak of the women who one day delighted in what they called my boyishness and the next whispered disparagingly about it, and especially the men whose eyes hardened and lips curled when I didn't field their flatteries and advances—how I wished these and numerous other people could have seen me negotiate Toronto's icy pavements while the wind drilled painfully into my forehead, or battle the two blocks to the streetcar in a whiteout, or seen me trudge home in ankle-deep snow carrying heavy bags of groceries. Living in Canada, Sydney said, with its complicated protocols and rules of conduct, is a test indeed to the mettle of anyone who arrives there from a tropical country, indeed anyone from anywhere who lands there with more determination than credentials. Being able to survive in a country like that is a recommendation of all who arrive with the earnest intention to become a grander person than would have been possible had they remained elsewhere, of all who come despite the fear that it will be a feat to achieve anything at all without the structure of culture and family, without the armour of one's connections. You found out in no time, Sydney said, that the clout your good name carried back home in the village, or on the entire island of Trinidad—an island that could easily be tucked into a bay in Lake Ontario—was useless there. My own negotiation of Toronto, Sydney told me, was indeed a testament to my mettle, and Zain, who one summer visited Toronto especially to see me, acknowledged this. She stayed for a week in my bachelor apartment, and drove about the city in my nineteen-year-old second-hand car whose body had been rusted by the salt used on the roads in the winter to melt snow. She told me—I who had known nothing of life's hardships before leaving Trinidad—that I had indeed taken the harder way, and that she admired and even envied me for this.

I was moved by the surge in Sydney's energy as he spoke. His voice grew steadily stronger. It was as if a force rose out of him and he was determined to once and for all relate his story.

On returning to Trinidad, Zain had gone to see Sid's parents. She thought she was telling them of Sid's courage when she said that it was quite something to see Siddhani Mahale, daughter of Dr. and Mrs. Mahale, living in a rented bachelor apartment in a rough part of the city and driving an old rusted car. Mrs. Mahale immediately called Sid, but not to commiserate. Instead, she delivered a lecture on how she herself had lived through seven winters in Ireland when Sid's father was in medical college there, how a little adversity never hurt anyone. If she, who had been thoroughly spoiled by the comforts and privilege of an old and grand business family, could do it, then anyone could. The real shame, said Mrs. Mahale, was that Siddhani had friends calling them up to tell them of the conditions their child was living in, as if it were their fault.

Of course Sid hadn't asked Zain to mention the conditions in which she lived, and wasn't at all pleased that she'd done so, but her mother's response enraged and saddened her. The gulf that existed between Sid and her parents—on account of her inability and refusal to conform to their idea of what a good daughter was—widened. On hearing about Mrs. Mahale's retort to Sid, Zain wasn't slow to add her own: that Mrs. Mahale, while in Ireland, had a husband at her side and the knowledge that she would soon return to Trinidad, and that when she did it would be to live the favoured life of a doctor's wife. Perhaps adversity was good, Zain remarked, but only if it didn't kill you first.

After Sydney reported this to me, he became wistful. He closed his eyes. It was already past nine-thirty, quite late for him. I waited for what seemed like an eternity, and tried to suppress the disappointment that had again begun to swell in me. A voice in my head grumbled, So are you going to sleep now? Is that all you have so needed to tell me? Is that what you so revved yourself up to say? That life in Toronto was difficult? I was suddenly angry. Are you assuming, I silently glowered, that from this I would see why our family was destroyed, why you went and did *this* to yourself?

I made a gesture to get up when, to my relief, Sid began speaking again, and contrarily, I found that it didn't matter that he again told me about Zain. As long as he kept speaking, I could hope for illumination.

Sydney said, sadly: In the end, Zain was the one who was brave. You see, she didn't leave home, Jonathan. She remained right here in Trinidad. Right here, spinning her top in the mud of all that was steady, familiar, and expected of her. That is, I see now, what true courage is. His fist landed on the bed with a thump of admiration.

When I lived in Toronto, he said, I used to write to Zain here in Trinidad and tell her how I missed "home"—missed Trinidad, that is. Zain would chide me over the phone for being a "no-whereian." She would say to me, You made your choice, so forget about this place when you're over there.

What choice did I make? I asked. I had *no* choice.

We'd be having a good tiff by this time. She emphasized the word *always* when she said that one always has a choice. Whatever action you took, she said, that was the choice you made. I replied that quite often one's choices were limited by society's expectations, and that sometimes choices were made for you by others. She raised her voice at me. It doesn't matter how the choice was made, she shouted, it's where you are right now that matters, so for God's sake, Sid, get on with it. *She* had; she'd got on with it, she said. She'd applied to the university in Trinidad and studied there. She'd married a Trinidadian man, and having done that, she'd built a business with him, she'd had a family with him. They'd built their own house, they'd joined clubs, they went out to parties and they entertained at home. Return to Trinidad, she said, or forget about Trinidad and settle down in Toronto once and for all. You can't live in two places at once—it's like having two lovers, she said. You're bound to be unfaithful to both.

At first Zain wasn't so much sick of hearing about my regrets and wishes, Sydney said, as she was worried that I'd never be content. But, over time, she came to understand my ambivalences, my perennial disquiet, and why in a city of several million people I was always so alone.

Sydney became quiet again. But this time I was more patient. He seemed to consider something, and having come to a decision he pulled himself higher up the bed into a sitting position. I helped arrange the pillows to support his back. When he was comfortable he said, The time for me to tell you everything has come, Jonathan. It was Zain who "facilitated" all of this (the quotation marks were his, made with the first and second fingers of each hand flicking at the air, and as he said "this" he looked quickly down at his torso and back up again). If she had been alive when I made that walk in the snow, I wouldn't have had to ask; she would have made it her business to come with me.

I was curious to know what had become of Zain, but I felt a rising dread. If Sydney was about to cast light on how he had come to transform himself, I was not entirely keen to hear that story now. Of course I wondered, but my wondering was not prompted by the kind of curiosity that sought answers; it was prompted by disappointment. I did not really believe that there was an acceptable story, and didn't need or care to hear one attempted. I could already feel my embarrassment and impatience rising. I was in a caretaking role with Sydney, and as such the tables had turned between us. But our relationship was still predicated on the original one in which he had parented me, and surely there are things that a child, regardless of his age, does not need, does not want to know about his parent. I wanted our original relationship preserved.

Sydney said something, but the cicadas outside the bedroom window must have multiplied tenfold and were making an uncommon and piercing ruckus, drowning out his words. I got up, intending to go to the window, but Sydney grabbed my arm. Don't go, Jonathan. Stay with me, he said. Please, just sit with me. Let me tell you everything. Please try to listen.

His small cool hand on mine still had the power to calm me. The dreadful whistling subsided. Before I could think to still myself, to steel myself, I had already turned my hand over, and this time he rested his in mine.

We sat like that for an unpleasant minute as he stroked my hand. I don't know why I let him, but in that time, so long in the moment and so brief in my memory, I resigned myself to his will. I suppose I had started down this path when I came to Trinidad looking for Sid, and I could not now abandon him on this last leg of our journey.

Throughout much of that night Sydney spoke, slowly but urgently, and as he laboured I felt that it would be selfish of me to bother him for answers to the questions that, more than thirty years later, still harassed me. In the end, what I discovered I really wanted from him was not stories, nor even answers, but the turning back of time.

Most often Sydney spoke directly to me and I was his sole audience—but every once in a while it was as if he and Zain were alone, and he was talking to her. I felt then that I was an intruder, but I mustered my resolve and continued my vigil. Despite these shifts in tone, he was remarkably lucid—a fact to which I now return, even two months later, as I chastise myself for not getting him medical attention earlier.

Eventually, he drifted off to sleep and I, curled by then at his side, was transported to a different time in our lives: I am wearing only a white cotton diaper and I am sitting on the wide, cool stone sill of the veranda wall of our house in the Annex in Toronto. My legs stretch straight out so that my flexed heels face the house opposite ours. One of Sid's hands is splayed across my torso, holding me against her body. I am leaning into her body, looking out towards the car-lined street in front of the house. Her fingers against my bare chest and belly are covered in a plastic film of red, yellow and green acrylic paint. There are red-brick late-Victorians on either side of our house and along the street opposite. The far side of the street is lined with parked cars whose metal trimmings catch and then disperse the light that dapples through the leaves of mighty trees.

3

Whenever I look out at the cruise ships in the Gulf, I imagine tourists from those ships returning home and saying, "Yes, I know Trinidad, I have been there." I, too, have said, "I know Trinidad," but by this I mean that I know first-hand the daily quotidian: On one of my visits here the German shepherd that belongs to Sydney's neighbour across the road (the house surrounded by the curiously high concrete fence that is menacingly and artlessly crowned with rolls of barbed wire) escaped and attacked the small dog of another neighbour. I know that the small dog had to be put down. I know that the owner of the German shepherd wears dark sunglasses regardless of the time of day or the weather. He doesn't say good day or good night to anyone. Lancelot and Rosita have no proof, but are nevertheless certain he is a drug lord. They say everyone knows that he is protected by the area police. Perhaps I can say I know Trinidad because I am privy to neighbourhood rumours and intrigues, and because

I can look out at that house across the road and wonder if its owner cares that death had not so long ago crouched on our back stairs.

On one of my earlier trips here, the youngest son of Mrs. Allen, the guava cheese lady who comes around on Saturday afternoons with her tray of sweets, won a scholarship in the CXC exams. The boy, Wilson, was sent by his mother to ask me to attend a special service at the local Roman Catholic Church for all the boys from his school who had passed the exam. Since then, the boy has been in touch with me by e-mail regularly and before I arrived this last time he informed me that he'd been accepted at the Cave Hill Campus of The University of the West Indies to study law. God's blessings on a hard-working mother, Rosita said to me gravely.

The people who live in the area are not people I saw once, in passing, on a visit here. I know what they look like from the front, from the back, from the side. I have spoken with them. I know their voices. I have heard things about them. They know things about me.

I know, too, the cool muscular smell of mildewed cracks in the floor tiles of the bathroom of a private, crumbling residence—this one; the fright of cockroaches lurking at the dry mouth of the drain, their antennae waving intelligences to each other. I know the smell of thyme, *chadon beni*, garlic, ketchup, soya sauce, sesame oil and burnt sugar; I can see the crystalline amber shards of the seasoning mixture stuck to a wooden spoon that stirred a chicken in a frothy pot in the kitchen of a private home—this one. I know how paint on concrete steps plasticizes and bubbles in the sun and splits with a surprisingly sharp, audible crack when poked with a fingernail. I know what it is to need to give a sponge bath to a sick man when there is no water in the taps and the two tanks at the back of the house have gone dry. I know how a garden of plants that tower to the height of a house here, but are stunted in pots inside houses where I come from, can wilt and crisp in the dry season and miraculously spring to life again in the rain, and how odd it is to be served food in good china and to sip rum or Scotch and coconut water from cut-glass tumblers even as there is no electricity for days, and for weeks no water in the taps—except for a possible brief reprieve in the most inconvenient hours of the night, when both, without notice, might become available, causing people, myself included, who throughout the neighbourhood are attuned in their sleep to the most distant rumble of the awakening taps, to scurry and gather pails, pans and drinking cups to catch as much as possible. All this and more I have come to know about life on this island over the course of nine years.

Yet, when I looked at Sydney I felt I was no different from the wishful but misguided tourist who thinks he can know a destination by reading a few paragraphs in a guidebook about its history, its flora and fauna, and then visiting it once for a handful of days. Perhaps I have a little more reason than most visitors to say, "I know Trinidad." But Sydney, the person I knew from the first day I was able to know anything, had remained, until those last days we were together, elusive.

What I now understand, at long last, is that a person can tell you simple stories to fill lacunae in time, but these stories will be nothing more than words ordered one in front of the other, like beads on a jeweller's beading board. You, the listener, might take away a few images, but their significance is diminished because context is absent. But Sydney was right: stories are many-sided. To truly understand, one needs to know, for instance, the rumours and gossip and even the lies about the story. And one needs to know seemingly unrelated things, such as the identity of the protagonist's neighbours, and what colour of light is cast by the street lamps, and how the streets appear in winter and in summer, and what are the era's most popular songs and films, what advertising jingles played on the radio stations, and what health and social services are in effect, and what are the immigration policies, which scandals have made the newspaper headlines, and how are the nation's sports teams faring, and what is the price of a taxi ride across town, of a kilo of tomatoes at the farmer's market, a hot dog on the street corner or, here, a doubles, or a shark-and-bake sandwich. Even the knowledge of what's happening continents away—which governments are falling or forming—adds light, and so gives shading and nuance to a story. Once this full palette is known, the beads on the beading board might be arranged differently by different beaders, but the completed necklace, although a delightful surprise, can also be said to be predictable and inevitable. When in the past Sydney would tell me his stories, stories that were full of these kinds of details, beginning always with that walk he had taken in the cold and ice from Bergamot Avenue to the Irene Samuel Health and Gender Centre, his words fell like glass coins in a bottomless bucket, ringing against the bucket's sides but never landing.

I awoke when Sydney did, about four hours later, in the early morning. He insisted on having breakfast in the dining room, and so Lancelot and I tried to dress him, but he was too weak and eventually lay back in the bed. He had asked for a boiled egg and a slice of toast, but when the dish arrived he nibbled on less than a quarter of it. I showered and dressed, then returned to his room. Rosita and Lancelot brought us drinks and sweets—tea, eggnog, sweet rice, raisin bread, Crix crackers and cheese. Sydney nibbled and sipped and eventually he began to speak again, his voice lower now; at times I strained to hear. It stays with me, how in such dire circumstances Sydney's speech had an exacting urgency. He knew that this was his last chance and he wanted to be clear, to say everything that had to be said.

It was only then, when he was, I realized, at last wrapping up his story of the walk to the medical clinic, that he chose to reveal that Zain had not simply died, but had been killed during what appeared to be a burglary at her home. I was taken aback when he said that he suspected Zain's murderer was known to her, and that, furthermore, if he were right—and he was convinced that he was—he also knew who this person was. He'd never told this to anyone before, he said, but now he dearly needed the peace that could only come from saying what he thought had happened to Zain. I worried that he was too weak, but he would not acknowledge my concern. Instead, he spoke throughout the long day, his story punctuated by periods of silence when I thought he had fallen asleep, only to realize, by the details he then revealed, that with each short rest he took, he was gearing himself up—rather than down—preparing himself to delve deeper into the well of his most personal memories and desires, his mind and his storytelling brighter and sharper than ever.

Here, then, is one of the stories that had so heavily weighed on him. I've tried to set down his words as best as I can remember, but forgive me if in doing so I have put in a conjunction or two of my own, or have inserted parts of the story I had heard on previous occasions and other parts gleaned from my reading of the notebooks Sydney left me—rejigging, reordering, culling, all for clarity and with no malice or intention to assert my own interpretations. Forgive me, too, if I put in Sydney's mouth here and there the most minimal of details, such as the colour of the landscape and scents of the place I have come to know well, for although my intention is first and foremost to give voice to Sydney, the writer in me has begun to take flight again.

———

SYDNEY'S STORY
(as he told it to me)

Zain and I were living our adult lives far from each other, but whenever I came home to Trinidad for a visit we would get together and, invariably, she would ask me to tell her what "made me so." She would hold my face in her hands and search me with eyes that were like fingers, like lips. She knew that to do this to me was a cruel luxury, but it didn't stop her.

I, for my part, knew that on a small island, in a place like this, I could not misbehave, especially with my best friend. This knowledge had been reason enough for me to leave the island as a young woman and retreat to a place where, if I fell for such a look and such a touch, I was on my own, in a place where I had no family, friends or community to offend. But in all my years away, no one ever touched me or treated me like Zain did. Was this peculiar to Zain, I often wondered, or was it the way of women from our culture? And was it only they who could ever satisfy me? If that were so, I knew my future in Canada would not be easy.

During one particular month-long vacation twenty years ago, I went between my parents' house in the south and Zain's house in the north where she lived with her husband and her two children, both then at university abroad. The month had begun happily. Zain and I were like youngsters again, driving all over the island, going here and there on our own, not returning to the house until well after dinnertime. Angus didn't mind us roaming about. He was traditional and conservative in some ways, but liberal in others. He trusted us not to get into too much trouble. The month passed quickly, and I returned to Toronto. I had been back only one week before my dear friend Zain was dead.

I could recount any number of blissful days during that month, but one stands out. It was late when we left Zain and Angus's house, around five or so in the evening. The sun was dropping fast, and she and I were headed into the Tucker Valley. It was frightfully liberating, the two of us driving on that road alone, through pastures and fields, at that time of evening. But we weren't alone; we were together, and when Zain and I were together we were, or so we imagined, invincible, carefree, daring. Not daring of ourselves, but of others. *Just you dare; you won't know what hit you!* We drove into the valley slowly, taking in the incredible beauty of the wide-canopied samaan trees on either side of the roadway. Rosettes of bromeliads and delicate orchids clustered around the trunks and branches of the trees, and Spanish moss clumped and hung like wet lace curtains. As the passenger, I could gaze at all of this, and at Zain too, her hair so beautifully coiffed, her makeup and her nails shorthand for how she was to be treated.

Ours was the only car on the road for a good distance into the valley. Then we rounded a bend to see that a hundred yards ahead a small white car had stopped in our lane, and another car, also white, had halted in the oncoming lane. Together, the two effectively blocked the road. Zain was telling me about Cynthia, her maid. Long ago,

Cynthia had answered an advertisement for employment that Zain had placed in the paper, and when Cynthia saw the house, when she met Zain and the two children, she'd simply announced, "I am taking this job. I will start right away. Show me my room." Zain was saying that by the time we got back, Cynthia would have made coconut bake and salt fish. Cynthia was a really good cook, and she was black, Zain said, so of course she didn't make bake like an Indian. Cynthia's bake was black bake, she added impishly. "Hers isn't limp and bland like a thick *sada* roti. This is bake in which you can actually taste the coconut. A wedge of it between your thumb and forefinger is firm; when you hold it up to your mouth, Sid, it meets you like a man."

I heard her laugh, but my focus was on the two cars, their disturbing configuration: we couldn't get by on either the left or the right of them; the road was edged by tall bush on both sides, and a couple of feet beyond this edging were ravines too deep and narrow for a car to manoeuvre. We would have no choice but to stop. I was thinking of how my father, and so many others, had repeatedly warned me that if you're the only one on a Trinidad road and someone tries to stop you, if they hit your car, or even if you hit someone on the road, you mustn't stop, for God's sake don't stop, just drive straight to the police station. And I was thinking that the police station was behind us and that there was no easy way to turn the car around. I was noticing that the sun had already gone down behind the hills. The dense greenery was swiftly losing its lushness and definition. There were fer-de-lance, bushmasters and coral snakes in the forest, I thought, and people weren't just mugged in this country, but they were raped, they were kidnapped and they were murdered. We were two women, alone, on a quiet road in the country. Above my panic I heard Zain say, "But you wouldn't know what I am talking about, would you. Don't tell me you like flaccid bake?" Although I kept peering ahead, curious that the situation didn't seem to unduly perturb Zain—she had continued driving, a little slower, but without any sense of trepidation—I shook my head in feigned irritation, for the slyness of the smile she wore indicated that she was anticipating my reaction. I strained to see if the drivers of the two cars were communicating with each other.

Aware now of my distraction, Zain paid attention. She said, "But what these people think they are doing? They can't just stand up like that in the middle of the road. How do they expect me to pass? They are going to have to move." And just as she said that, as if they had heard, the cars began to move, the one in our lane carrying on now abruptly and swiftly, the one approaching us moving more slowly, the driver peering into the field to his left even as he was rolling forward. Zain remarked that they must have seen some animal or other. She touched my shoulder and said, "Sid, don't believe everything you hear about how much crime there is in this place. Relax a little. There is crime everywhere, but you have to live, don't you?"

The two cars picked up speed and I exhaled. I asked Zain to turn off the air conditioning so that we could open the windows and listen to the sounds of the birds and smell the lush greenness. Ahead, a flat field of low uncultivated grasses, patches of bhaji and of pigeon peas extended well back to a middle ground of broad-leaved trees like teak, papaya, breadfruit, soursop. And rising quite suddenly now in front of us was the Northern Range. A small sign, posted so low we could have missed it, informed us that we were entering the park of Macqueripe Beach. Zain looked at her watch and said, "It's still early. Cynthia won't have dinner ready yet." The sky was by this time yellowish silver.

"Let's go," I concurred.

We drew near to a guard's hut on the side of the road, with a gate that could be raised and lowered, and a sign that warned of a 6 p.m. closing, at which time all persons must have vacated the park. It was quarter to six. There was no one in the hut. Zain asked, "You think they mean it?" From behind us came a car. As it overtook ours Zain put her hand out to stop the driver. "The sign says the park closes at six. You know if they serious?" she shouted. The woman in the passenger seat laughed. The man driving said, "No, it don't have nobody that does come and check." The woman added, "I coming here plenty and I never yet see nobody in that hut." They drove on, the man shouting back, "Doh 'fraid, follow us, we going for a swim."

And so we drove on and the field ended. Suddenly the forest was right up against us. Dark trees met the road now. Out of the blue, Zain asked, "What about Jonathan? Are you in touch with him?"

"Jonathan?" I asked, surprised.

"The little boy—well, he'd be a young man now, I suppose—the child you were bringing up with that English woman. Was her name India?"

"She and I haven't spoken in some years," I said. "India did not want him and me to have contact."

"Yes, you told me that in one of your letters long ago. But that is still so? It must be so hard on you. But he's no longer a child, so what does it matter now?"

She was, of course, right. I shrugged and said with finality, "I guess it's complicated."

She let the matter rest and we carried forward in silence, but an unease washed over me; I felt suddenly ungainly, my body ill-formed. As if she sensed this, Zain put her hand out and rubbed my knee.

Thankfully, the road soon ended and we were at a parking area. A few men, women and children milled about. Before us, beyond the paved area, was the perpendicular rise of the mountain. Stepping out of the car, I looked up to see the mountain's top and almost lost my balance. The face of the mountain, I saw, was embroidered with an infinite variety of textured shapes and shades of dark green vegetal tentacles waving out from the face of the wall, linked together by nets of wild philodendron vines. It was frightening, to be so suddenly and unexpectedly halted by the forest of the Northern Range, and this added to the sense of danger I felt about Zain and me, two women from "nice" families, being out here on our own, so late in the evening. On the other side of the parking lot, through a row of cedar trees, was a narrow view to the sea. The light on the open water was startling. It was still bright light—daylight—out there.

We found a stairway and made our way down—Zain in her low heels, and I in my runners, feeling as usual like some deformed-yet-loved thing in her presence. People were hurrying past us. "Come on," she said, picking up speed, skipping down the steep stairs. We arrived at a bay where small waves formed tightly and then broke. The man and the woman who had spoken to us from their car were already standing in the water, the woman in a dress, the skirt of which she had tightly gathered around and knotted in front of her, the man in navy blue pants that reached his knees, the hem of the pants wet from the leaping water.

We stood close enough that the man called out, "You make it in time to see the sun."

Zain answered back in her usual quick fashion, "Yes, you know how to give directions."

His wife had been grinning, but at Zain's retort her lips tightened.

The man said, "Well, it was a straight road, no turn-offs, you can't get lost even if you tried."

Zain answered, "You know how long I trying to get lost, and I just can't get lost? Is a good while I trying, man."

The woman turned away, and the man, his smile forced now, looked quizzically at Zain. He glanced at me, he looked back at Zain, and then turned his back to us.

Out ahead, Peninsula de Paria, a flirtatious finger
of neighbouring Venezuela, pointed directly at beautiful
Macqueripe Bay, sprawled across much of the horizon
save for a slip into which the sun would soon drop on an
open horizon line. Several people had cameras at the ready.
Neither Zain nor I had carried a camera. No photographs
of us together, come to think of it, had ever been taken.
She and I stood side by side watching. We didn't speak.
As Zain gazed out at the horizon, I wondered what the
moment meant to her. It occurred to me that I could think
of it as magical, and make a promise, a wish, a commitment,
but I turned instead to watch a woman and two children,
their backs to the drama of the sky unfolding, being pho-
tographed by a man. The children's antics escalated as they
waited for the man, likely their father, to take the picture.
He was admonishing them to behave, to be still. Then he
became animated and said, "Now!" The camera clicked.

The sun had hit the water. Zain's eyes were fiercely set
on it. She seemed calm and, for the first time that evening,
serious. A minute or so later, we turned our attention to
the scene around us. With our backs to the horizon, the
trees were now softly lit and in sharp focus. What a surprise, a gift it was, to realize that the hills on either side of
the bay were splashed generously with chaconia, which had
been obliterated earlier by the harsh light, sweeping arms of
redness reaching outward as if to fan the bay. And the sky
directly above was the most translucent and yet luminous
shade of phthalo blue I'd ever seen. We stood staring up and

Zain gripped my arm, pointed to the sky over the parking lot, and said, "How strange. So blue in this direction after sunset. And what a strange shade of blue. Almost green."

Even as I saw what she saw, and marvelled, I was watching to make sure that her touching my arm had gone unnoticed by the strangers around us. I stepped forward, moving slightly out of her reach, and said, "It's the colour of the Barbados sea as seen from the air."

She asked, "Do you know what makes the sky blue?"

I opened my eyes wide in a gesture of invitation, and she obliged, laughing, because she knew I was making fun of her, and as she wove in words the tale of oxygen and nitrogen and argon gas and dust particles and light waves and electromagnetic fields and colour wavelengths and frequencies, I thought, you are the mother of two adult children, the wife of a businessman, you are a Trinidadian woman, you are an Indian woman, a Muslim woman, you live here in this country, but who are you, really?

Zain said, "You're not listening to a thing I am telling you, are you?"

"I heard every word," I lied. "Now, tell me what makes thunder."

Her eyes suddenly brimmed with tears. She tried to smile, but it was as if her face had broken. I wanted to put my hand on her cheek, but I dared not. I wanted to take her hand and pull her to me, but that would have been foolish. Any other two women on this beach could have interacted so, and others would have seen one woman comforting another. But I didn't look like other women. I indicated with my head that Zain should follow me and I walked as casually as I could, toward the stairs, back to where the car was parked.

It was when we were climbing back up the stairs that we saw the men with the snakes. The stairs were poorly made, angled downwards, and as you ascended you had to not only step up, but also grip the rusting railing tight and *pull* yourself along so that you didn't slide off. And those stairs were wet, too, made slippery from bathers returning to their cars. We were concentrating, and we weren't looking ahead. Zain was ahead of me, and immediately behind me were three young women chatting loudly—I don't remember about what, but I do remember their high-pitched voices, their raucous, daring laughter. They were a new, different breed, I remember thinking. Zain and I had never been like them. I thought they were a bit too loud, and at the same time admired them for it. Zain was making her way up at a good pace. One of the laughing young women snapped suddenly, in an arresting voice, "All yuh!" and her companions went momentarily silent. Zain and I were instantly alert. I looked up to see what was happening, and in that moment Zain cried out and twisted her body back almost to face me, blocking the view with her hand. The women now uttered various shrill sounds of fear and displeasure. I looked back at them and they, too, had their views blocked with their hands, and so I wasn't sure where to look. But I could see the face of the one who had called out: it was stone serious, and she was staring up ahead. And now I turned and could see, coming down the stairs towards us, four men. They were young and of Indian origin, all with short squarely cut hair that stood stiffly in the most traditional way, and two of them wore long fat snakes about their necks and chests. The young woman shrieked, "Move aside!" The men looked at her. They were bounding down the stairway lithely, as if the snakes were beach towels. "Move aside, get to the side," she shouted at them, more authoritatively than before. They finally obliged, stepping now to the far edge of the stairway to make more room for us to continue quickly past them.

"I 'fraid them things. Don't make joke with me around them things, you hear!" the young woman said as she passed them, the voice that had been so high-pitched and bright some seconds before now dark and thick. As I had passed, I'd turned to get a good look at the snakes—an unusual thing for me, as I am one of those people who can't even bear to look at the image of a snake, much less the real thing. They were so thick that the outline of their scales was quite visible inside patches of cream demarcated by black, and brown patches also outlined in black, and ochre patches of irregular shape, and yellow and black spots. The snakes had the full roundness of motorcycle tires, and did not seem to be limply resting, but rather to be quite alert; the pointed head of one was angled towards the beach front. Their underbellies could be seen in parts and here they were white, the scales less smooth. The eye that I saw in swift passing had a light brown glassiness. Although I am terrified of snakes, when I saw that Zain had hunched her shoulders and turned her back to the men, utter disgust on her face, I wanted to embrace and comfort her. But of course I did not dare to do so, not even around this new and liberated brand of young women. I feared that I, and not the snakes, would become the centre of attraction.

Darkness fell fast, as it does in the tropics. On the way back to the car, Zain turned off onto the golf course road. Farther ahead, she stopped. She turned off the lights and the engine. We were engulfed in pitch-blackness. "What are you doing?" I asked, my concern about safety in such a remote area juggling in my mind against the remote possibility that she was creating an opportunity for something more between us. "I have something I want to tell you, Sid," she said. And then she told me the news that would eventually haunt me, and it haunts me still—that she had come to know someone, someone who had come to mean a great deal to her, and whom she wanted me to meet.

Unaware that I had stopped breathing, she continued. She and this someone had met in the grocery, in the lineup at the cashier. They'd been seeing one another for some months now. Angus didn't know, of course. And she'd told him, this new man, a great deal about me.

I knew I needed to say something, but all I could manage was an insipid "Well, that's a bit of a shock."

Zain repeated—as if I might not have understood—that this man meant a great deal to her and that she wanted me to meet him. I couldn't answer. After a moment's strained silence, she apologized for asking me, and started up the car. On the way back to Cynthia's bake and fish, Zain told me, as if trying to explain, all the usual sorts of things—he was handsome, smart, attentive and was living on a big beautiful boat that was permanently moored in the harbour near the yacht club; he was caring, he was lean and muscular, and his skin glowed red from the sun; he was gentle and rough at once, but his roughness was never to hurt her, only to weaken her with delight, and on and on. I had heard more than I cared to know. I responded only that I hadn't realized she and Angus were having problems, to which she answered, "Well, that's the thing. Angus and I have no problems. He loves me. And I love him. It's just that there is no mystery for us anymore. I don't think Angus could survive without me, and I can't bear the thought of him being alone, but I can't bear, either, the thought of not being with Eric. I hope you will agree to meet him."

I didn't respond, and Zain didn't bother to ask me again—she simply arranged a meeting some days later on a trip she and I, just a little cool with each other now, took. It was not until we were a few minutes away from the Coal Pot Café in Salybia–Toco that she informed me Eric would meet us there.

There must have been something more to him than I was able to see, perhaps something only revealed in private. To me that day he appeared less handsome, less grand, than she had reported. He was clearly uncomfortable and I guessed that he was meeting me only to please Zain. Still, I did not find him particularly attentive to Zain and, to my discomfort, she asked him several times if he was all right. Over lunch he asked me, "So, you are related to Dr. Mahale?" I said Dr. Mahale was my father. "Yes, I know that," he replied. I could see Zain waiting for an expansion of the subject. I, too, waited, and when Eric said nothing more, I ventured, This is such a beautiful area of Trinidad; I haven't been to the beaches up here in almost two decades, and I am so happy to be here.

It was a poor attempt to make small talk. I asked if he came here often. Eric said only, "No." I asked where he lived. "Up by the yacht club," he said.

Zain jumped in, reminding me that Eric lived on his boat.

I tried again. "So, do you call that home?"

"If home is where you rest your head at night, then I suppose so."

I asked how he made a living.

"So you are her guardian, now?" he asked with barely veiled hostility.

Zain laughed, her embarrassment apparent, and playfully punched his arm. She said, "But why you being so coy, boy?"

He said, half laughing, "This can't be for real, man: this is an interrogation."

Eric offered me no more, and I gave up. He talked with Zain about the drive from the yacht club to Salybia–Toco, asked her if she had heard from someone whose name I didn't catch. Later, at the beach, I sat on the sand and allowed myself to be mesmerized by the terrifying ragtag tumble of waves and currents from the Atlantic Sea while Zain and Eric walked hand in hand down the length of the dune. On returning Zain dropped to the sand beside me, but Eric stood facing the sea, arms crossed on his chest. I decided to try one last time, for Zain's sake. I stood up and joined him and asked if he ever brought his boat here. He answered with one word: Never.

Zain got up and went to the water's edge. Eric and I stood in silence for some minutes. Then he left in his car.

He is not always like that, Zain told me. She couldn't understand what was going on with him. On the way back to her house she brooded, and I, peeved but intent on not revealing my disappointment in her choice of a person with whom she might cheat on dear Angus, intent, too, on not showing my own feeling of betrayal, or my fears about why Eric was so rude to me, laid my head back and dozed.

The second time I met Eric involved, to my dismay, similar deceptions. Zain had taken me to her gym, after which we were to go out for lunch. I hadn't bothered to ask where we would go as I no longer knew restaurants on the island. But my heart fell when I saw that we were heading to the yacht club. Halfway through our lunch at High Tide Restaurant, Eric strolled in and joined us. He was well known there, and obviously liked the attention the restaurant staff paid him. This time he was closely attentive to me. Perhaps Zain had taken him to task about the way he had acted before. I was not fooled, especially as the topic he chose to engage in with me was my personal workout at the gym. Just as such a topic between a man and a woman was less about the workout than a way of coming around to speaking about the other's body, I was used to the subject being broached by a hostile kind of man so that he could entertain the inevitable, simple-minded supposition that I was pumping myself up so that I could appear masculine. Of course, my guard went up, and rightly so, for Eric soon admitted that I presented him with the rare opportunity to ask what it was that turned a person into someone "like me." His questioning eventually went too far, and I was relieved, grateful—and impressed—when Zain brought it and the lunch to an end. She had, in a flash, seen Eric as he was: small and unlikeable.

A couple of days later, the next time I saw Zain, she told me that she had confronted him on his boat, where they had a row. Eric didn't, he told Zain, like her being "thick" with me. She was pleased with herself that she'd stood up for me: she'd shouted, she said, that under no circumstances would she tolerate bigotry and insults towards any of her friends or herself, and furthermore no one, not her father, not her husband and certainly not he, had the right to be so parochial, so domineering and boorish as to tell her who she could and could not be friends with. But the matter didn't, of course, end there. He grabbed her by her upper arms and shook her, and then he pushed her. She was so shocked that she didn't fight back. I thought that was a good thing, and told her so. This new side of him had frightened her, she said. She left him as quickly as she could, and later that same day, once she'd found the privacy, she telephoned him and ended the relationship.

Just before the end of that trip—about ten days after the incident with Eric—Zain and I spent our last day together. It was a Tuesday, the day on which, every week, Angus ate dinner and played poker after work with friends at a club in Port of Spain. When Angus returned—which would be, he said, about ten thirty, give or take a drink or two— they would drive me down to San Fernando to my parents' house. Zain and I ate dinner, went to the guest room and propped ourselves on the bed next to each other. We had pushed in the door, but not fully closed it. Zain wanted to explain why she had been open to an affair. She reasoned that Angus was her first and only love, that they had been together now for so long that they were like siblings, that she wanted some mystery in her life, some excitement, to be seen again as a sexual being. I was flattered—and saddened—when she said that it was I who had sparked that desire in her to be loved again.

We lay back in the bed, like old times, her head on my shoulder and my arm around her. She wanted to be loved and seen as a sexual being, but I would never be, I saw, the one to give her these gifts. She nodded off and I dozed and woke and dozed and woke, knowing this was the last time I would see her on that trip. As I held her, it came to me that I had never regarded Angus as a threat to my relationship with Zain—he was, instead, my aide—and I was relieved that Eric, the real threat, was no longer in the picture. I could hold Zain and, regardless of the truth, imagine that I was the only one giving her the attention she craved. I could pretend that out of this could well grow more. I convinced myself there was no harm in my imagining or pretending.

Then I heard a noise outside the door. I lifted my head. Someone was there. I pulled my arm out from under Zain's neck. She awoke and we both sat up quickly. We heard footsteps running up the stairs, then the door at the back of the house shut. I whispered that we should call the police, call Angus. But Zain insisted we should first go and look outside. By the time we reached the gate we could hear a car driving away, although we couldn't see it in the dark. Zain was silent. She didn't appear to be frightened. She was, rather, seething, but offered me no explanation for her reaction. I asked her if Eric had a key to the house and, with some relief at being able to admit it, she said he did. It was my turn now to be enraged. I asked if she had gone mad, and she nodded. Although Angus travelled for work, she explained, she'd always refused his desire to hire security guards for the house while he was away. She felt that an alarm system was enough protection even though she seldom bothered to engage it. Eric worried about her for the same reasons as Angus, and felt that Angus was "slack" in not hiring a security company regardless of what she wanted. A couple months ago he'd gone with her to a nearby hardware store, taken her house key from her and copied it, so that if there was any trouble at her house while Angus was away— or even if she was frightened, for any reason—he would be able to come over at once. It was a matter of trust between them that he would never enter the house without her prior knowledge and permission, and of course would only do so when she was there alone. Angus had always given in to her, and Eric's protectiveness and insistence made her feel simultaneously vulnerable and taken care of. She found she liked the idea that someone would step in and do what needed to be done, not only without her having to ask, but against her wishes. So she let Eric make the copy.

I said nothing, but I was appalled. For a moment I felt that I didn't know who Zain really was. She hadn't yet had a chance, she concluded, to get the key back from Eric after their fight on his boat. She would deal with it the very next morning.

When Angus returned he sensed our unease and insisted on knowing what was bothering us. I said I was upset because I didn't want to return to Canada; I no longer wanted to live in a place where I didn't have family and where I wasn't part of a community. Zain busied herself fixing him a plate of food. She and I were quiet, but Angus did not seem to notice. After he ate, we readied ourselves for the long drive south, back to my parents' home.

Just before we left, Zain called me into her bedroom. She held my hands in hers and said in a low voice that what Eric had done that night was wrong, but that I wasn't to worry. I made her promise that she would arrange to meet him only one more time, for the sole purpose of getting back her key, and that she would do so only in a public place, in the daytime. Then she went to her dresser, opened a drawer and pulled out a bulging white envelope, which she handed me. She told me that for years she'd been saving whatever U.S. currency she came across and that after our many conversations she knew what she wanted to do with that money.

In the envelope were two rubber band–bound bundles, each one holding thirty one-hundred-dollar bills. Six thousand dollars in all.

She would not accept my protests, insisting that I was to use it to do whatever would make me more comfortable in myself and in the world.

Angus and Zain drove me back to my parents' house. And that was the last time I saw Zain.

I returned to Toronto, and over the course of the next few days she and I spoke on the phone a couple of times. In one of those calls she told me that the day after I left she'd gone to the trailer on the yacht club grounds and confronted Eric about the key and the intrusion. He had laughed with incredulity and ridicule, as if she were mad.

One week after I left Trinidad, one week and one day after she and I had lain on the bed in her guest room, I was awakened by a phone call early in the morning. When you live in another country, far from your aging parents, every call from them causes a lurch of fear. A call outside the usual schedule can stop one's heart. My parents knew this, so they would begin each call by saying, "Hello, Sid, everything's okay here. Are you well?" But this time my mother's first words were, "Sid? It's Mum." I waited some seconds for the usual reassurance. None came, and so I braced myself for news about my father or my sister, Gita, Gita's son, Devin, or husband, Jaan.

"I hope I didn't wake you," my mother said.

"What's happened?" I responded.

"What are you doing?" answered my mother, and this made me sit up in fear. I repeated my question sharply. She answered, "We have some bad news. Something has happened."

"Is Dad all right?" I asked, getting up out of the bed.

"Yes. It's not our family. We're all right."

So, what could be that bad? I wondered. Her tone was not one that suggested her reason for calling was mere gossip.

"What are you doing right now?" she asked again.

"For Christ's sake, Mum. Just tell me what happened."

"Well, I'm worried that you're alone. Are you alone?"

"What happened?" I shouted.

"It's Zain."

"Zain" was suddenly a name that seemed strange, unfamiliar. For a few seconds, I didn't know who my mother was talking about. As realization dawned, my legs buckled and I sat back down.

"There was a home invasion at her place yesterday. She was alone at the time."

"What happened?" I asked, but before she could answer I spoke again. "What do you mean a home invasion?"

The house had been broken into, she said. Ransacked.

I knew that robberies were never what they appeared in Trinidad. The room was spinning and I started to shake. I couldn't summon the words to ask if Zain was all right. A small voice somewhere within me asked, "What did they want?" Mum didn't answer. I knew then that Zain was dead.

"Oh God. Don't tell me. Please don't tell me," I cried.

I heard my mother saying, "I'm so sorry, Siddhi. I'm so sorry. I wish you weren't alone."

Between sobs, I had sense enough to ask for details. "Was it really a robbery?"

"It's very strange, Sid. The house was trashed, apparently, but according to the reports in the news, the police are saying that nothing was taken."

We were both quiet for a moment. I am sure that what was in my own mind was also in my mother's: the only thing that really mattered had, in fact, been taken.

"When did this happen, Mum?" I finally asked.

"Last night," she said.

"What day is today?"

"It's Wednesday," she said. "I think Zain had to convert to Christianity when she married Angus, so it will be a Catholic funeral. But I don't know when it will be. As it's a murder, I mean. The police will have to continue—"

I interrupted her. "Tuesday night. That's when Angus plays cards in Port of Spain with his friends."

My mother said simply, "Yes."

Somehow we managed to end the call.

My mother had promised to call again as soon as she had all the details for the funeral, but when she reached me a day later she had other matters on her mind.

"Siddhani, I hope you won't mind, but I have something to ask you. Just a minute, I want to shut the door." There was a pause while she stepped away, then returned. "You there? I want to ask you something, but I don't want you to get annoyed, you hear? I am not asking this to quarrel with you. I think I know the answer, but I want to hear it from you."

My heart pounded. I thought I knew what was coming. I had already decided that Zain's murder was the work of Eric or of someone hired by Eric. Perhaps Eric had been caught and had said something to the police, to the papers, to the world, about Zain and me lying in the bed in her guest room.

Had the police arrested anyone? I quickly asked my mother. She said no, and then, bluntly, "I want to ask about the two of you, Siddhani."

I was relieved and panicked at once. She waited, and I remained quiet. She tried again.

"Well? Look, you're really mashed up about this thing. You're all alone up there. I don't know what to do. Were she and you—you know what I mean? Did you like her? Well, not *like*. Come on, you know what I mean."

My mother, I saw, was for the first time willing to talk to me—in an obtuse manner perhaps, but as best as she could—about this aspect of my life. But I dared not answer.

"Look, Siddhani, I am not asking to get annoyed," she reiterated. "I'm just worried about you."

Like the air released from a full, taut balloon, fear rushed out of me, and I was left oddly appreciative of this new interest and concern. I stumbled over my words, telling her that Zain "knew" about me. I trembled as I admitted that I'd always had strong feelings for Zain, but that she and I were never anything more than friends. And I hastened to add that, in any case, Zain hadn't been "that way" herself. I told my mother that Angus "knew" about me too, but even so he hadn't in the least minded Zain and me being friends. Even if Zain hadn't been married, I said, she wouldn't have been interested in me in that way.

Normally, I would not have liked to admit any of this; I would have preferred that anyone who wondered would never know the truth for sure. But on this occasion, still unable to fully process the fact of Zain's death, I felt an overwhelming relief at being able to voice all this to my mother.

I went on to explain that it was because of my intense friendship with Zain that I had come to realize I wanted as my partner in life someone who didn't need an interpretation of my home-ways, my home-vocabulary, who would know what I meant if I said, "I feel like a good lime tonight," or who understood without explanation what made a comforting homemade meal for a Saturday night, what food and rituals were fine for a Sunday lunch, for a picnic, for Christmas lunch. My mother remained silent throughout this rush of words, and I was emboldened to say that I wanted to be with someone who, no matter how this body of mine aged, would love me and continue to want to take care of me; I wanted to be with someone who would notice that the hem of my pants had come undone and, without asking or telling me, would have it mended; someone who would see that I had run out of toothpaste and would, without asking or making a fuss about it, pick some up on her way home. I told my mother that it was Zain, the woman, the Trinidadian, the wife, the mother, the friend, who had made me see the incongruity between what I was and what I wanted. And it was Zain who had made me realize that I would probably be alone for the rest of my life.

I stopped then, unable to go on, openly weeping. After a long silence, my mother replied simply that she would book the ticket for me to return for Zain's funeral.

———

The flight back to Trinidad to attend Zain's funeral seemed interminable, and yet it wasn't nearly long enough. I would arrive in a Trinidad where Zain no longer existed. We would not get in her car and drive off on adventures. I would never enter her guest room again. My face would not be touched by her long thin fingers. I remember thinking that it was useless to chastise myself and say, *If only I could have known the last time I was with you that I would never see you again*, because I couldn't imagine how such a sentence might be finished.

Throughout the flight I repeated, under my breath: "I am going to your funeral; I am going to Trinidad to attend your funeral." I recalled the dream I'd had during the previous night's terrible sleep. It was one I had dreamed a thousand times before: Zain and I stand in a room full of people, quite far from each other. Yet I can feel her skin against mine. Then we're in a bed. I know she's my friend, but she's lying in my arms. We're in a constant state of moving towards each other, and we look at each other's lips, but our lips never touch. A hollow plastic pipe, the kind used in plumbing, has replaced my backbone. It runs from my vagina to my chest. Its large hole makes a whooshing sound as air rushes through it unimpeded. I keep reaching behind my back to try to touch the hollow space, but it is as if I am backless. I want Zain to enter the pipe and fill me up so that I know I exist. When I wasn't remembering the dream, I pretended that Zain sat next to me. There was an intense knowing between us. It was the same knowing I had felt the first day of high school when I met Zain and she pinched my arm.

The airplane landed in Trinidad at five thirty in the morning. I had been here only weeks ago, yet I felt as if years had passed. Day broke as I stood waiting in front of the arrivals building at the airport. A heavy greyness, portending rain any minute, hung in the sky. But then the low clouds on the distant horizon took shape with the light and slowly transformed into the outline of the Northern Range. Ahead, the parking lot emerged. A wide umbrella of almond trees shaded the doubles vendors who had already stationed themselves beneath, and from the branches of the trees the sound of quarrelling parakeets crescendoed with the dawning day. I watched the light creep over the mountain ranges, incising deep vertical ridges and bringing out of the darkness the rich variety of trees. I shook my head hard, trying to make sense of the fact that all this before me was just as I had left it mere days before, but Zain was gone for good. Trinidad was still Trinidad. But Zain was not Zain. This was not as simple and obvious a thought as it may sound. No, it was a baffling, shameless, outrageous thought. How could Trinidad exist without my dearest Zain? As a result of this revelation, everything I experienced and thought on that particular journey to Trinidad, to Zain's funeral, felt stark and transparent. I saw the country, and the tenuousness of my place in it, as I never had before. I stood apart and watched.

A line of cars idled in place. Their drivers stood outside, leaning on car doors, ready to jump back in and make the circle if some authority were to move them along.

As I waited for my ride, my eyes wandered away from watching the sunrise over the mountains for no more than five minutes, and when I looked again, recognizable forms had emerged. My tongue danced inside my mouth: *banana, silk cotton, poui, immortelle, cannonball, breadfruit, mango, caimete, bois canot, nutmeg*—the words themselves becoming an umbilical cord. I picked out the roofs of houses, the silver of an unpainted galvanized roof, the fleck of a red one, one turquoise, and here and there light green patches of cultivated plots.

My father had insisted upon coming to meet me. I would have been happier if he had sent the driver to pick me up. Despite the reason for my trip this time, I couldn't shake the usual discomfort that I would not be rewarding his effort with a son-in-law and grandchildren in my tow.

I had considered dressing more formally than usual for this journey home, out of respect for Zain. But Zain had once, quite a while before, met me at the airport when I was wearing a pair of baggy blue jeans, a golf shirt printed with horizontal stripes in red, yellow, white and green, navy socks and blue leather Campers. She commented in her usual teasing way that if I had clutched a large book or briefcase across my chest, I would have passed for an impossibly cute young boy in desperate need of sartorial guidance. I was, of course, pleased, and Zain thereafter became interested in trying to help me dress in that very manner. So, I had decided to wear this outfit, even though I had long outgrown the style. Against my chest I clutched a green all-weather knapsack from Mountain Equipment Co-op in which I had placed all the letters Zain had ever written me.

One might imagine that as I waited for my father I was

preoccupied with thoughts of my dear dead friend, but self-consciousness, born of the habit of self-preservation, got the better of grief. I observed my fellow passengers, but so as not to have it confirmed that they were indeed judging me I did not let my eyes catch theirs. I was not, however, beyond judging them myself. This was again a matter of survival. I decided that the majority of the women passengers had dressed to show off their big-city accomplishments to the families they had once left and were now returning to. I saw that some had not removed their fancy leather and jean jackets with heavy fur collars, despite arrival in the tropics, that others had décolletage bedecked with gaudy pendants dangling from chunky necklaces, that several had hair that shone as if wet, piled high on their heads, while others had hair cornrowed so elaborately that one could construe the wearer's desire to make it known that it was possible in Canada to have one's hair done better than in Trinidad. There were flashy sparkling handbags, some in faux alligator skin, some in ultra shiny brown leather, some in ceiling-white plastic. I had also noticed among the returning passengers two women who were, I was willing to bet, "like myself." All three of us, I saw, took pains not to catch each other's eyes. We looked at our luggage, our watches, the hills, the changing sky; we read our passports and checked our return tickets.

We were all, I thought, counting on the probability that, simply by living in a big North American city, we would be greeted as warriors on our arrival back home by those who knew us and those who didn't alike. Greeted as champions.

I was a champ for giving up the perks of living with family, among friends whose families had known mine for generations, among people familiar to me from primary school days. I lived now without the deep comfort of neighbours who cooked more food than they needed for themselves so that they could parcel it up and bring you some. I had left behind strangers who, passing on the street, bid each other good day, and people who put off their own chores to lend you a hand. I had given up all of this in the hope that I would no longer have to live a lie, that I could, at last, come into my authentic self. So on this particular occasion I had dressed as I always did, to announce my individuality and assert that I had indeed found authenticity. No one here needed to know the truth or to question whether such authenticity was achievable. But, deep inside, I had a sudden burst of clarity as my thoughts turned to Zain: I understood that on my previous visits to Trinidad I had hoped that Mum, Dad, Gita, Jaan, and even Zain would admire me precisely because I had become yet a little more unrecognizable, a little more mysterious to them—but the price I paid for that illusion of mystery was steep.

At last Dad arrived, pulling his burgundy Jaguar carefully into a parking spot. The car had barely come to a stop before the trunk opened automatically, revealing an empty, immaculately clean, royal-blue carpeted area. Dad stepped out slowly and walked around the car to the sidewalk. Daylight had arrived in earnest by this time, the sky as blue as it would be, the glare strong.

With a lit cigarette between the fingers of his right hand, my father lightly gripped my shoulders, pulled me to him and patted my back. The greeting was over in a second. He dropped the cigarette on the asphalt, stepped on it and twisted his foot. The soles of his gleaming patent-leather shoes were thin, the warm weather here and the dependence on cars not warranting thick-soled protection. My father's performance with his cigarette was deliberate, a sort of preparation to lift my suitcase into the trunk.

"It's okay, Dad, I will get it," I said. "It's heavy."

I reached for the handle but he was firm. "No, no. Don't be silly."

In my peripheral vision I could see waiting passengers, taxi drivers and porters watching. My gesture, I surmised, had likely insulted my father. I backed away. My father gripped the suitcase handle, heaved upwards, but then struggled with the final lift into the trunk. I reached under and lent a hand up. Once the luggage was in, he shoved and shoved to move it to the far end of the trunk. Without looking at me, he mustered all the congeniality his pursed lips would permit.

"Well, we hadn't expected you'd be returning so soon."

Our drive home ought to have taken an hour but instead took more than twice that long. We were often at a standstill on the highway, sometimes going a full fifteen minutes without a single car budging an inch on the southbound lanes. I suggested turning off the engine, and realized I sounded exactly as I had hoped I wouldn't: almost immediately upon arriving I was imposing my North American–acquired righteousness regarding environmental issues. Dad countered that the heat off the asphalt and the exhaust from the cars in the lineup would be too unpleasant. After a while we noticed that the only cars coming through on the northbound side of the highway were police vehicles. Something major, we assumed, had stopped traffic both ways. Life will carry on, I thought, with both resignation and the sense of being cheated, and there will be events that will overtake and overshadow what has befallen Zain.

My father declared, as if it were his idea entirely, "I think this will put a strain on the air conditioning. I'm going to turn off the engine. We can turn down the windows, just for a few minutes. You don't mind, do you?" The question was rhetorical—he had already engaged the controls. Drivers and passengers, all men, had come out of their cars, strangers standing between the two lanes of cars pointing south, their chatter drifting through the open window, expressing resignation about being late for this or that, some lamenting they had left home so early especially to beat traffic, that they had not even had breakfast yet. Heat, like a curtain, blew into the car and with it the sting of exhaust, woodsmoke and spices from the curry powder factory located nearby. No birds could be heard but three corbeaux circled wide and slow high overhead. I wanted to ask if Zain's murderer had been found, but at the same time couldn't bring myself to mention her name just yet. Instead I suggested listening to the radio for possible news about what could be causing such a major jam. From station to station there was only music—Indian music, calypso, American pop music, advertisements. My father and I made uneasy small talk.

Finally, I could wait no longer and asked what had been on my mind. "So, any more news about what happened to Zain?"

He simply shook his head in resignation, and I tried again. "Has anyone been caught?"

"We're living in a barbaric society, Siddhani. There is no respect for life here anymore. The government doesn't respect the people, so they don't respect themselves or anyone else. The police haven't made a single arrest in any of the last dozen or so robberies, all of which have ended with at least one murder. Do you know how many murders we have had this year so far? It is June, and there have been 245. Just under 40 murders a month. More than one a day. This country has gone to hell."

I persisted, bringing the conversation back to Zain. "Do we know what was stolen from the house? I mean, was anything actually taken?"

My father looked at me directly for the first time since I had arrived. "Well, the news reports are still calling it a home invasion. I don't really understand what that means. We haven't heard that anything was stolen. I don't know what this country is coming to. It's so odd that nothing was taken. Nothing material, I mean. One can't help but wonder if Angus is involved in something shady and this was some sort of revenge, payback, you know, that sort of thing. It is surprising who is rumoured to be involved in high-level crime in this country. You hear about judges, the police, government ministers and certainly businessmen. We meet these people at cocktail parties, and the way they carry on— you know they must be involved in something. After all, the economy hasn't been so good in Trinidad for years now. No one can legally make the kind of money to have the life-styles these people have."

"I know Angus, Dad. Angus isn't involved in anything. He's not that kind of man, at all. I phoned and tried to speak with him, but he didn't say much; he was just crying. He said he didn't even know how the kids were doing. They were all numb."

My father turned practical. "Your mother sent flow-ers to Zain's parents and to Angus and the children. I've arranged for Tank to take you to the funeral. He'll wait for you, for as long as you want. I've told him that while you're here he'll be at your disposal. I think Gita might be coming over tonight. Yes, your mother mentioned that, actually."

The jam on the highway continued. I thought about turning the window down to ask the driver beside our car what he saw from his vantage point, but felt I should ask first if this was all right to do. My father said at once, "Good idea. Let me ask him." He leaned across me to call through my window. The driver, a balding man with a moustache and wearing a sleeveless mesh vest, was already looking at us, as if he had anticipated the interaction.

He smiled and said, "Dr. Mahale, I say to myself is your car self. You going good, boss?"

My father smiled in return. "How are you, man? A hell of a thing, this traffic, eh?"

I knew from his tone that he hadn't recognized the man. Our neighbour said that as far as he could see, nothing was moving, and that the lanes on the other side were clear.

When the man turned away, I asked Dad if he knew him, and indignation and pride were bound up in his one-word answer, "No!" He leaned down discreetly and looked at the writing on the side of the truck. It said, in green letters, *Ramdeen Transport*. "I know of the company, you see their trucks all over, but I don't know this man personally. In any case, he is probably just a driver."

He turned the engine on so that the air conditioning would cool the car. A minute later he turned it off again. He did this several times.

Suddenly, a wave of annoyance washed over me, and just short of snapping, I said, "I don't understand how you can stand this sort of thing, Dad. Why do you all put up with such inconvenience and so much slackness? It's probably an accident due to speeding or another murder. Somebody's been killed, probably. But that's just par for the course here, it seems."

"It's unbelievable, isn't it," my father calmly agreed.

"Yes, but how can you put up with it? Nothing changes in this place."

"Things are improving, Siddhani. Things do change, but slowly. It's harder on people like you who go away and see how things are done elsewhere. I'm sure it's all relative, though. You must have the sense over there that change comes slowly too. Don't you?"

I realized that what I really wanted was to talk more—more openly, more directly—about Zain's murder. But I couldn't. It was easier this way.

"I don't understand why you stay," I said. "How come you and Mom don't leave?"

"We're too old for that now. That sort of move doesn't make sense at our age. All our friends are here, my golfing friends, your mother's family connections, which mean everything to her. We'd have to make friends all over if we went somewhere new, and at our age that won't be easy. The weather too. You know, I can't stand the cold. That's why we haven't left. You know what I always think about when I imagine living abroad? Slipping on ice in front of my own house. Having to shovel snow and scrape ice myself. And, yes, slipping. From what I hear, people do things for themselves over there. I can't imagine cleaning my car myself, or even my golf clubs and shoes after a game."

"But why didn't you leave years ago, when you were younger?"

"Oh, Sid, it's not that easy. I am 'somebody' here. Everybody knows me. People know who we are. With my connections I get things done overnight, not only for us, but also for other people. I don't think I would have had that kind of clout in Canada or the States. Life is easier for us here than it would have been even in England. If we'd wanted to go to the States or to Canada I'd have had to take my medical exams all over again, to start over to build a practice. I suppose I could have done something entirely different, but we're living the life we've always known. Can you imagine me behind a counter in a convenience store? I'd rather die. Or live here." He chuckled, then continued more seriously, "You know, it does bother your mother and me that you can't live in Canada the way you can here. No one over there, I am sure, knows who you are, whose child you are. We still wish you'd come home and settle back down here. Life would be easier here for you. Don't you think so? It's not too late, you know. If you wanted to return I would make a few calls and you'd have a choice of jobs in no time."

I opened my mouth to reply, but at just that moment, people began getting into their cars, and the thrum of engines started up. I knew there was no use in responding.

We started off slowly, and as cars began to stream past on the other side as if a bridge over a causeway had been let down or the guard at a rail crossing cleared, the traffic in our lane picked up speed and carried on without a hitch all the way down the highway. We saw not a single thing that could have warranted such a halt.

Dad used his controls to turn up our windows and he switched on the air conditioner. I allowed myself to sink into the seat and into sleep. It was only as we arrived at the turnoff from the main road that would take us into the residential area where my family had lived since I was seven years old that my father said softly, "Sid, we're here."

I came reluctantly out of sleep, wanting to stay in the place I had gone to, where I had just said to Zain, "Look at the crabs," and she had answered, "That's you, Sid, that's just how you move." I had heard her correctly, but I responded lightly, "Did you say stealthy, like a cat?"

"No, you fool," she said. "Sideways. Sideways, like a crab."

I teased her: "Oh, you have to talk louder. The waves and the wind. I can't hear you."

As I woke, she was chiding and teasing, "You have to clean your ears. I can't talk any louder. You want me to lose my voice or what? You move like a crab, is what I said. But learn to walk like me. Like a cat. One foot in front of the other."

The sunlight, the stunning silver of the sea ahead, jolted me into the day, and I caught my breath. We were at the very spot where, as children, my sister and I would be awakened from the sleep we'd fallen into on the long return drive from Port of Spain or the beaches at Mayaro or Maracas. Again, despite my recent visit, I felt as if I were seeing everything for the first time. The old jacaranda tree in the Atkins' yard was in full bloom. The De Francos' tall white undulating fence, their rambling concrete house, disappearing and reappearing through a forest of landscaping, was not as shamelessly imposing as I'd always thought, but suddenly as reassuring as a cup of fragrant morning tea. The street off to the side, just before the De Franco house, made me remember—as it always did—poor little Johnny Maingot. I was eight when Johnny tore off his left-hand ring finger. It was his fifth birthday and he was wearing the ring his parents had given him as a present. At the party he tried to scale the chain-link fence around his family's house. He fell, but the ring caught on a loose piece of wire. His father rushed him to our house, imagining that Dad could reattach the finger right there in the home surgery. I hadn't seen the accident but, oh, so many years later, I still have a picture in my mind of every detail, even the finger tearing off on the fence, as if I had observed it all. I had wondered at the time if, because it was his left-hand ring finger, this meant that he was no longer marriageable. As it turned out, Johnny got a girl pregnant when he and she were in their last year of high school. They married and he took a job as an insurance salesman in one of his parents' friend's businesses. I knew this because my mother kept me up-to-date on news about everyone.

Just ahead was the Gulf, its water an uninviting grey-brown. The sky was clear all the way across. It was one of those days when one could see from my parents' property the faint blue of the northern arm of the island where Angus and the children were, and where Zain used to be. I turned my window down halfway and felt the breezes, heard the bird sounds and dogs barking.

The metal rollers of the automated ten-foot-high sliding gate grated along their track. Musa and Bunny, the two family dogs, came running down the side of the house.

The back door was unlocked, and Joan, who had worked for my family for several years, came out. She hugged me in such a way that I knew she was telling me she was sorry about

Zain. I nodded in greeting to Bhoodoosingh, our yardman. He mumbled back, "Mornin', Miss. You come back already. I sorry to hear about your friend." Bhoodoosingh brought in my bag, leaving it just inside the door to my bedroom.

Now Mum came briskly towards me, her hair groomed and makeup fresh. She offered a warmer hug than I had received from Dad.

She gave an unsure half-smile, biting one corner of her lower lip as she said, "Are you all right? How was the flight?"

Her look held so much that was unspoken, and it made me want to cry. Seeing this, she quickly said, "Come, let's go and eat. Joan made breakfast for you."

Mum, Dad and I headed down to the breakfast table. Dad kept a notepad and ballpoint pen on a butler's cart that was parked behind his chair. He took up the pad and, putting on his glasses, read quietly. Then he set it down next to his plate and alternated taking in mouthfuls of food with listing his day's tasks. After a while, he looked up and asked Mum about her supply of pills. Mum replied that she had enough to last the week. He took off his glasses and looked at me. What were my plans for the day? he asked. I said I had no plans. I was tired. I might take a nap. My father mentioned that he'd had the pool cleaned yesterday for me. It was lovely out there and I should go in today before it was dirtied with ash from farmers illegally burning cane. And did I need Tank right away for anything?

I thanked him and repeated my desire to stay close to home. My father put down his knife and fork and stood up.

He patted Mum on her head, squeezed my shoulder and left for the day.

Mum called Joan, and the two of them began discussing what was in the fridge that needed to be used up and what was to be bought in the grocery and in the market that day. I sat in the kitchen for some moments, listening to their voices against the purring of the large fan that kept the area cool.

Then I rose and went to my old, familiar room and lay on my bed—Musa and Bunny having taken up their usual positions at the foot of it. Cool air pumped noisily from the outdated air-conditioning unit. The room's concrete walls had been painted recently. Drawn curtains over the windows, which were protected by wrought-iron grilles on the outside, kept out the heat of the mid-day sun and darkened the room. I switched on the ceiling light. It shone through a thick square shade of frosted glass on which were etched in fine gold lines Snow White, Cinderella and a fairy godmother, all united by waves of silver-painted ribbons. This had been my bedroom since I was ten years old. I thought: I am in the country of my birth, in the neighbourhood and house I have known since I was a child, in my own bedroom. My mother is outside, and the gardener I have known since I was a teenager is in the yard. This is my home.

Still, I felt more alone than ever. More alone than I had felt in Canada where I had no relatives, where I travelled the same streets daily and yet hardly ever crossed paths with people I knew, where I lived in rooms that stored no childhood memories. Which was my real life? I wondered.

The one in Trinidad, where we had the same neighbours for more than forty years, where I knew people who could tell me what I was like as a child, where a stranger at the mall would stop me and chat because I looked so much like my mother or father, or identical to my grandmother? Or was my real life the one I lived in Canada, where there was no one to be compared with, or to disappoint?

A strand of grey cobweb hanging from the ceiling billowed in time to the pulsing air-conditioning unit.

I suddenly wondered why I had bothered to return for Zain's funeral. Hardly anyone in Trinidad knew the true closeness I had with Zain. It occurred to me that in all the years I had visited her I had spent time at her house and eaten meals with her and Angus and sometimes the two children, but she and I would never meet up with friends of hers or of mine. Save for this last time. Save for Eric. Granted, I myself had never initiated getting together with other friends, but the fact that neither had she hit me now like a revelation. Could she have felt some small reserve about being seen to be friends with someone like me?

In the eyes of all who would attend the funeral, who was I to her? No one there would know the depth of my grief, the primacy of my presence. Who would know how she had touched me and let me hold her in the privacy of her guest room? If I were asked if we had ever kissed, or been sexual with each other, I would truthfully say we hadn't, but my answer would elide the intensity of our bond and the intimacy that at times had blinded me, and that she had felt too. Zain had secrets, and Eric and I were among them. What did it say about me, I wondered, that I knew about Eric and that he knew about me?

If a suspicion had ignited in the recesses of my mind when I learned from my mother's terrible telephone call that Zain's murder had taken place on a Tuesday night, it now, suddenly, flared: because of what Eric knew, because of how he felt about me and people like me, because of how violently hateful he'd been about Zain's closeness with me, because the murder had happened on a Tuesday night and not any other night, because I no longer felt I knew Zain as well as I had thought and therefore wasn't certain that she'd actually broken off the relationship with Eric as she'd told me she'd done, or that she'd got the house key back from him—because of all this, I knew beyond doubt that it could only have been Eric who had ransacked the house and taken Zain's life. Perhaps he hadn't meant for it to end the way it did. Perhaps he didn't even do it himself, but I was convinced he was behind it. I hated Eric. No, I didn't simply hate him; thoughts of him turned into images of his body parts rotting, flies buzzing around his intestines as maggots twisted and turned and evolved into more flies that laid more eggs in his entrails.

A worrisome thought intruded on these ghastly ones: might he actually show himself at the funeral?

There was a knock on the door. Mum came in carrying her own glass and sat on the edge of the bed. She immediately noticed the billowing cobweb and sucked her teeth in irritation. "But I told Joan to clean out this room properly.

Joan doesn't look up, and she doesn't look down. I bet she didn't sweep under the beds either." She inspected Joan's work in the room as she spoke. "Why don't you go down and lie in the billiard room with the sliding doors open all the way? It's the coolest part of the house. That would be better than being cooped up on your first day home in this room with the air conditioner on, wouldn't it?"

Now Joan entered with a glass of lime juice for me and a plate with a slice of fruitcake. "Joan," Mum said crossly, "but I thought I asked you to give this room a thorough cleaning. You didn't bother to cobweb? You'll have to do it, eh."

Mum finally turned to me. "You're pale. Are you all right?"

I contemplated telling Mum what I'd been thinking: that I thought I knew who Zain's murderer was. But I immediately saw that if I were to do so, I would have to explain, and in doing so I would divulge Zain's secret affair with Eric. I would also have to reveal to my mother that Eric had expressed his disgust for me, for people like me. I would have to tell Mum that I had been lying on the bed in Zain's guest room—that Zain had been lying there with me, and that she had rested her head on my shoulder as she slept, that my arm was around her—when someone—it could only have been Eric—entered the house and saw us like that. I imagined Mum translating the word *seen* into *caught*. I felt shame as I thought of all this, shame that I was the subject of Eric's scorn and hatred. I would surely cause my mother to feel shame, too, I thought. In any case, such a serious allegation would likely lead Mum to call my father at his office right away, and my father would only insist that we go immediately to the police. I saw in an instant the suspicion I would bring on Zain and her family, on myself and my family. In the end, it would likely be said that it was my behaviour, that it was *I* who had caused Zain's murder.

My mother had correctly surmised that I was consumed by thoughts of Zain, and responded to my silence by rubbing my leg to comfort me. We sat like that for some minutes, in silence. Then she said, "Imagine how Angus and the children are. They must be so mashed up."

I did not answer. She turned to being her pragmatic self again, and asked, "Did you bring something appropriate to wear to the funeral?"

I muttered that I had.

"You're not wearing pants to it, are you?"

I decided not to argue with her so soon after arriving and merely said that I had made sure to bring something suitable.

She told me to give my clothing to Joan to take into the laundry room, as it was Fatty the ironer's day to work. She continued, "If you go down into the billiard room, keep the glass sliding doors open all the way, but don't unlock the wrought-iron gate. You'll get the sea breeze there. And you'll see what I've been doing with the garden without having to go outside. Whatever you do, don't unlock that gate. It's safer that way. Or why don't you go into the pool? The sun has gone off it now."

I questioned the logic, knowing full well that the rules applied to the goings-on in this house were always determined by my mother. "So, it's not safe to open the door, but it's safe to go out there to the pool?"

"Well, Bhoodoosingh is out there. No one will bother to come where there is someone working."

Mum was uneasy. I could see that her mind was busy. Her hand was still resting on my leg. She tapped my leg, suddenly, as if it were a door, and looked at me searchingly. "Sid, I was wondering, whatever happened to that little boy? Jonathan. I don't hear you talking about him at all."

She never ceased to surprise me. "I haven't seen him in years," I said. "I last saw him when I left his mother. What makes you ask?"

"I sometimes think of him. He was such a nice little child. He liked you a lot. You were with him for, what? Ten years? Why don't you see him?"

"I would like to, but it's not so simple."

"You see, this is what I don't understand. That child must have suffered when you just disappeared on him like that."

I realized, in an instant, that by honing in on Jonathan, my mother was expressing, as best as she could, her worry about me in this time of my loss. Still, I sat up sharply. "I didn't just disappear, Mum." But before I could defend myself, she carried on.

"That is the problem with those kinds of relationships. I don't understand how you could bring up a child like that and then just move on."

"But straight couples do it all the time."

"Don't be ridiculous. They don't do it all the time. In any case, that is what marriage is for."

Aware that we were now locked in our usual dance of push and pull, and grateful to her for this backhanded caring, I lightened up and teased. "Oh, so you're advocating on behalf of lesbians for the right to marry, now?"

My mother sucked her teeth and got up. At the door she turned, the compassion that was being so indirectly conveyed by her words evident in her drawn features. She said, "If you had stayed in that relationship, you would have had a child of, what? Sixteen years, now? You wouldn't be going into your older years on your own. You would have someone in your old age." No doubt embarrassed by this display of emotion, my mother couldn't leave it at that. She had to add, "You're not getting younger, you know. And you're clearly not looking after yourself. Look at you. You've seen how slim Gita is keeping herself, and she has a son! I don't understand all of this instability, this kind of life you people live."

Like a child, I yelled, "Mu-um," ready again to engage with her, but she walked out and closed the door behind her.

It was unlikely that Mum would follow me out into the sun, so I decided to camp out by the pool. On that day, the light seemed brighter than I had ever known it to be. I found myself having contradictory and mawkish thoughts:

how dare a day without Zain be so radiant, and could such
brilliance be the result of Zain looking down, beaming
on our little island? The lawn was an even dark green in
colour, and each fat blade of grass lay against the next in a
haphazard yet perfect pattern carpeting the earth beneath.
The garden had grown thicker and older, more lush. A new
planting here or there was a pleasant surprise and I made a
mental note of each: they could be a neutral topic of conversation between my mother and me. The bougainvillea
I remembered as a small shrub growing out of a pot now
trailed over the pool's back fence and was covered along the
top with indigo flowers. Hibiscus, datura, ferns, ornamental
grasses, dracaenas, and heliconias known as sexy pink, were
all perfect, like specimens from a botanical garden. They
were Mum's pride, and I felt my own swell remembering
the name of each. A grey-green lizard about six inches long
ran along the midrib of a low-hanging branch of one of the
dwarf coconut trees, the toes of its feet splayed. It lifted its
upper body, pushed itself up on its front legs and turned its
head to watch me. We stared at each other. It blinked first.
Clouds so thin they were almost invisible passed in front of
the sun, and the brilliant light dimmed ever so slightly for
a second or two before becoming blindingly bright again.
When we were children we were often warned not to look
directly at the sun. We'd go blind, we were told. But such
light compelled one to turn in the direction of its source.
I did so, and reflected on how Zain and I had gotten away
with so much when we were together. She was my foil, my

alibi, the screen behind which I could be myself. Now what?

The lizard dropped its elbows, lowered its body back onto the leaf's spine and stared straight down its skeletal nose. The skin under its neck, lighter in colour than its back, was fleshy. I thought of Jonathan, sixteen then, probably too old to care about lizards.

More than once, even as I reflected on Zain's death, painfully aware of her absence, I made the move to rush back inside the house to telephone her and announce that I'd arrived home, to ask her to come and fetch me and take me for a drive around the country. I was in my parents' house, in my childhood home, but I was lost. What was I here in Trinidad, without my dearest Zain?

Everything within the gates of this property, I reflected, is mine to share with Gita. The pool, the ample wrought-iron chairs and tables, the bird baths, the avocado tree, the lime tree, the mango trees, the anthurium lilies, the orchids, the philodendron as large as a living room in a downtown Toronto apartment, the dracaena reaching up as high as a billboard, even that lizard, the butterflies, roaches, spiders, mosquitoes, beetles, bees and birds. These are all more mine, I thought, than not. They are more mine than all the birds in Toronto, than the snakes and turtles at Leslie Street Spit, the orange-and-black butterflies bobbing about my second-floor balcony in early fall will ever, *can* ever be. More mine than the yellow-jacket wasps that tap their antennae on the screen door of the balcony of my apartment on Bergamot Avenue in Toronto's East End.

The pool was the first built in our neighbourhood. Now it seemed so much smaller than it had when I was a child and swimming its length had been a test of strength, courage and worth. Half a dozen strokes and I would conquer it now. The water was crystal clear that day and the sun ignited the ripples caused by the breeze. Everything sparkled.

I sat on its steps, taking in the warm sun and reflecting that I had been living "abroad," away from my parents, for about twenty years by this time. Mum and Dad had been very young when they had Gita and me, and I was now older than they had been when I immigrated to Canada. Yet I was their child when I left, and so many years later, with so much distance between them and me, I continued to be their child, an obvious fact that seemed almost incomprehensible and miraculous, for I was in many ways a stranger to them, and they to me. I reflected that no walls had been torn down or built up in our house, the flooring remained the same, the parameters of the yard were unchanged. But the trees I remembered as saplings now had trunks I could barely wrap my arms around. The house had been painted numerous times since it had been built some thirty years before, but always in the same off-white colour. Some pieces of furniture had changed, but the living room was the same as the day I first left for Toronto, and so was my bedroom, and my parents' bedroom, and the library in which Gita and I had studied and where Dad still kept a desk—except that it now held a computer. The physical aspect of the place had not changed. And neither had our relationship to one another. Yes, I was still their child, and my parents were still my parents, regardless of all that we did not witness of each other's lives when we were apart.

What might I have become had I not left? Was remaining in Canada an act of courage or was it timidity? I certainly didn't feel like a returning champ in front of my parents. I slid into the warm water. Keeping my eyes open, I dived under and splayed my hands on the concrete at the bottom. I thrust my feet up, pointing my toes to the sky. I stayed like this for several long seconds. When I stood again, my eyes stung, and cool air hit my body, and an acute awareness of my present washed over me: there on the pool's ledge was a sweating glass of lime juice made by my family's housekeeper, there just beyond was the yellow-green of the dwarf coconut trees waving up to the transparent blue of the sky, and there, farther off, was a variety of birds, carrying on like competing vendors in a market. In Toronto, no one save India and Jonathan, neither of whom I was in touch with, could have accurately pictured me in those surroundings. My sense of belonging was as profound as my feeling of aloneness. I dreaded attending the funeral I had come for.

I arrived at the church twenty minutes early, and yet all the pews in the church were full. People stood at the back, along the sides, and clogged the main entrance and the two side doorways. I took my place at the back, hidden. I scoped out every corner, and moved a bit this way or that so that

I could glimpse from behind pillars. I carefully scanned the face of every man in the church, my heart thumping in fear, and in my distraction I missed most of what was being said throughout the service and the eulogies. But Eric was nowhere to be seen. I even stepped out of the church partway through, and circled the building looking for him, before squeezing back inside. When I was sure he wasn't present I joined the queue and paid my respects. I rested my hand on the blond, highly polished wood casket. It was smooth and slippery, and unyielding, and I had to tell myself that if I began to cry, I would surely fall apart and I would be unable to put myself back together again. I would bring unwanted notice to myself. I imagined myself being watched instead, and was able to walk past her casket knowing that that was as close as I'd ever be to Zain again.

I went to Angus, who sat in the front pew with Zain's parents and the children, Aliya and Peter. He had not known that I had come back and when I approached he stood and wrapped his arms around me. I wanted to say something, but I couldn't speak. He pressed me to his chest and kissed the top of my head. I remained in his tight embrace for what seemed like minutes. Neither he nor I spoke. Aliya asked in a barely audible voice if I was coming to the cemetery. I hesitated, and she asked me if I would instead stop by their house that night.

When I left the funeral, I asked Tank to drive past the yacht club. I knew where Eric kept his boat, and that it could be seen from the road. His boat was not visible, though, and this further confirmed my suspicion. Just to be certain, I had Tank drive in to the yacht club. I had him stop at High Tide restaurant where Zain and I and Eric had eaten a short time before, and where Eric was known. As if I were a regular, I asked the waiter who met me at the door what had happened to Eric's boat. She told me that he had come in two days ago to let them know that he was taking off on a trip up the islands; by the end of the day he'd pulled up and out. "Just like that?" I said, and she answered, "Yeah, that's how all these boating people are."

That evening I did visit Zain's house, as Aliya had requested, but I could not bear to stay long. The passageway that led to the guest room both called out to me and repelled me. It gnawed on me that I had failed to do something, something that might have prevented Zain's murder, something that might have led to an arrest. Weakened by remorse and guilt, I did not have it in me to be more polite, or to consider that Angus, Aliya and Peter had little choice but to carry on living in that very house. I left without eating or drinking any of the offerings. Within days, I returned to Toronto.

All this, I hope, will count as some sort of answer for you, Jonathan. But there is, of course, more to tell. There is the walk.

The very week I was back in Toronto, I went and saw a doctor and began the process of counselling. I had my body measured and my mind assessed. I knew that I would not do anything to myself while Mum and Dad were alive, and that perhaps they would live for such a long time it would mean I'd never reach my goal. I am somewhat ashamed to say I waited for that freedom. In the meantime, I was encouraged to join a peer group who were at various stages of the process that some of them called *transitioning*. In such a way, I became part of a community where I met people whom one did not usually, in those days, see in the streets. I met men whose gender, height and sturdy limbs were ill-disguised behind long hair, hair that was coiffed into exaggerated women's styles. They wore makeup, nail polish, dresses and women's shoes with heels. They went by women's names and were referred to, with remarkable ease, as "she" and "her." I was quite drawn to one person in the group, a Chinese woman who had chosen to be female. At first, I would stare at her, in vain, to try to see traces of the man she once was. She was the only person in the group whose voice and demeanour did not betray the fact that she had started out as a man. She had not, I saw, merely changed her physical body; it was as if she had studied and taken on the thoughtfulness and graciousness traditionally expected of her new gender. I was moved by her, and yet there were moments when, regarding her, I felt sadness, and saw that whatever she had gained by this change must certainly have come at a cost. The people in this group often talked about the price they had paid—the loss, that is, of family, friends, employment—but they always concluded with testimonials about having achieved a rare inner peace.

I also met women who went by men's names. The women wore their hair short, not as a woman might, but with an exaggeration that paralleled that of the men with women's hair. Some of these women were well along in their process of transformation and had already had their chests reconstructed surgically. Others bound their breasts. They wore boys' or men's clothing, and shoes that were clearly a size or two bigger than their feet, and, regardless of their age, had the attractive awkwardness, the intriguing mix of bravado and shyness of teenaged boys. Neither the men nor the women were flamboyant like cross-dressers and transsexuals, but they moved about, at least in our sessions together, with a quiet confidence I admired. Whenever I entered the room where we gathered and I saw the ones who were no longer women but were not men either, my chest would heave, and from deep inside would well a confusion of emotions. I would be breathless with the excitement of recognition. I would want to collapse with relief at the prospect of my own change. I would feel envy and impatience that I was not further along on my own path. But I felt fear, too, that in becoming like them I would find too late that I had given up more than I had intended to, fear that there were steps on the journey that, once taken, were irreversible.

As time went by, and I was provoked by the group to become clearer and firmer about my needs, my goals and my reasons for this journey, I knew that I did not simply want to embrace within myself what some in the group called "a female masculinity." This seemed to mean taking on the appearance and manner of boyish and masculine women, and I already fit that mould. What I felt in my very bones was that I could no longer live my life as a woman; I no longer wanted to be identified by others as a woman, and treated, as a result, in predictable and predetermined ways. It was easier to change myself than to wrestle with society. Above all, I desperately needed a kind of annihilation, and a rebirth. I did not want to stand next to a woman and feel, ever again, that I had to guard my love for her, or that I dared not touch her in public in the ways I wanted. Never again did I want to cower, or to be with a woman who in private would allow me to love her, yet in public would feel shame or fear to be seen with me. I did not want to live in a body that was scorned by men, that triggered the need in others to subdue it—to subdue me. I did not want a body that attracted hatred and brought harm to those women I cared about. A body that could not protect her. Looking back now, I realize that no one had ever asked me directly if I wanted to be a man, for I would have had to answer "no." I remember saying, however, I could not bear the body in which I—this "I" quite separate from any body—existed. I suppose that was good enough for my peers. Perhaps many of them shared my sentiments, but our options then were black and white, between this and that. The grey area of freedom we longed for existed only in dreams. I was coaxed to dress, to negotiate streets and to engage in encounters with people as if my surgical and hormonal transformation were a *fait accompli*. And regardless of how strangers might have viewed me, I felt the power of this.

Even as I found strength among these people, I knew we had little in common besides the goal of physical transformation, and after a couple of unfulfilling attempts at romances with "peers," I allowed my circle to grow smaller. My parents passed away some years later, one not too long after the other. I returned each time for their funerals. My feelings, in the end, were complex and confusing—being without parents conferred on me a new kind of aloneness. I felt, to say the very least, naked and lost and frightened, as if my parents and I had been inseparable. But lurking alongside these real and deep feelings was excitement, impatience and a blind hopefulness.

And so, one snowy morning, I made my way, walking alone, from my apartment on Bergamot Avenue to the clinic where my body's transformation would begin. I legally changed my name from Siddhani Mahale to Sydney Mahale, knowing full well that I would—more likely than not—thereby cut myself off from all whom I had so dearly loved. I was embarking on the chance to appear on the outside as I wished myself to be inside. I would reinvent myself in my own image, on my own terms and, finally, enter a life of fulfillment.

If it weren't for your search for me, Jonathan, you and I would not have reunited. And if, in the end, anything was fulfilled, it was not through my actions. It was because of you. Your presence in my life is the bigger part of that fulfillment. The smaller is to tell you this story.

———

It is only in writing down Sydney's story that I have gradually understood the truth: Had he simply come straight out with an explanation or a defence delivered in distilled sentences—for instance, if he had bluntly said that our family broke up because my mother wanted a different kind of lover for herself and parent for her son—I would have heard only a string of words held together by the conventions of syntax. What would I have understood by this?

Or, had he said directly, "Ah well, Jonathan, you see I changed myself so drastically because I expected it would be easier for me to cut a path in the world with women, and love, and art exhibits and sales, and shopping for clothing, and just existing in society, and I thought that it would afford me a surer respect. I thought, that is, that it would help me to rise tall in the eyes of people like your mother," I would certainly not have understood.

Had he explained to me that he returned to Trinidad after living in Canada for more than fifteen years because there wasn't a soul he could ask to accompany him to the hospital, I might have granted that this hinted at something profound, and was perhaps darkly humorous, but I might also have thought that he was lacking in fortitude.

Had he taken a minute, or even a day, to share with me that he'd returned to Trinidad because the changes he made to himself had not made life easier for him but had only alienated and isolated him further, I might have thought that he was weak and cowardly. I might have been scornful.

Had he told me in a brief sentence or two about the

day he lay on his bed with a fever, so sick that he couldn't go
to the drugstore to get the simplest aids such as throat loz-
enges and a box of NeoCitran, and decided then that it was
time to return to Trinidad, I might not have wanted to hear
of his isolation and might have buried myself in my writing.
But then again, this might not have been a bad thing, for it
has been nine years, from the day I found Sydney here in
Scenery Hills, since I have been able to produce a worth-
while piece of sustained writing.

Had he told me long ago, when I first inquired about
Zain's whereabouts, that he thought he knew who had killed
his best friend, I would have been horrified that he had not
taken his suspicions to the police and would have insisted
that he do so immediately. I would not have understood the
repercussions of such an act for a person like Sid, much less
the consequences of a friendship with a person like Sid for
a woman like Zain. I would not have understood that, even
in death, Sydney wanted to preserve Zain's good name and
that of her family.

Sydney knew that I had to hear *all* of the stories, in a
seemingly digressive way, for *any* to make sense in the end.
But more than this, Sydney knew what I myself did not, not
then: that in my presence he was on trial. He cared enough, I
understand now, to give me through his stories every nuance
of evidence so that I would make my judgement fairly.

4

By nighttime, Sydney could only whisper, but his memories burned bright. He had talked, stopped and seemed to reflect, and then carried on in little spurts, for hours. It was clear—and fair enough, I suppose—that there were things he kept to himself, but still, a fuller picture of this storyteller who had once been my other mother had emerged. When he was satisfied that he had told me all that he had wanted me to know, his breathing became shallow. He no longer asked that I hold off from calling for help.

He was in the hospital for three days. I spent most of my time there, returning to the house only twice to wash and change.

Rosita came to the hospital at mealtimes and returned to the house in between. The first time she visited she brought Sydney and me a breakfast of rotis wrapped in tea cloths and a dish of potatoes she'd fried with onions and cumin. She brought the good plates, knives, forks and glasses and orange juice she had herself made that very morning. She set it all out as if we were at a picnic and announced, "No sugar in anything." Sydney seemed pleased. We both ate, I shyly but with much appreciation, the aroma of the potato dish enveloping us, making a family of the three of us in the sterile room.

Afterwards, Rosita was gently persuaded by a nurse that the hospital would provide Sydney's meals according to the in-house nutritionist's recommendations. Pique flickered across Rosita's face, but only those of us who knew her saw it. It was Sydney's kindness to her that he refused to allow the nurses to help him with his food and drink, and it was Rosita who from then on fed him. She quarrelled, naturally, about what she saw as scandalous ineptitude on the part of the hospital's cook. "This hospital don't have a cook. Whoever make this food is no cook. This food tasteless for so. How they expect people to get better eating so?" she muttered. I humoured her, saying that it was probably meant to encourage patients to get well so that they could get out of there fast.

Sydney was happy with the attention and company. Between him and me there existed a new closeness. He had bared himself to me the previous day, but I held no power over him. Although he was the one who had done the talking, his divulgences had the effect of making me equally vulnerable before him.

Sydney was a novelty at the hospital. Nurses, including ones who were not assigned to his care, came into the room.

They gawked at him. And I saw them watching me too. From their awkwardness and uneasy half-smiles, I imagined they were curious about my relationship to this Indian-Trinidadian man who had once been a woman. Questions, however, were not directly put forward, except when one nurse asked, "You know him good, eh?" I offered that nurse no other explanation than my own half-smile. More than once I heard a snicker from a nurse or a doctor in the corridor outside Sydney's room, or the tail end of laughter, and worried that it was at Sydney's expense. But when I thought about going out and confronting the situation I realized that I wasn't one hundred percent certain the laughter was directed at Sydney. I had never cried "prejudice" before and certainly didn't have evidence or the vocabulary to make a convincing case for the accusation. I considered simply stepping into the corridor outside the room, standing there with my arms crossed and a stern face, but I decided that I might alienate those who could have an effect on Sydney's health and life. Still, I cannot deny that I felt some shame and confusion about what he—or should that be *she*—had done to his—or *her*—body, despite all that he had so recently told me. In time, the jeering ceased. Or perhaps I simply stopped listening to it.

The first morning at the hospital, after Rosita returned to the house, I was touched when Sydney, still weak but able to sit up a few minutes at a time, asked if I would shave him. I had not touched his face since I was a child. In fact, I had never before touched "his" face. I set a small basin of cool water on a trolley, alongside a towel and a thin lavender washcloth, a can of shaving cream, a disposable Bic and a small bottle of bayleaf-scented aftershave lotion, all brought to the room, on request, by a nurse—and I began. I cupped his face in my hand and thought of Zain. I held him by his jaw to turn his head. How Zain must have loved Sid. She might not have called it "love," but she must have felt it. How could she not? The scent of the fried cumin and the onions from breakfast that had mixed with the usual hospital smells were obliterated by the astringently sterile, yet oddly reassuring fragrance of shaving cream. I lathered Sydney's face, perhaps more than was necessary, with the tips of my fingers, stealing all the time—from the past, the present and the future—that the sense of touch, burdened with such a task, might grant, and perhaps it was only my wishful imagination, but I believe I felt the old familiar bones beneath his skin. I felt the weight of what he had shared with me the day before, and the weight of his life. As I pulled the Bic up his neck—here he raised his head, exposing it for me—I felt a purer love for this man than I had known before. Throughout the time I shaved him, no less than four nurses stopped by to watch. And now, months later, it is the coolness of his skin, the contouring of his face, the sudden, not-too-late, somatic intimacy that stays with me.

That day, Sydney asked me if I would be so good as to make sure that there was food in the house so that Rosita could cook proper meals for those of us there. My job was simply to check with Rosita, and I was to give Sankar money—he told me where I would find it—for whatever was needed and to send him to fetch it. On two occasions over the next day and a half, when Rosita, Lancelot and Sankar came to the hospital, Sydney asked me to pass him his bag, took out a few dollar bills and requested I go to the hospital's cafeteria to purchase Solo soft drinks and a package of Teatime tea biscuits for them. I was moved, realizing that he was in sickness as he had always been in health.

Doctors came and went. Sydney was wheeled away for X-rays and an ultrasound, and after each interminable time he was wheeled back to his room, where I waited. Nurses came and went too, and I believe that over time they warmed to us. One doctor, a small black man with tortoiseshell glasses, called me into the hallway outside the room and asked what my relationship to Sydney was. I fumbled before telling the white lie that Sydney had been like a father to me from the day I was born. In the fraction of a second that he considered my answer, I prepared myself for what might come: curiosity, argument, lectures, opinions and judgements. I was ready now to fight. But when the doctor spoke, it was to inform me that there was pneumonia in Sydney's lungs, that this was the main problem, the priority. He reassured me that Sydney was strong, Sydney was stubborn, and it was only a matter of time before the tablets worked.

I was as momentarily relieved at this news as I was gradually disheartened. I wanted to believe the doctor, but couldn't shake the idea that I knew better. How was it that I, but not the doctors, could see that there was little chance he would recover? I had heard somewhere—perhaps I'd read it in novels, or seen it in movies, or had heard from friends who knew first-hand—that when an older person or sickly person contracted pneumonia it was usually that, and not the primary illness, that did them in. Looking back, I feel a gnawing guilt: had I, on hearing that it was pneumonia, become so afraid that I weakened both our wills?

During the hospital's visiting hours that evening, two men, one with heavily kohl-lined eyes, the other wearing a loose, light scarf around his neck, his right-hand pinkie fingernail long and painted the colour of a wet cherry lozenge, visited Sydney. As ill as he was, Sydney was pleased to see them. I had not met any of his friends before and was moved by the graciousness the three men exhibited towards one another. Beyond his greeting, Sydney said no more than a word or two. The strain of doing even this was evident. The two men tried not to expose to him how ill they saw him to be. They chatted as if they were paying him a visit on his veranda in Scenery Hills, including Sydney in their conversation by looking at him as they spoke, one making comments and posing questions, as if directly to Sydney, the other answering as if for Sydney, the two sounding as if they were three. The one with the kohl-lined eyes went to Sydney, pulled a little black plastic comb from a bag draped on his shoulder and arranged Sydney's thinned hair. The man rested the tips of his fingers under Sydney's chin, lifting Sydney's face a fraction to take a good look. He licked the tip of one of his ring fingers and ran it across Sydney's eyebrows. He appraised Sydney again. He said, "You're as handsome as ever, my dear man. Nothing can take that away from you—isn't that so?" The other answered in the affirmative. Who could not have been pleased at Sydney's smile, weak as it was, at this show of attentiveness? When I saw that they were ready to leave—the painted-pinkie one had kissed Sydney softly on his lips—I exited the room to allow the three some minutes alone. In the corridor I asked, doing my best not to impart too impolite a curiosity, how they knew Sydney. The one with the kohl-lined eyes replied that they had all attended the same health clinic. I reflected on how Rosita had taken it upon herself more than once to telephone Sydney's sister to inform her of Sydney's turn, but was told each time by the housekeeper that Gita was unavailable. These two men, then, were Sydney's only visitors.

Their visit had a decidedly buoying effect on Sydney. For some hours I entertained a false hope of his recovery, and when with a strong voice he started to speak again of the day he had walked to the Irene Samuel, I anxiously listened as if it were the first I had ever heard of this walk. I listened, too, for signs that he was mentally competent, that he was regaining his health on all fronts.

But once this bout of storytelling was over, the end was all too swift. Time seemed to stand still and race at once. It was unbearable, by nighttime, to watch the man who had regaled me with his stories sunken against the bed, vulnerable under the pale blue cotton sheets, unable now to whisper without pain. He uttered single words, *water, breathe, chest, light, nurse,* and he said my name, not always to alert me to his wishes, for sometimes when I answered, he looked for a few seconds into my eyes and then shut his. Eventually I reclined, as best as I could, in an armchair that was kindly brought by an orderly for me, and, to my surprise and shame, more exhausted than I realized, I slept through the night.

The following morning, when I pressed the doctor to explain why there was no improvement, but rather, why there was an obvious decline—for Sydney now had count-less tubes and monitors attached to him, and his breathing was aided with oxygen—he urged me to have patience. The pneumonia was not recent. It had set in for some time now. The medications, the antibiotics, required time. The oxygen, he assured me, was being administered only as a precau-tion. The doctor insisted again that Sydney was a stubborn fellow, that Sydney wasn't going anywhere in a hurry. Never before had I experienced such a sobering apprehension of my own impotence.

Those of us who loved Sydney were no longer in a tem-poral eddy. It had become clear to Rosita, Lancelot and me, even if the doctors would not say so, that time was running out. Rosita and Lancelot joined me and kept watch. I stood at Sydney's side, afraid now to turn away for even a second. I wiped his forehead with the thin washcloth, not because it needed wiping, but because that was all there was to do.

Towards the end, as he breathed shallowly into the oxygen mask, he seemed like a stranger to me, neither Sid nor Sydney. But still there were moments when it was as if curtains parted and revealed my beloved Sid in the bed, aged, but as she would have been had she never taken those hormones. Then the curtains would shut again and the face would become not Sid's, not Sydney's, but that of a stranger.

There is nothing more difficult than standing in a room doing nothing. We were simply *there*. That is all. Rosita, Lancelot and I. We were there, an arm's length away from Sydney, a touch away, and we could do nothing. I was not even "waiting." I was just present, and for some time I marvelled at the horror of our human powerlessness to effect change. I had always taken it for granted that being present was the same as being at the ready, as having agency. But, there I was, present yet impotent.

A memory eventually came to me, a gift really, for it lifted me out of the miasma of the present. A smile broke on my face, and I saw how closely related are smiling and crying. When I was a child, Sid used to say to me, "Yes, Jonathan, but how do *we* feel about it?" The use of the plural came about after Sid was chided by my mother—*we the English*, she'd said, *do not admire indulgences*—and I was corralled into a conspiracy of good-humoured mockery. When India was not in her study writing, she watched and listened to Sid and me with narrowed eyes and pouted lips. Sid would stretch out the *ee* in the word *feel*, and I would laugh at the way she did this. "How do *we fee-eel*?" I was old enough to detect some play in the use of the "we" even if I didn't fully understand what was being played at, but I was too young to incorporate it into my own answer, so I used the singular "I." I would concentrate at length, aware that I was being asked not only to have a feeling but to express it in words. Because it was Sid who was asking this of me, I wanted to be as honest and as clear and as creative as possible. I took the task very seriously. Sid sat for as long as it took, staring into my eyes. I looked back into hers, and saw her expectation and pleasure. I pondered how I felt, and found words and phrases and accurate explanations that surprised Sid and delighted me. I knew I had to begin my answer with *I feel*, and so, imitating and elaborating on Sid's imaginative excesses, I once said, *I feel as if there is a big blue sky in my heart, and in the sky in my heart, even though it is daytime, there is a meteorite shower, and the shower is shaped like a bouquet of flowers, and it's exploding in every colour that exists in the world.* Sid went scrambling for a pen and a piece of paper. She wrote down what I'd said and pinned it with a magnet to the fridge door. To this day I clearly remember that particular image I had concocted to describe my happiness. Later, I overheard India say, "What are you trying to do to Jonathan, Sid? You're too indulgent with the child. He should learn that to yield too readily is not something we do or admire." Now, so many years later, it occurs to me that my mother might not have been the disciplining parent I thought her to be then; perhaps she was nervous about, or simply jealous of, the closeness and playfulness between Sid and me.

At the end, Sydney had the presence of mind to ask that his oxygen mask be moved aside. His breaths came shallow and quick. I was holding his hand when he half opened his eyes and looked at me. He whispered, one slow word at a time, that when I was a child my hair was as yellow as corn. Some minutes passed before he spoke again. "It's so dark now," he said, and I assumed he meant that the room had become dark, which I knew was the sort of thing that people are said to experience when the end is near. But he followed that with, "It's like your mother's. Dark like hers." This was, finally, all that I had ever wanted from him. I felt small, self-centred, upset that it had come so late and deeply grateful all at once. He shut his eyes again, and what seemed like several minutes passed before he looked at me and uttered, "You look just like India." He squeezed my hand and said, "You didn't take after me one bit, did you, Jonathan?" It wasn't a question. There was a sort-of smile on his face. I heard myself plead that I did. He sighed and closed his eyes. He seemed to sleep then.

About half an hour later, he opened his eyes and again looked directly at me, urgently, and then he spoke what would be his last words. I saw in his eyes the panic, and heard it, too, in his voice, when he said, "Zain, Zain." I stroked and patted his hand. I think he relaxed. It soon became clear that he would not awaken again. Rosita and Lancelot were asked to wait outside the room by the nurses, who were now present all the time. I was allowed to stay at Sydney's side. I found myself whispering, shamelessly pleading like a desperate child or a forsaken lover, "Please don't go just yet, Sid. Sydney, hang on just a little longer, please."

I brought my lips to his ears and brushed them against his skin as they formed the words, without sound: Sid, I want to say it plainly: Not a day has passed when I didn't think of you as one of my two mothers. My love for you has never faded.

But I betrayed myself in that moment. For even as I felt an unfathomable love for Sydney, I felt the hurt rise again, that old hurt of having figured so little in the stories he had recently told me, and the new hurt of there being no chance of that changing now.

At the official pronouncement of Sydney's death, I cursed the wall of irreversible time and my own stunning ineffectualness. I was left with his body in his room—I don't know for how long—and I indulged myself in all the feelings for which India, my other mother, would have had little patience. I went to the window and pressed my aching forehead against the glass. While the driver of a car in the parking lot below tried and tried again to reverse out of the space in which he was caught, I thought about how this was India's loss too. And then I had an out-of-place and out-of-time realization, entirely irrelevant. Yet tears fell down my face because of it, and I went and stood at the foot of the bed in which Sydney lay. I wrapped my hand around Sydney's blanket-covered foot and watched him from there, doused in regret that he, that she, would never see my mother's family's house in Marrakesh. In that moment, it seemed that this irrelevant loss was the most important and regrettable thing.

In a flash I recalled being on our rooftop terrace in Marrakesh. It was just after sunset. On one side of the city the sky was a dark, luminous blue, and on the other it was the colour and sheen of a golden hued pearl. The call to prayer had ended a quarter of an hour ago, but hung in the air still. I leaned on the surrounding wall and watched the cobbled street below. Having cleared during the call, it was coming alive again with men and women and children. I recalled, too, the sense I used to have when I was up there of India's presence on the far side of the terrace that wrapped around the courtyard below. I would stand where she couldn't see me, look out and wish that Sid was there with us. I used to think that Sid would understand the people down on the street, that she might even be able to speak with them in their language, that she would have made friends with them.

All of this came in a moment, and along with the regret that Sydney had never seen that house in Marrakesh I felt, inexplicably, a strong remorse, as if this were my fault. And yet, neither India nor I had been to Morocco, to that house, in more than three decades. I hardly ever think of that house anymore, and when I do, I imagine it taken over by the care-taker's family or occupied by squatters. It was that absurd anachronistic regret which brought home the fact that Sid and Sydney were gone for good.

In my pants pocket was Sydney's *bayrah*. A nurse had taken it off his wrist on his arrival and handed it to me. Now I squeezed the circle of heavy gold with all my strength. We had intuited, Rosita, Lancelot and I, that this would come to pass, but I saw that, even so, death is untimely, and in the very moment one is inevitably unprepared.

It wasn't the diabetes or his weakened heart that had killed him, the doctor told me. It wasn't the years of injecting his body with low levels of testosterone. It was simply the pneumonia which had gone undetected for too long. *Who* had not detected it, I asked, my voice low in volume, but raised in pitch by at least a fifth, betraying my astonishment and disbelief. I broke the silence that followed by saying, "I thought you said that Sydney was strong, I thought you said that he was stubborn." The doctor said nothing. I persisted. "Is this just the kind of thing you always say?"

"It happens," the young doctor with the heavy-rimmed glasses explained wearily and turned away. No one was to blame.

PART TWO

5

One could walk a straight line from the house to the spot
by the retaining wall where I used to park Sydney in his
wheelchair. How awkward this past tense, and how strange
that one so quickly takes it on. But I meandered, delaying
my arrival. Once there, I circled it. From our spot—did I
imagine this?—came a hint of the cedar and lavender hair
oil Sydney used to use. He and I used to spend count-
less hours sitting there. In the early hours of morning we
would watch the pale yolk of sun breach the faint east-coast
horizon and the ensuing spectacle of rapidly unfurling sky
over the breadth of the island. Sydney used to point in the
direction of the southwestern end and the names of villages
down that way would dance like mercury on his tongue: *Los
Gallos, Icacos, Bonasse, Fullarton.* If he was on the patio and I
in my room, and some drama of sky and sea were unfolding,
he would call for me to come and watch with him. In the
evenings, if it was particularly clear, we would face the other

side of the island and wait to see the sun, like a maraschino cherry, plunge behind and silhouette the Peninsula de Paria that defines the neighbouring Venezuelan coastline. And it was here, the ever-changing spectacle of land, sea and sky as backdrop, where Sydney used to painstakingly relate his stories to me.

Today, there was no such spectacle. Rosita brought me a cup of coffee and then presented a large brown envelope. My name, *Jonathan Lewis-Adey*, was scrawled across it. Sydney had months before entrusted Rosita with the task of locating the envelope, if and when this particular moment should come to pass, from a drawer in the desk in his room and delivering it into my hands. The envelope was a repository for two others, one of which, a fat one, was addressed again to me. Inside, among other documents, was a letter. *My dearest Jonathan*, it began.

My heart beat faster. I expected this greeting would be followed by an acknowledgement of the original relationship between us, or of the newer one that had begun when I first started visiting Sydney here in Trinidad nine years ago. But the words were simple and straightforward and, save for the superlative in the greeting and the line immediately following—*I am sure that, of all people, I can count on you in particular to look after my business*—the letter was without sentiment.

Sydney wasted no time addressing the details of his "business." I was to first inform Gita, his sister, of his passing. There were phone numbers for her and for her husband, and for Pundit Brahmanandam Rao, who would officiate at the funeral. Pundit Rao, the letter said, would instruct me in organizing the ceremony's details. Sydney had already made his arrangements with a funeral home, whose director would procure the death certificate and the other necessary legal papers. His funeral had been paid for—there was a receipt (attached to another enclosed set of papers) dated six months earlier—but its details were to be worked out by the pundit and me. I had only to stick to the budget, Sydney advised in the letter, not because there was no more money than he had paid, but because further expense was unnecessary. Then came the names of the pallbearers. I was not, I noticed, to be one of them. There were numbers beside their names. They had not been asked yet, naturally. That would be one of my forthcoming duties. Sydney had even gone so far as to draft the copy for his obituary that was to be printed in the newspaper.

> Mahale, Sydney. 1950—. Foster parent to Jonathan Lewis-Adey of Toronto, Canada. Parents: the late Dr. Amresh Mahale and the late Mrs. Sita Mahale. Sibling to Gita Patil, in-law of Jaan Patil. Employer of Rosita Debisingh of Mathura, Lancelot Mitchell of Diego Martin, Sankar Dass of Princess Town. Ceremony at home, 21 Hibiscus Drive, Seaview Lots, Scenery Hills, to be followed by cremation at the Caroni River, —. In lieu of flowers please support the Priority Fund at the Trinidad and Tobago Baphomet Private Health Clinic.

I had only to fill in the relevant dates and time. I was instructed to open the other attached papers and did so. Among them was a handwritten will, witnessed by Kareen Akal Sharma, a name that meant nothing to me, notarized and dated only a few months previously. I scanned it quickly. It was a simple will, with several mentions of my name, and as far as my limited experience with such matters allowed me to discern, it appeared that I was to take the larger share of his estate, which included, besides the house and financial investments, a number of notebooks in which, he wrote, he had jotted down bits and pieces about his life and which I had full permission to read and to use in whatever way I saw fit. Gita's son, Devin, along with Rosita, Lancelot and Sankar, Kareen Akal Sharma and the Priority Fund at the T and T Baphomet Private Health Clinic were left smaller sums of money.

It is a strange honour to be the beneficiary of anything, particularly at the expense of the life of a person you love. I swung between feeling considered, remembered and, dare I say, loved and overcome by shame. This was, I suppose, the price one paid to be the inheritor of another's life. There was a key to a safety deposit box in that envelope too. The smaller second envelope, which I did not open, was addressed to a Mrs. Ula Morgan, under whose name was the full address of a bank in Diego Martin. Sydney's letter dictated that I was to present myself, with appropriate identification, to Mrs. Morgan at the bank. She was expecting me.

I paused to wonder when this package that included

Sydney's will and his letters had been prepared, and for how long Mrs. Ula Morgan had been expecting me. Although I had fulfilled Sydney's expectation that I would come when called, I felt an unnecessary terror that this had happened only by chance, for had it not been for Lancelot's manner on the telephone, had it not been for my correct reading of his unconscious formality, I might just as easily have second-guessed him and waited a little longer before incurring the trouble and expense of a short-notice flight.

Although I had been directed by Sydney to immediately call and inform his sister, it was my mother, India, I called first. I was surprised by her attentiveness. She asked for details about the three days in the hospital and the upcoming funeral. When I told her that responsibilities for the arrangements were falling on me, I recognized her pensiveness and worry in the silence that followed. She asked if I needed her. I was moved, even as a small recalcitrant part of me felt that she might have assumed rather than asked. So I said that while I was able to handle the situation on my own, perhaps she might want to come to the funeral for Sydney's sake. There was a pause. Then she replied that he would not have expected it, and besides, Graham—her common-law husband of some twenty-odd years—had not been well lately and she would not feel comfortable leaving him. We exchanged a few polite words before saying goodbye. Some minutes after the call ended, I felt a twinge of regret that I had neglected to ask what was ailing Graham, but I consoled myself that had it been serious she would have told me.

I dreaded the telephone call to Gita. Sydney had lamented that he and Gita were in touch with each other only because he took it upon himself to make short monthly telephone calls. I had a brief reprieve when my call was received by Gita's housekeeper, who revealed that the family was in England to take care of arrangements for their son Devin's first year in university. The housekeeper promised to waste no time in contacting them to tell them of Mr. Sydney's passing.

Some hours later, Gita telephoned. As I fumbled in my explanation of who I was, she interrupted: "Yes, yes. I know who you are. You were a child when you came with your mother to Trinidad." She made no further attempt at familiarity. She said flatly but politely that as unfortunate as it was, there was no point to her or Jaan returning for the funeral, as they would have to make the trip back to England again immediately. They had not finished all they were doing for Devin there. The phone call ended abruptly, unsatisfactorily.

I was in such a state that the smallest thing could have caused me to brood, and this was not a small thing. But I had to bear up and carry on. Responsibilities, ones that my life until then had not prepared me to handle, loomed. I had never before attended a funeral, yet I was suddenly responsible for organizing one. The pundit Sydney had retained assured me on the telephone that he would meet with me the next day and guide me every step of the way, and that it would all be quite simple. All six pallbearers responded to Sydney's request as if it were an invitation of the highest honour. I consoled myself that perhaps I had not been afforded the same honour because I needed to take charge of the general arrangements, and perhaps that was an honour in itself.

Dinner that evening was a strange affair. The table was not set and the food was not placed on it in serving dishes as usual. Instead, the dishes remained on a counter in the kitchen, covered from flies with a tea towel. Rosita handed me my plate and a knife and fork, and I helped myself. I sat at the table, but not in the seat that had come to be mine. And I positioned that chair off to the side, so that I did not face the empty table. I poked at the food on my plate and had a mouthful. Then I poured myself a Scotch and coconut water and went outside to the wall at the edge of the garden. Night had fallen fast. It was already close to twelve hours since Sydney had died. With each passing minute the gulf between then—the time, that is, when I had been with Sydney—and now—the time when I would forever be without Sydney—widened. The pang I felt was partly familiar and partly not. That is, I knew well the time when Sydney was like a beacon to which I always travelled. But this particular present was foreign to me, and I didn't know how, exactly, to exist in it. I sipped my drink and said aloud, "This is where I bring Sydney. We sit together here in the evenings and chat." And then I tried out the new present: "This is where I used to bring Sydney. We used to sit out here and chat." I said, in the familiar way, "Sydney loves to look at the lights below." Then I said, and listened carefully to the new, cold sound of it: "Sydney used to come out here with me. We used to sit out here. Sydney so very much liked the lights ahead."

Nights here, after Sydney and I had eaten our dinner and the kitchen was cleaned and the servants had gone their respective ways, it had become my habit to telephone Catherine. There is one phone in the house, a corded phone located in the kitchen. At least during each call, Sydney used to make his way slowly, on foot, to the fridge for a glass of coconut water or a bowl of the jelly, holding on to the counters and walls as he pulled himself forward with his arms. I sensed his ears trained on my words. What he would have heard was the restlessness of someone who was not without a lover, yet who was, in effect, alone. It always took me several days to a couple of weeks after returning to Toronto to reignite an appreciation for Catherine. She and I have been doing this recalibration for two years now. We have never broached the subject of marriage, but we presume a kind of partnership between us. There is, I am sure, more to us than habit. If she were to meet someone else, I don't really know what I would do. And who wouldn't prefer to be the one leaving, rather than the one left?

That first lonely night after Sydney was gone, I waited until Rosita had retired to bed. From Lancelot's room on the other side of the garage came the low sound of the radio. Only then did I telephone Catherine. I used our old trick: one ring and I would hang up, after which Catherine would return the call so that no cost was incurred on the exorbitant Trinidad end. We would later share the bill. Out of habit I spoke in a low voice, all the while half expecting, despite the irrationality of it, that Sydney might overhear or enter the room. His absence loomed large throughout the house. In my two years with Catherine I had not yet revealed to her the full story of how Sydney and I were related. She knew only that Sydney—not Sid—had been India's lover for the first ten years of my life, and that, despite the years that had passed since, and the distance between where we lived, I considered him a parent. This was all she knew, and, to my relief, her curiosity had not been piqued. I now told Catherine that Sydney had died and described how, even as I spoke them, those words seemed strange to me. I related how the doctor had announced, "Well, Jonathan, Sydney did his best. He tried his best, man. But in the end he just couldn't make it." I asked her if it was more honest and mature to state it plainly as we tended to do, at least in my own Anglo circles, in Canada—to say, that is, that a person had died—or was it better, more respectful and kinder to soften the unfairness with euphemisms: he or she hadn't made it, had passed away, or as Lancelot cried out in the hospital room, "Sydney gone, Jonathan, his Saviour take him and now he gone and he leave us behind"? Perhaps all of these are more accurate, I said, and *died* is the shorthand and the euphemism.

Catherine, after an awkward silence followed by an attempt at wordless sympathetic sounds, said, "Will you be coming home right away, then?" I caught myself explaining, as if I were asking permission, that Sydney's only sibling, Gita, was out of the country, so it had fallen on me to make the funeral arrangements and "tie up the loose ends here." Attempting to express her sympathy and support, Catherine offered that she thought I was unfairly put-upon to deal with such an unpleasant task that was not my responsibility.

This was my fault: Catherine knew nothing about— *about*, another euphemism and so loaded—Catherine knew nothing about Sydney; I had not shared with her stories of my childhood with my mother's lover. I ended the phone call feeling more profoundly alone than I have ever felt, with unusual burdens and obligations, and imminent responsibilities.

By the pale yellow glow of the lamp on my bedside table, I read Sydney's letter numerous times. *My dearest Jonathan.* How I held on to the possessive *My*, and the superlative *dearest*. How I burdened the phrase immediately following that greeting with my own deep desires: *I am sure that, of all people, I can count on you in particular.* And how I was pained by the formality of Sydney's closing words: *With the deepest appreciation for the trouble I am asking of you here.* Despite my grief I took umbrage with that phrasing, the choice of the word *trouble* suggesting more distance between him and me than I had ever thought existed, and therefore a slight. But he had ended with *As always, Love, S.*, and this buoyed me. I feel sure that the word *always* was meant to precisely convey, beyond his passing, his sentiments regarding our relationship. And the word *as* was surely meant to reassure me of both the past of that relationship, and of the fact that it had continued uninterrupted after he left the house in which he had lived with India and me. The signatorial *S* was employed, I felt certain, so that I might end his letter however I wished: Sydney or Sid. *As always.*

I could not sleep. I wondered how it was that night turns over, as it does, without sentiment, that time cannot be stopped or slowed, and that seconds pass and suddenly it is minutes that have passed, and then hours, and soon it will be days and then weeks that have passed. Morning will come, I thought, because that is what it does. And when it comes the sun will shine and the tropical sky will burst with disregard and blueness. Clouds will drift by, because that is what they do. Tourists who have returned to the cruise ships tonight, after a day of shopping in the city or bathing at the beaches, will not have had their hearts broken here and yet they will think they know this place. Tomorrow morning hummingbirds will come to suckle on flowers right beneath these windows, and squawking parrots will pass over the house headed for somewhere else. Stands of bamboo in the hills behind us will wave like giddy teenagers at a charity carwash, and the flames atop the oil rigs will not stop pulsing. They are pulsing brazenly right now.

6

Recently I have found myself calling upon whatever divine beings there might be, thanking them for Rosita, who was then, as she is now, a gift. For example, I had thought that I would wait until after the funeral to go and see Mrs. Morgan at the bank. In my mind, there was no longer any urgency. But Rosita assured me that there would be no rest over the days to come, before or after, as there would be many things to attend to, particularly because I was "from abroad," as she put it, and would eventually need to return to my own home. I agreed to go the following morning.

I had been restless throughout the night. Five o'clock in the morning arrived and I had hardly slept. The birds in the trees were creating a ruckus. When I went into the kitchen, Rosita was there cleaning, as if it were spring or the night before a Trinidadian Christmas. I sat on the veranda and watched the sea and the sky turn from volatile shades of rubellite to a placid glistening grey. Kiskadees conferred with one another in the shrubs. Parrots in the hills behind the house bickered, every so often a small group of them bursting into awkward flight, headed towards the Swamp. I followed one of them with my eyes—a vain attempt to relax, to let go, even if just for seconds—and then another, and then another, until the last black speck it became disappeared into the glare of the sky.

When I returned inside, Rosita had prepared breakfast and set the table as usual, but this time there was only one setting, one placemat, one plate on which sat a matching cereal bowl, and there was one teacup (the usual teacup which I, a coffee drinker, have never used, yet which is always there for me), one cloth napkin, one knife and one fork, one cereal spoon, and one juice glass. The formality of the setting that had previously amused me now unsettled me. I had not questioned Sydney's insistence on such formality, but I found it fussy and it did not suit me personally. I knew that I should not, at the moment, ask for the table to be set otherwise.

Rosita and Lancelot had already eaten their own breakfasts, but when I sat down they joined me; it was the first time we had ever been at the table together. In our silence Sydney's presence was evoked. Rosita was unable to suppress her tears.

The banks in Trinidad open at 8 a.m., so I showered and dressed and waited for Sankar to arrive at the house to take me there. After a few minutes, I went into Sydney's room, and then into his bathroom. I opened the cupboard beneath the sink. There was the usual: bathroom cleaning supplies, shampoo and soaps, toilet paper. There were, too, two large boxes of individually packaged syringes, and smaller boxes of individually packaged needles. I opened the medicine cabinet. Its narrow shelves were lined with orange plastic bottles of varying sizes, containing pills. On the labels were his name: *Sydney Mahale*. On the inside of the door of the cupboard was taped a sheet of paper on which his daily schedule for taking his medications was handwritten. I knew that the cupboard would one day have to be emptied of the medicines, but for the moment it felt as if the bottles with his name on them were a substitute for Sydney's existence here, and I dreaded them being discarded. I went to the armoire in his bedroom and unlocked it. I retrieved his knapsack and placed it on his bed. From it I took the stack of letters, and carefully untied the red string that held them together. The first was a yellow sheet of foolscap paper folded into quarters to make a greeting card. A rose was hand-drawn and coloured in red on the front piece. The interior was decorated with S-shaped squiggles made with red- and green-coloured pencils. It read:

To Sid,
Happy Birthday,
From your best friend.
P.S. By now I am sure you know the wisdom of having me as your best friend. The reason I permit you this honour is because of that very wisdom. Happy Birthday, my best friend.

From your best friend,
Zain

I once asked Sydney how he knew Zain, and I remember watching him brighten as the cogs in his brain engaged. He had just turned sixteen, he said. He had transferred over from St. Jude Convent to Zain's school, San Fernando Presbyterian Girls' High School. Sydney began to glow as he recalled that first day.

The girls, including Zain, from the class I was to enter, he told me, had lined the never-ending corridor to the Lower Sixth rooms. The corridor had been narrowed by the severity of their crisp starched-white shirts, heavy cotton navy-blue ties, immaculately pleated navy skirts, navy socks and heavy black shoes. Some of the girls had leaned one shoulder into the wall so that an insolent hip jutted into the aisle; others rested their upper backs against the wall, braced by one leg bent at the knee, a foot flat against the cement. Many covered their mouth with their hand as they spoke, some pressed lips to the ear of another, and all trained eyes on me as I passed, the *shoosh shoosh shoosh* of whispered judgements falling against my back and shoulders like light belt straps.

Yet I managed a brave smile, Sydney recalled. I knew the lineup was to see—not to welcome—me, to see who this new student transferring to San Fernando Presbyterian Girls' High School in her final two years was.

The teacher walked ahead of me. "Okay," she said. "Enough of this. You all behave yourselves." No one budged.

At my other school, each girl would have straightened her-self—if she had even dared present herself like these girls in front of a teacher in the first place. Behind my smile, my heart had all but stopped beating.

The classroom I entered was empty, yet the room felt stuffy and airless. Mrs. Augusta walked me to the desk assigned to me. She turned to one particular student and called out, "You. Yes, you. Come here, please. Introduce yourself." I hadn't noticed this girl in my march down the corridor. But then, I hadn't looked at anyone directly, hadn't picked out any faces. The girl Mrs. Augusta had addressed turned to me and said, "I am . . ." But either I didn't hear or she purposely mumbled her name, so I had to ask her to please repeat it, and she said her name loudly and slowly, with irritation—*Zain*—her eyes boring into me. It was as if she were daring me: *Comment on it, just go ahead.* Instead, I said my name, adding, "Pleased to meet you." If raised eyebrows could smirk, Zain's did.

I had been one of the more popular girls in my other school, but now, even before the bell to begin classes rang, I was feeling disheartened. Clearly, the niceties that had earned me points at the convent school were held in disdain here.

Mrs. Augusta let out a sigh of exasperation and said, "Come now, enough. Zain, I am going to leave it to you to show Siddhani around. I expect you to help her with every-thing she needs. If there's something you're unable to do, come directly to me." Zain sucked her teeth, but only enough to be able to get away with it, and said, "Oh gosh, Miss. Why me?" Mrs. August ignored the question and said, "Okay, stop the theatrics now, and behave like a proper young lady."

Zain boldly answered back, "You mean, even if I am not?"

Mrs. August looked at Zain sternly but said nothing. I was impressed. That sort of back chat would have been enough for detention where I had come from.

When Mrs. Augusta left, Zain faced me. She sneered. "So, you got expelled or what?"

The lineup of girls outside, awaiting the bell before entering, was intimidating, and so was Zain, even though I felt myself perversely drawn to her.

"No. I want to do art for A Levels, but it isn't offered at my other school, so I got a transfer here." It irked me that my tone sounded slightly pleading.

Zain stared hard. She was taller than me by about two inches. I could not read her silence. Then, in a flash, she blurted with equal measures accusation and caution, "Likely story. You see those girls out there? They will find out the truth about you in no time. So no point lying."

I so wanted her—the desire to conquer my adversary something I had learnt early as a survival manoeuvre—to believe me. My composure thankfully remained steady and I stated flatly, without irritation or fear: "There is nothing to find out. I am telling you the truth."

I could read the expression in her eyes instantly. She was curious, and I was disarming her too soon for her liking. I was as amused as I was disappointed at how easy this had been.

She did not take her eyes off mine, and I could feel mine tickling with discomfort. She raised her hand to touch my arm, and I felt triumph wash over me. But instead of a friendly touch Zain pinched my skin. I surprised myself when I instantly flipped up that same arm and gripped her wrist hard. I said, in a soft voice, "Don't do that." There was no smile on my face now.

But that was when her facade broke, and she was suddenly grinning. I felt her body relax. My grip relaxed then, too, but I did not let go of her hand. I remained unsmiling, suddenly frightened, but not of her.

All this Sydney had related to me in bewildering detail, and his words flooded back to me now. I read the letters as if parched, eager for any bit of new insight into Sydney, unable to let him go. I cut the stack of letters and removed another.

How can you not think Mrs. Rodriguez's son is not THE most handsome boy you've ever, ever, ever seen? I think I am totally in love. I am feeling wild and giddy. Why on earth didn't I take Rodriguez's Commerce class? I could have gotten to him through her, don't you think? His name is Paul, but they call him Dizzy. Dizzy?! Hmm, I wonder if that is because of what he is, or what he makes others.
Zain

The one immediately following read:

I don't care, I will convert. Do you think I have a chance? His mother knows I have brains. He can find out for himself what else I have to offer. Which is a lot.
Zain

I read several more consecutive notes.

But, Sid, you are such a prude. Have you never been in love with a single fellow? How can you not think Paul is a total catch?
Z

I know I have a lot to offer because I have a very fertile imagination, which can't be said of you.
Z

You are not the first to say I am self-centred. And you are not only a prude, you are very stuck-up. I don't know why I give you so much of my time. I don't understand you. You spend all your free time with me, but you don't let me know you. You don't open up at all. What are you hiding?
Z

Well, it feels like you're hiding something. I tell you everything that is going on with me, and you hardly ever tell me a thing. I think about you all the time,

Sid, but you don't consider me ever, do you? What
does it mean to be a best friend? You have to share
yourself. Not just your damn sandwiches and your
homework, but YOURSELF. Should I be reconsid-
ering this friendship?

Do you like the flower? I left it for you. But don't
just leave it sitting on your desk, you moron. Put it
in some water. There are jars by the sink in the art
room. It's from Mum's garden. Do you like it?

Z

I put these back and cut the stack again, this time farther along. I neatly arranged the two parts on the bed, so that
the letters could be positioned again in their proper order.

Dear Sid,

It's been three days since you left, and I know it
takes longer than that for a letter to arrive, but I
can't wait to hear from you. What is Canada like?
It's cold, of course, but how cold? Have you seen
snow yet? Have you met any other Trinidadians?
I am so worried that you are going to replace me
overnight. I can't believe you're starting university,
and I will now be a year behind you. I wish I didn't
have to work this year.

Angus comes over almost every day after his
work. Mum has dinner ready for him now when
he arrives. I don't know how I feel about that.

Sometimes proud, sometimes like she's pushing my family on him. Dad still doesn't talk to him much, but he doesn't take his eyes off him either. They still won't let me go out with him, except to buy corn up the hill, or for coconuts in town, and then we have to be right back. Angus said he will convert to the Muslim faith if that is what it takes (you might remember that he is R.C.). Sometimes I am so in love with him, and then there are strange moments when I don't have a clue what love is. Sometimes it's like something in an advertisement, and if you have it, or if you give it, then you're very cool and have a lot of prestige. If you don't have it, or if you don't give it, you're a failure. Everybody is supposed to get married, so I suppose I will one day too, and Angus isn't a bad fellow. He is applying to go to university next year. Mum knows this, but not Dad.

OK, I want to tell you something—I don't have anything to compare this to, but I love it when he kisses me. His kisses have become what I would call a little more urgent lately, and they've become open-mouthed. That I like a lot. I can't go into detail about how I feel, because I am shy—yes, me, I am shy, and yes, with you—but I am sure you will find out very soon what I am talking about, if you haven't already. Have you? I can't believe you didn't let Bindra kiss you before you left. You don't know what you're missing. You are so cold-hearted sometimes. That fellow would give his life for you. But if you're not interested, then you're not interested, I suppose. Who are you waiting for, anyway? Don't go and fall in love with some crazy white Canadian, just because you might be lonely. You have to come back here and marry someone from here. I wonder if Bindra will wait for you. Perhaps distance will make your heart grow fonder. A lot of people would want their son to marry into your family. You're lucky. But Angus is the one for me. It is only a matter of time before Angus and I get on with it, I imagine. If we get married, you will have to come back for the wedding, OK? I can't believe the things I tell you. I hope you don't show my letters to anyone.

OK, write me as soon as you can. I hope you have already, and that this letter and yours to me are crossing paths.

Your best friend ever, and forever,

Zain

My heart quickened. The irony was not lost on me—how could Zain have known when she wrote these notes and letters that they would, long after her passing, mean so much to someone she had never met? I was learning now *from her* about Sid. It hadn't occurred to me before that there might have been a time when Zain did not know that kissing this fellow, Bindra, would not have brought Sid any pleasure. It could only have been painful for Sid, traumatic, to have to hide, especially from her closest friend, the fact that she was aware even then that she wouldn't marry or live a traditional life. But I also knew that, in the end, Zain did not abandon Sid.

I reflected on the words before me and on what Sydney himself had told me of his adventures with Zain, and I felt, for the first time, gratitude and a kinship with her. We were, I saw, the warp and weft of his life, and as incongruous as it might have been, I felt something akin to excitement begin to creep over me.

I read the letter that followed, hungry for more about both of them.

Dearest Sid,

Dad still isn't talking to us, and that is causing hard times at home. He refuses to accept that I have taken an apartment up here in Curepe, near the University. Angus still lives with his parents and he drives up for his classes. Of course, he stays over often. Mum knows that Angus stays over, but she hasn't told Dad. She doesn't have to. He has it in his head that Angus and I are living together and that I am a fallen woman. Ha! I wish! Well, I am, sort of, aren't I! I am worried about Mum. Poor thing. She and Dad hardly talk to each other, and I am the cause of it. But, thank God for telephone service coming to the cane field; I talk to Mum every day, two and three times some days. She still ("still"? This will never change!) makes all Dad's meals and sits at the table with him while he eats, even if they don't speak a word to each other. I can't imagine being with anyone like that for an entire lifetime.

Anyway, enough crying. I am sad you didn't come for the wedding, which just shows that you are strange, and will probably never change, and I guess I have no choice but to accept you as you are. And if you're trying to get rid of me, I won't give you the satisfaction. That is just the kind of person I am. Anyway, we love the bedspread you so kindly sent. It is on the bed right now, and already all kinds of wonderful things have happened beneath it and on top of it! Use your imagination. Angus wants to be a different kind of man, he says, so he makes breakfast on Sunday mornings. Eggs. He can't cook roti, or *choka* or anything like that, but he can boil an egg, and do toast. And he actually ties up the garbage and takes it downstairs every night. I can't believe how lucky I am. (I am half joking, of course.) (But half serious too.) (Men really are a different species. I think they need us more than we need them, which is to acknowledge that we do need them, or at least their bodies! Yes, I am enjoying that part a lot. An awful lot!)

School is going well. I am still planning to do medicine, but that is one area where Angus and I have disagreements. It's really the only thing we ever have disagreements about. I don't think it's such a big deal, but it's the only thing we fight about. I really don't understand. His father talked him into taking over the business, and he talks about me working in the business, regardless of what degree I get or what I say. I will have to show him who is the boss, but there is time for that. I am enjoying being bossed (just a little bit bossed) at the moment.

So, I hope one day you will tell me what you are learning about yourself. It isn't very fair to just say, "I am finding out so many things about myself, and my ways in the world are beginning to make sense to me, where they haven't, either to myself or to others, before." Just what the heck are you talking about? I am interested—I know sometimes I give—or rather gave—the impression that I wasn't really interested in what you had to say, only in telling you about myself, but I have to admit I wonder all the time what you're doing, what you're seeing, what you're feeling and thinking, who you're becoming, and if we'll always be friends when you come back here, after being in such a big strange place. Just don't get strange (or should I say strangER?), OK?

I have to go study now, and then get dinner, but please write me back and tell me something very specific and detailed.

I love Angus, of course, and deeply too. So, now
that that is out of the way, I can tell you I love you,
and you won't think I am strange (I think there are
some people like that at the University, but each to
his own, her own, whatever!). So:

I love you,

Zain

P.S. Angus sends his love too. He is so sweet.

———

At the bank that day, Mrs. Morgan expressed her sympathy,
as if I were Sydney's closest relative. How much did she
know about Sydney? I wondered.

In the safety deposit box I found another copy of
Sydney's will, the deed to the house, bank share certificates,
and share certificates for National Golden Flour Mill and
for Tabor Cacao Industry. In a small cream-coloured envelope pocked with what looked like age spots was a tiny yel-
lowed black-and-white photograph with scalloped edges.
It showed a little girl in a short frilly dress, a tall, young
and rather dashing man and a plump, very well-dressed
and good-looking woman. The man, suited, stood on a
step holding the child, who sat atop the broad platform of
the staircase pillar, while the woman stood at ground level,
one hand on one of the child's plump legs. The child, who
could not have been more than two years of age, had long
black hair pulled back in a ponytail and bangs. Her hands

were clasped and she grinned as if she were the happiest person on earth. On the back, written in a faded turquoise ink and a hand that took pride in penmanship, were the words *Siddhani with Dad and Mum. Mum is pregnant here with Gita.* Looking closer I could see that Mrs. Mahale was more than simply plump. I couldn't for the longest while take my eyes off Sid. I could see nothing in the face of the child in that photo that might have suggested she would one day want to change her gender. Beside the photo in the deposit box was a royal-blue velvet pouch held closed by a gold cord. Inside were delicate pieces of gold jewellery—part, I thought, of Sid's inheritance from her mother, but nothing I could imagine Sydney ever to have worn, save perhaps for when he was that rather pretty little girl.

And there were a few newspaper clippings. Quickly scanning them, I recognized the story. How could I not? Ninety-six hours before, Sydney had laid bare what had weighed so heavily on his mind for twenty-five years, and here was the story in my hand, as it had appeared in the news: "Spice Baron's Wife Murdered in Home Invasion." I confess I had often thought—without malice, I must add in my defence—that Sydney was an old person doing what old people did: he was reminiscing, stuck on a single story, perhaps even a single point of view, and I was his trapped audience. But as he finally laid out the full story for me in the hours before we took him to the hospital, I had seen why he'd insisted on telling it to me, and why he hadn't brought it to a close earlier. Now, in my hands, were the news reports of Zain's murder.

And last, there were the three notebooks. They were all of the same size, held together with a thin leather cord. I undid the cord and opened one of the books. I knew the handwriting well. I read the first sentence, savouring the familiar neat calligraphy that slanted backwards like men straining on the rope in a game of tug-of-war. But a little farther on I tumbled in a riptide of emotion, surfing one moment with elation that in my hand were words Sydney had written himself, and in the next dragged under that I could not ask him what he had meant by this or by that. In a sense, these, and not the ones he spoke during those last days, were now his final words. I braced myself and read:

When we were in high school, Zain was so much brighter than us all. I could never understand why she didn't use her scholarship and study medicine as she had always wanted to do. And I have never been able to understand her father not wanting his daughter "doing that kind of work, man's work, showing off with her brains." I couldn't understand at the time how she let him dictate what she should do. It is only now, after experiencing what it is like to live in a foreign country on one's own, without family, that I understand. God, Zain, the choices we made. Both of us. Would we have been happier with other choices? Or are hardships just part of any choice?

Are hardships simply more difficult to accommodate while advantages are more difficult to see?

And then, how to explain Zain becoming a Catholic, getting married? Did you really go to church, Zain? I can't imagine Zain, of all people, genuflecting, crossing herself, taking communion with her hands pressed in prayer. Zain, I bet, was more like a Muslim forced to convert during the Spanish Inquisition: Catholic in public, but Muslim at home and in her heart.

I was thrilled she invited me to the wedding. But I hadn't told her about myself, and in Canada I had become used to dressing as I pleased, used to wearing slacks and jackets and flat shoes with socks. Can you imagine a woman in Trinidad going to a wedding dressed like that? I was so much more at ease not having to cater my looks and voice and mannerisms to back-home expectations of how women "ought" to be. I no longer knew how to flatter men. No, I would have been out of my depth, out of place at Zain's wedding.

Whenever I returned to Trinidad to visit Mum and Dad and Gita, Zain would invite me to her house, and I would be the centre of attention with her two children. They were intrigued that I, who had no husband or children of my own, who lived in another country while my own parents and sister lived in Trinidad, was their mother's close friend.

I put that notebook down—exhaustion kept at bay by a faint breathlessness more often associated with elation—and I opened another. Considerations of privacy, and the invasion of such, might have given someone else pause. But he had willed the notebooks to me, and explicitly given me permission to read them.

Some sections of sidewalk along the mostly residential blocks on Eldon Street had been taken care of with diligence—cleared and salted, salted and cleared, twice a day when the accumulation came down like this. But for the most part I had to take short footsteps, bracing myself on one leg before planting the other, along a packed, uneven path narrowed by the snow shovelled from residents' driveways and walkways, snow that in turn had been piled up along the sides from the clearing of the main roadway. This is the kind of winter people will say is the worst they've seen in their five, or ten or thirty, years of living in the city. The worst in their entire lives. The most snow. The coldest temperatures. The fiercest storms. The longest winter. They say this year after year. The treachery. I was terrified of slipping and losing my grip on the knapsack. As I write this I am suddenly reminded of the men with the snakes around their necks. Do you remember, Zain, how they appeared as we were walking back up the steps from the beach just after the sun had set that evening at Macqueripe?

How I wish you were with me these days, Zain. How I wish you could accompany me on my trips to the clinic to change the bandages. How I wish you could see what I look like now.

At just this juncture, Mrs. Morgan knocked on the door to the room to see if I was all right. I closed the book reluctantly. I had come unprepared, so Mrs. Morgan gave me a promotional cloth-bag with the name of the bank printed on it into which I emptied the contents of the deposit box.

Back home, I shut myself in my room and pulled out the books again.

You begged me to come down. Come for a month and stay with Angus and me, you said. You told me you felt like a large bear in a small cage. I'd cheer you up, you said. Neither of the children were at home anymore. In any case, they had their own lives now, and it wasn't right to burden your children. It was just this thing happening inside. Inside of your body and your brain, and you felt like you were going crazy. Trinidad was a small place. Everyone knew everyone. Your friends were Angus's friends. You felt there was no one you could talk to. But you could talk to me, you said. I'd cheer you up. Speaking on the telephone wasn't enough. If only we lived in the same country, you said.

You knew that I did not have a dime. I could not afford spontaneity. I could not contemplate a trip. But without telling me, you organized the return ticket and sent it to me. How the tables had turned in our lives. An open ticket, Toronto to Port of Spain, Port of Spain to Toronto. I only had to fill in the dates.

You were such a different person on the telephone from the one you were in the flesh. It was as if, on the telephone, all my senses concentrated in my ear and I could hear your voice in a way that I couldn't when we were in each other's presence. On the telephone I heard in your voice how unhappy you were. In one of your letters you shared with me your plans—too many for a single person to carry out in a lifetime. You had met a German woman who had been a famous swimming instructor and choreographer. She was in Trinidad with her husband, who was teaching at the University. You asked the woman to give you synchronized swimming lessons. She knew several women who were also interested in synchronized swimming lessons, and the two of you were planning a show in one of the coves in Chaguaramas. Then, in a phone call just a few days later, you informed me that you were thinking of taking piano lessons. You knew of someone who was selling a piano. In that same call you said you wanted to start up an organization to put musical instruments in the hands of underprivileged children, and you might even start a school of music for them. A children's symphony. Symphony camp. Sunday concerts in the Botanical Gardens. A gemology course for yourself. Jewellery making. Artisanal bread making. A chauffeuring business with all-women drivers. You wouldn't drive yourself, of course, but you would own the business and run it. You told me all of this, but you didn't tell me that you were seeing a man named Eric.

And now I was engulfed in a confusion of emotion again. I could no longer deny it: I recognized it to be the longing, the readiness, the need—the *insistent* need—to begin to write again.

I put the journal down. I was increasingly anxious, aware there were a million and one things to be done, and I was the one expected to take charge. But I felt myself overcome by anticipation—not anticipation of all that was to come in the next few hours, but a sense, an eagerness, that I was about to begin my life anew.

I thought about the earlier times when Sydney would relate stories about himself or about Zain. I used to become quickly impatient, wanting ones, instead, that showed our connection. Did it take Sydney's death for me to become more mature? I opened the envelope and removed the will and the newspaper clippings. I flipped through the clippings again, as if doing this were the most urgent task at hand. Sydney had once shown me photographs of Zain. As far as I remembered, those photos showed a simple-looking—neither attractive nor unattractive—young woman. From her eyes one might imagine, especially after reading her girlish letters, that she possessed an acerbic humour. In the newspaper photos she appears to be plump and well-groomed in the manner of the women of the Indo-Trinidadian elite. Her hair, parted on one side, has some lift to it as it falls in great neat waves to her shoulders and frames her well made-up face. The rise in social circumstances that accompanied her marriage and prevailed throughout her adulthood had, I imagined now, given definition to the features that seemed in the earlier photos nebulous. Sydney had told me that there had been no romance between Sid and Zain. I believe this to be true, but I believe, too, that Sid had loved her, and so had Sydney, long after Zain was gone. I pulled the clippings together neatly and replaced them. In his storytelling, during the days when he and I were together, and, now, via the bequeathing of his and Zain's writings and these newspapers articles, Sydney had afforded me a consideration I had not predicted. Such foresight, openness and generosity overwhelmed me. If there was anything worth inheriting, I thought, it was these qualities. This revelation had the effect of making me want to sequester myself and begin to think and to write.

With one of the notebooks tucked under my arm, I went out to the wall at the edge of the garden where Sydney and I used to sit, and under a luminescent sky in the heat of the day I again read Sydney's tilting scrawl.

I would dream often that I was a little piece of thread. I, the thread that is, hardened into a filament of wire so fine I was practically invisible. I had existed for a long time inside of a blurry bump that was on the surface of something so big that I was unable to see its edges. Somehow, I punctured the bump. I, the filament, emerged out of the bump and a crust of dried birth fluids clung along my short length. As I, this filament, lengthened—and this lengthening was happening rather swiftly—those dried bits dredged and trapped new bits along the way, and I, the filament, took on some width now. Suddenly I was longer than a tape measure, and was covered over and weighed down by the accumulating crust.

Soon, in less than twenty-four hours, this encrusted filament will arrive at what I think of as the eye of a needle through which it—the unrealized strand of me—will pass, and forty-two years of accumulated crud will be scraped off—or so I hope—and on the other side of the needle a person will emerge. I am on the brink of personhood. It is strange, and not entirely believable, that a journey that has taken a lifetime could so suddenly reach its culmination, twenty-four hours from now, simply by me arriving at the door of a hospital. It is strange, and not entirely believable, and, I fear, a little foolish to expect.

As I read, my emotions, urges, desires, beliefs surged one way and then the other, and I seemed to have little control over them. My interest in writing seemed at some moments to be a much-needed anchor, and at others to be almost unsavoury.

I looked out beyond the silver sea towards the area of the island that had beautiful names and reflected on the fact that for nine years I had been coming to Trinidad for no other reason than to spend time with Sydney. A full day and several hours had now passed with no Sydney present. And yet, I was tied here.

I remembered how, when I was a child and had visited this island for the first time with India and Sid, Sid's mother had the cook prepare us a dinner one evening of small greyish-green freshwater fish. I remembered the tough skeletal covering, armour really, of the little fish whose name I would never forget, the *cascadoo*. The *cascadoo* had whiskers and was unlike any fish I had ever seen, not more than twenty centimetres in length, and rather frightful looking. The cook had curried about a dozen and a half of them. They remained whole in the dish, from head to tail, and we were to eat them with rice. I watched Sid push the scales up one of them, sliding her knife from tail up to head, and was appalled by the thick yellow flesh that was revealed. She encouraged me to try it, but as I was about to follow her lead, Mrs. Mahale recited a local saying: "Those who eat the *cascadoo*, the native legend says, will, wheresoever they may wander, end in Trinidad their days." I was immediately terrified that if I ate even a morsel of the curry sauce in which the fish lay, I would die before the end of the trip. I refused it. India picked at one, declared it prohibitively bony and left most of it. Now I wondered, if I had indeed, however accidently, ingested the feared morsel of *cascadoo* that had been served to us that night, and was bound to stay here on this island. Sid had so enjoyed the ugly fish, sucking on the scales that were wide and long like toenail clippings, and on the fine threadlike bones to which the flesh clung in lumps. I remember the mound of scales, tails, fine bones and cartilage from the heads piled high on Sid's plate, not a speck of flesh left behind. Had *she* been destined, then, to return to Trinidad and remain there until the end of *his* days?

And now Sydney's house seemed claustrophobic like a wood and concrete *cascadoo*. I knew nothing of the island, I told myself. Yes, yes, I had been to various parts of it, and I had seen the supposed drug lord across the road numerous times and met Mrs. Allen and her son a few times. But still I felt I knew nothing. I had no meaningful friendships here, and now that Sydney was gone, no further attachments. My connection to the island would soon loosen. I would do everything I could, as swiftly as possible, to wrap up all Sydney's business here and leave sooner rather than later. This was not a holiday house, and for me Trinidad was not a holiday destination. I had no need for a place here. I thought of India the day we left Marrakesh to return to Toronto, waving wistfully to the wet-eyed staff as they waved back. As the taxi pulled away, India said to me, "Do you think, Joji, that they're saying, '*Au revoir*, Madame, *au revoir*, Master Jonathan,' or 'Go on now, off you go. Quickly'?"

Of course, the staff here at the house in Scenery Hills were unlikely to have said to me, "Go on now, off you go. Quickly." To point to a mundane example: on one occasion during those first days after Sid's death I was making my way to the stove when Rosita intercepted my path and reached ahead of me for the kettle. She prepared the coffee I wanted but had not yet asked for, and certainly had not expected her to make. At a different time, this might not have been worth noting. It would have been the natural order of things. But we were in that state where every action seemed to have greater intensity than usual, and to take on special meaning. I felt that Rosita was, in that instance, taking care of me rather than performing her usual duties. It is certainly possible that I am misguided in thinking that there was now a nuance in our relationship that meant, having become the inheritor of Sydney's role, I was not simply the employer nor she simply the worker. I can only swear that the act was done with the kind of caring I had only known, before then, from Sydney.

In moments like these, I felt with unwavering certainty that I had to keep the house, had to keep Rosita and Lancelot on. But such moments were still only fleeting.

Quite suddenly, as I was facing the Gulf—my back to the house—I had one of my now-frequent revelations: I must immediately call Catherine. I was struck, as if by lightning,

with the thought that after Sydney's passing there was
nothing to come between her and me any longer. (And I
was instantly presented with further evidence that my presence was not being wished away by the staff: I had thumped
my forehead with the palm of my hand by way of excla-
mation, saying aloud, "Of course!"—and not a second later
Lancelot was behind me, his hands on my shoulders, guiding me to sit as if I were weak and infirm, and cooing that I
needed to take it easy. I protested—perhaps too brusquely—
that I was fine, I was fine; I'd simply had a revelation and
hadn't realized he was right behind me. He stayed at my
side, thoughtful, and then said, "Is so when people you love
dead and leave you. You does stand up just so, and realization coming at you fast-fast, like bullets from a gun." That
was yet another instant when I felt keenly how one has no
privacy in this place, and doubted my ability to live among
people who were so aware of my every move and need.)

Once I was free of Lancelot's hovering, I parsed my
thoughts. I had always been so preoccupied with Sydney
that I had never really attended to any of my relationships—
not with my mother, friends or lovers, and, most recently,
not with Catherine. Catherine was a good person. She was
loyal. She was fair. She had a job she enjoyed, and interests
of her own. She was the kind of person with whom one
could reliably build a life.

It was quite clear to me that she had to come to Trinidad.
She had to stay here at the house with me while I sorted out
details and made arrangements for these people who had

worked here. It would allow her a glimpse into this side of my life. It would be a way of reconnecting with her, of showing her the closeness I shared with these people—the kind of closeness that I yearned for, at least most of the time—and, once we were back in Canada, she and I could begin our life together. And I would begin to write again.

The longing to write was the only thing I was not having second thoughts about. I reminded myself that in one of the letters Sydney had left me he made special mention not of the furniture in his house, not of his paintings nor his boxes upon boxes of photographs and not of his trinkets, but of the notebooks he had used as diaries. He explicitly stated in the letter that I should do with them as I chose. Sydney knew I was a writer and he knew I was having difficulty writing. Surely, then, with this particular mention, with this bequest, there was more than a suggestion, there was an outright invitation—a request, even—that I use the material of his life to create my next work. Was this not so? And wasn't his story integral to mine? Wasn't his love of Zain and sorrow over the tragedy that befell her also my story now? Yes, back in Canada, Catherine would do whatever it was she usually did, and I, finally able to write, would bury myself in this new body of work.

But in short order my enthusiasm for reconnection dissipated. I imagined us in our little corners: I in mine, writing with measured contentment, but not knowing, and not needing to know, what she was doing in hers. When my book was finished, what would we do then? Catherine, the woman I lived with, would read my book, and she would learn about her lover—about me—from the book he had written while they were living together in the same house. Where could we go from there?

7

Too soon, I was obliged to put aside the notebooks and attend to my new household reponsibilities. I kept the books locked in my suitcase, which in turn was locked and stored inside the closet in my bedroom. Such caution was necessary, I felt, because of Sydney's alarming speculation about Zain's death, but it was an inconvenience, too, as I thought of the notebooks often and was drawn to reading them—to indulging myself in Sydney's words, which, naturally, were delivered to me in his voice—at all hours throughout those first days when nothing was as usual. They were my only constant. I began my days with them, and ended with them. In between, I took refuge and sought answers in them.

I began to feel unfairly put upon when my attention was needed, it seemed, for every little matter. Although the keys for the linen cupboard were in Rosita's care—everything is stored in locked cupboards here—she wanted permission from me to remove guest towels and a tablecloth that had never been used. I wondered why she wanted them at such a time, but felt that I—who had previously never been more than a visitor in this house—had no right to ask. Sankar wanted to know if he could drive the car since it was registered in Sydney's name, and Lancelot needed me to make a decision about whether or not the landscaping firm that usually came on that particular day of the week ought to carry on as usual. I was to telephone the company and speak with the manager. I did so reluctantly; I was not settling easily into my new role.

All the while I ruminated on what I had learned about Sydney from reading the notebooks. I thought of Sid and India, and how Sid had so easily and lovingly done for my mother and me what she herself had been wanting from a partner. I know my mother would not have dreamed of reciprocating. But if she and Sid were so ill-suited to each other, why then had they remained together for so long?

At the next opportunity I retreated to my room to ponder this, and in the notebook came across an entry that made me realize there was more to Sydney's stories than he'd related to me himself. I was moved by the nuances in the words he'd written, nuances he'd chosen to omit when he'd spoken to me. I got up to lock the bedroom door, sat on the edge of the bed and read.

Zain, what made you so brash and bold? Why did you have to challenge convention? You were always making people face the worst aspects of themselves.

I have often wondered if you introduced me to Eric on that fateful visit because in Trinidad I had no real ties, other than to my parents and my sister, and it was unlikely that I would share your secrets with anyone. Did you think my presence in Trinidad afforded you an excellent alibi, a way to spend time more easily with Eric? Angus wouldn't have thought twice about us coming and going, and so, once you were with me, you could carry on seeing Eric with ease. Sometimes even now, so many years later, I feel betrayed by you, Zain. I haven't written this down before now because the implication has been too difficult for me to face. To think that you consciously used me is to put a tarnish on this friendship that meant so much to me. Perhaps you felt that since I had a secret of my own, one that you kept for me, I would be fine with knowing about and keeping yours. There is a shade of bribery about this—on both sides, I suppose.

When you first told me you'd met someone, you were so coy about it that I thought for a moment you meant you'd met someone who would be a good match for me. This person, you carried on saying in your wistful voice, was "utterly amazing, just wonderful, really very special, unbelievably interesting, unusually smart." I realized you were using the kind of superlatives one does when describing the object of one's infatuation, and suddenly I knew that

you were talking about someone for yourself. You
referred to your friend as "this person"—and for a
confusing time I thought that you might be having
an affair with a woman. I was almost blind with
jealousy. Perversely, my jealousy was only heightened when you told me that "this person" was a man
named Eric.

You told me how you had met, and since then I
have so often imagined the meeting that I feel as if
I might have been there in the grocery store, watching you: You are awaiting your turn in line, brows-
ing through a magazine, and the man behind you
draws close and begins to comment on the photos
of the celebrities in the magazine. I can see from
the way you turn and look at him that you think
him rather bold to be peering at and commenting
on your reading material. But on the surface you
are perfectly nonchalant, and chat back as if it were
the most natural thing in the world. You walk out
of the grocery without a glance backwards; but you
wait for the man outside in the parking lot, and
he walks towards you as if this meeting has been
planned. He is tall and lean, not a spare ounce of
fat on him, but muscled, and his skin is a reddish
bronze. You can see that he spends most of his time
in the sun. He puts his bag of groceries into your
cart and pushes it towards your car. Somehow he
already knows which one it is. He takes the keys

from you and opens your trunk, lifts your grocery bags in, shuts the trunk and hands back the keys. You say, So, I have to tip you, I suppose. I only have a dollar bill on me. I don't suppose you take credit cards? And he says, What about lunch, then? You follow in your car as he drives his own to the restaurant at the yacht club. There, he tells you that he is in the boat repair and maintenance business. After lunch, you follow him to his office in a trailer on the yacht club grounds.

Zain, how is it that we were in touch for a year, by letters and by phone, and yet in that time you never told me that you were seeing this man? You had been seeing Eric for more than a year by the time I learned about him.

It is impossible for me to forget that dreadful lunch the three of us had at the yacht club. For the second time, you used me to meet Eric—at least, this is how it feels to me. The staff at the restaurant knew Eric and they paid him a great deal of friendly attention, and he revelled in it. He also knew several of the customers, engaging in small exchanges with them while he sat at our table.

The conversation between us plagues me still. Eric leaned in and remarked that he'd heard I worked out routinely. I said, Yes, as does Zain. He said, "Yes, like Zain. But you have a lot more muscle than she does. Women here work out not

to gain muscle, but to lose fat." He reached out and
wrapped his hand around one of my biceps, and
squeezed it. He said, with a grin, "So, what's this all
about? What do you expect to achieve?"

I felt as if I had been punched in my stomach
by this question, but I smiled, shrugged and said
nothing. I saw you turn and look at Eric warningly,
but he didn't look back at you. He lifted his empty
beer glass to the waiter as he said to me, "Well, I'm
listening. Tell me about yourself."

"What can I tell you?" I responded, my guard up.

He said that he knew some things about me, that
he had always wondered about people like me. You
started, and said, "Eric, what's going on with you?
Come on, you're going to embarrass her." But he
brushed you off, saying that it wasn't often one had
the chance to find out real answers to real questions
such as these. "If you're really okay with yourself as
you are," he said to me, "then you shouldn't be afraid
to answer some questions."

I said nothing. He said, "So, what is it that women
might see in someone like you?"

You snapped then, telling Eric that he had crossed
the line, but I said, "No, it's okay. He can ask what
he wants." I turned to him. "You first," I said. "What
do they see in someone like you?"

Your eyes lit up. "Yes," you said, "tell us: what do
women see in you?"

He said, "Well, first of all, I am a man." He paused. "And you, Zain—you above all know what that means. Am I not a man!"

You became still. I was speechless; blood had rushed to my head. But Eric was not finished. He addressed me again. "I was wondering. Were you molested as a child?"

I didn't answer, and he said, "I mean, is that why you want to be a man? I'm giving you the benefit of the doubt here, you see. I mean, what has caused you to be the way you are? I'm just wondering." His calm quiet voice and smile could not mask his hostility.

And then, Zain, you began to laugh. You shook your head and laughed. I shrank in my seat, and rather suddenly your laughter ceased, and you became serious. You pushed your chair back and rose. You snatched up your bag and turned to me. "Let's go. I've had enough of this; this is ridiculous. What on earth was I thinking?"

I followed you out while Eric remained sitting at the table.

I could sense then that you had seen something new in him. He had embarrassed himself, yes; but worse, his ignorance meant that I had felt shamed by him in front of you. You told me later that he called you up and pleaded that he had meant no harm by his questions. He was just playing, teasing.

That is what real men do, he told you—they tease
and heckle each other. I should have been able to
take it. He said that he couldn't understand how
a woman who was a lesbian could be "just friends"
with another who was not; it was nearly impossible,
he said, for a straight man and a straight woman to
be nothing more than good friends.

I looked up from the notebook at this, thinking of my
own struggle to understand who Sydney had once been, and
who he had become.

When had I first become aware of the variety of iden-
tities Sydney had embraced during his existence? It might
well have been during those evenings when he and I had sat
out on the veranda, or during those afternoons in the garden
by the wall. Perhaps I had begun to expect, and even look
forward to, hearing about these variances when I sat beside
him on his bed in his room, as a son might well have done,
and listened while, propped against pillows, he regaled
me. Was it in the dining room, eating Rosita's dinner: curried duck, *channa*, and *dhalpuri roti*—the heat of the slight
pepper in the curry causing me, to Rosita's and Sydney's
amusement, to sweat profusely and drink copious amounts
of soothing coconut water? Was it when Sydney remarked
how unusually hot it was that day and Rosita muttered
from the kitchen—reminding me for the umpteenth time
that she listened to everything and missed nothing—that
this was earthquake weather? Sydney lowered his voice

and confided to me that people here always said that, but of course, there was no such thing as earthquake weather; earthquakes occurred miles beneath the surface of the earth and had no regard for what was happening—heat spells, extreme cold, endless rain, or dry weather—on the surface of the earth. What interested him, he piped up opportunistically, were changes of seismic proportions that took place—or, despite conditions being ripe for such changes, that did not take place—in the minds, hearts and bodies of people, not beneath the surface of the earth. And this was enough of a preamble for Sydney to launch for the next hour or so into the story of his walk to the Irene Samuel centre.

Or was it a different occasion—during my third visit when I took him for a drive to the Queen's Park Savannah? I had not yet received any hint from him that he understood the hurt he had caused me. We sat on one of the park benches drinking coconut water we'd bought from one of the nearby vendors, and Sydney said, out of the blue, "There used to be, Jonathan, two or three snowfalls every year that brought the city of Toronto to a standstill—hardly ever for more than a few days, but the city was always ill-prepared. Is it still like this, Jonathan?" he asked. He remarked that side streets had always been low on the priority list of those to be ploughed. I wouldn't be surprised, he said, if it is still like that. You know, I have been noticing how the sea—and he pointed across the city, in the direction of the Gulf—seems to have risen more each year even as it has become hotter and drier in the dry season. Yet there is much more rain nowadays in the wet season. This may well be the beginning of another ice age, you know, Jonathan, he said, for it has been scientifically noted that ice ages have always followed not cold weather, as is usually assumed, but abundant rainfall. It is the rain that comes first. Then the cold.

I tossed off an answer, almost dismissing this topic, saying lightly that I didn't doubt it at all. The weather had indeed been rather strange in Canada these last few years—it could be cold or even hail in June, and there were now unseasonably high temperatures at the height of the winter season.

Sydney did not respond right away. He was pensive for so long, in fact, that I assumed this topic of conversation had been exhausted. But just as I was about to suggest we move along, he turned to me rather suddenly and asked, as if it were the most important question of the moment, Have the Toronto winters become colder, or have they become milder, Jonathan? Has there been a change? He paused again—waiting for my response, I thought at first. But he was clearly uninterested in any rejoinder from me, for I had barely begun to talk, excited at the prospect of sharing some details about my own life—in particular, to elaborate on how the winters had indeed become so tedious that there were years when, at the first hint of cold, I took off to the south of Spain, where I met artists and writers and beautiful interesting women, and where I spent time thinking and writing and did not book a flight back to Toronto until after the famous groundhog in Punxsutawney, Pennsylvania, and the less-famous one closer to home, Wiarton Willie, had made their prognostications; a digression which, I was hoping, would allow me to interject some lightness into our morning by imagining a similar annual Trinidadian celebration, held perhaps at a beach, with grand marshals in skimpy sequined and feathered costumes and food and music and speeches, where everyone would observe the behaviour of a crab emerging out of its crab hole, noting whether it came right out and took off down the beach in its sideways canter, or peeped out and retreated, thereby foretelling the timing of the rainy season—when he took advantage of my pause to jump back in and tell me about the particular morning that had been forever seared into his memory.

There was a winter in Toronto, he said, when one snowstorm followed another, and after weeks of this, the snow ploughed off the streets was piled so high on the sidewalks that you couldn't see the road over the top of the bank or the cars passing there. The city couldn't clear away the snow fast enough.

Seemingly unaware of any effect his words might have on me, he continued: But thankfully, the supervisor of the building, the same building into which I had moved immediately *after*, had done an adequate job, given the circumstances, of cutting a path that stretched across the full width of the stairs, right down to and including the sidewalk.

Sydney's use of the word *after* was like a blow: it immediately blotted out images of my Crab Prediction Day party, not to mention everything that he himself was saying. *After.* The way he used the word assumed—demanded—a *what.*

After *what?* And it was an admission of time on the other side of *after. Before. The same building you had moved into after what? What had happened before you moved into the building?* These questions twisted around each other in my head. I thought about how I had curtailed my trips to Spain and begun coming to Trinidad for this moment precisely: for Sydney to explain the time *before*, time that he had just so nonchalantly condensed and dismissed in that one word, *after*. I wanted him—I wanted her—Sid, Sydney, whoever, whatever—to complete the phrase *the same building into which I had moved immediately after* with the words *I left you. You* here being plural. And although no explanation would have sufficed, I wanted him to fully elucidate why he had left my mother and me. A sweat broke on my temples. But wary of exposing myself, I remained quiet, and Sydney carried on.

It was extremely cold weather, the kind of weather you and I know, he said. He gave me a complicit smile and mused, Had a person never experienced such temperatures, such wind, she or he would have a hard time imagining it.

He carried on, but I was disheartened at his obliviousness. He and I were like the ships in the Gulf sailing past each other in different lanes.

I was grateful that the sidewalks had been cleared too, Sydney said (passing my ship none the wiser). For you see, he said, I was about to embark on a walk from my apartment on Bergamot Avenue in the city's east end to the Irene Samuel Health and Gender Centre twenty minutes or so away. The heat register inside the glass-walled entrance of the apartment building thrummed. The area of the glass door around which my mitten-covered hands were pressed had frosted a size larger in two perfect splayed-hand shapes. My hands, he remembered, were already hot in the thick wool gloves I had pulled on the instant I closed my apartment door, and the cold off the glass had been welcome. I would have liked to stand there all day imagining, he said, that the heat of my body, so infinite, so powerful, could melt away snow and ice, and warm, if not the city, at least the entrance on Bergamot Avenue. I felt invincible that day, he told me, adding that Eastern philosophies teach us that a change in a single person can create a change in that person's entire environment. And knowing, he carried on, that I was on the verge of personal change—change of seismic proportions—I entertained fantasies of myself as the catalyst that would halt your Canadian winters in their track. But your winters are unstoppable.

Sydney laughed at himself for the audacity of such a dream, and despite my defensiveness and disappointment over his earlier unfinished sentence, and now at how he was shoving winters over onto me when I knew that Sydney held dual citizenship, Canadian and Trinidadian, and therefore winters and all that come with them were as much his as they were mine (the making of such distinctions is petty, of course, but I was not above pettiness in matters concerning Sydney), I was reminded of how he used to encourage me to wish for and to dream of the impossible. The implication was that the act of wishing and imagining was of equal value to—and sometimes of greater value than—the realization of dreams. I recalled how, when I was a boy, my mother would often be in her third-floor study writing, while Sid and I entertained each other downstairs in the large room that made up the dining and living areas. Sid would tell me, convincingly, that people could fly. She could teach me, she'd say, and with a swimming-like gesture—the breast stroke, I would later understand—we would thrust our heads up and our chests forward into the room, and with our arms we would slice through the air, catch it in our turned-out palms and sweep it back, and I do remember the air felt as thick and leaden as water might have felt. We would make our way through the rooms as if we were half swimming, half flying, me expecting liftoff any second.

A change in Sydney's voice brought me out of my reverie. He was speaking matter-of-factly now. The door had sealed between the warmth inside and the cold air outside, he said, and I had to shove hard to open it. It popped open against the seal, and cold air was rashly whipped up and sucked into the entranceway. Snowflakes somersaulted in, and upon hitting the ground transformed instantly into puddles of wetness in front of the heater. Cold air slammed like a hand against my face and nose and I gasped, unable for a couple of seconds to breathe. It was as if, in a flash, there had been a mini death, and a rebirth. If you understand, Jonathan, that I felt that day as if I were on a journey of death—a small death, and one of rebirth too—you would also understand why I saw the same in all of this cold and snow. I suppose I was looking for a rhythm and a pattern in the world around me to confirm the correctness of all that I had taken into my own hands, and all my pending actions. If you think I am speaking in riddles, Jonathan—and here Sydney turned and looked at me full-on—it is because I don't know how else to speak, having been trained to hide my unease beneath the more natural desire to be. To simply be. What luxury! As if he saw behind the mask of my stillness he patted my knee and said, Please try to let me tell my story as I must, in the only way I know how.

And, Jonathan, he added, you must understand that I am not trying to whip up unnecessary suspense. It is already there, always, but of course one wants relief after suspense, and I must admit that in a life like mine, there seems to be constant suspense and little relief, even now. Back then, I pulled the hood forward on my down jacket, yanking it low to protect my forehead, pulled on the straps of the knapsack to ensure its snugness, and stepped outside.

———

Women's voices in the kitchen brought me out of my room. I reluctantly went to see who was there.

Rosita's sister Carmen had arrived, and the two were preparing food. With the back of her hand Rosita was wiping away tears that were pouring down her cheeks. She had already chopped a large mound of onions, and was chopping yet more. Carmen had her hands in batter inside an oversized basin. The air in the kitchen stung my eyes and skin and was bitter on my tongue. Lancelot, groomed and dressed in a white shirt and black pants, came in from the garage carrying a case of soft drinks.

"What's going on?" I asked, bringing them all to a halt.

Rosita said simply, "The wake."

Emotional fatigue had no doubt got the best of me, for things that should have been obvious were clearly not. I was fumbling through the aftermath of Sydney's death and felt as if the immediate future was unpredictable, being revealed to me one event at a time. I was the only one, it seemed, who had never before experienced the death of someone close. And so my words slipped out, unfiltered.

"You've got to be kidding." I corrected myself clumsily. "I mean, is that what all the food is for, and that pop?"

"What you think, Mr. Jonathan? Is a wake tonight," Rosita said.

"Here? At the house?" It seemed I was unable to control my surprise and displeasure.

Carmen stopped kneading and turned to look at us. Lancelot had been stocking the fridge with the drinks. He, too, turned.

It was Carmen who, with a tone of amiable curiosity, broke the tension that had so suddenly arisen. "Oh, all you don't have wake for the dead in Toronto." It was a statement of understanding.

The bitterness in the air now stung my eyes and I began to tear up. The others continued to look at me, and rage surged in my voice before I had time to check it. "So, who invited people over?"

Rosita said, with more impatience than I had heard from her before, "You don't invite people. Is not a party. They come."

"Yes, they just come," agreed Carmen. "That kind of news does travel fast, and if people know the person who dead, or a relative of the dead, or somebody who know them, they does come. Is so it is. They just come."

"How many people are you expecting?"

The others chuckled, not with good humour but in disbelief, and talked over one another.

"You could have five people or you could have a hundred people."

"It depends if the person was a good person or not. If he popular, or if he is somebody."

"People does come to *maco* too. Some of them just farse. But not every body. Most people come to pay they respects."

The telephone rang. Lancelot answered it and handed it to me. It was Gita, calling from England. I pulled myself together as best I could. She came straight to the point: she and Jaan had decided that they would return for the funeral. They had already booked the flights. They were, however, unable to get sensibly priced flights immediately, and would arrive in three days' time. She said that she was sure that the pundit would agree that the funeral should be postponed to accommodate the arrival of the deceased's only relative.

Gita ended her call by saying, "Siddhani said, a long time ago, that she considered you to be a relative of hers. That being so, I imagine you will look after everything. We will come, but please understand that we won't be involved in the ceremony itself."

I had hardly put the receiver down, and was still reeling, when Rosita said that she and Carmen were going to finish up the cooking and then they would get dressed. Did I have any clothes I wanted ironed to wear that evening?

"What do you mean? Do I have to dress up?"

Rosita, without looking at me, said, "Well, is a wake."

"What time are you expecting people, and how long will they stay?" I asked.

"They will start coming all now so, and they will come every evening until the funeral," Rosita answered.

Every evening until the funeral. I thought of Gita and Jaan, and how they would not arrive for another three days. The funeral would, of course, not take place on the very day of their arrival. So, did that mean that there were to be three full evenings of people dropping by?

"And what about me?" I asked. "What am I supposed to do? I am not sure about this. Is there somewhere else they can go? Aren't wakes usually held at the funeral home?"

No one responded to this, but Rosita's mouth pursed and Carmen turned back to her kneading.

I took a deep breath and gathered my thoughts. It was important to show a little amicability; perhaps I could do so by inquiring if there was enough drink on hand. "What do people drink? Where is Sankar? Tell him to get the car ready. I'll go and get a bottle of rum, and perhaps a couple bottles of wine."

There was a charged pause, followed by a chorus of "No!"—the word inflected with horror and incredulity.

Carmen took it upon herself to say, "Hindus don't drink alcohol at wakes, Mr. Jonathan, and don't eat meat. We can't cook no meat in the house until one week after the day of the funeral."

I was not, at the best of times, a big meat-eater, yet I received this last as if it were an indication that all control over my own life had been taken from me. I had not asked for any of these responsibilities, and for a moment I fantasized about saying to hell with it all, to hell with *you* all, and leaving. I could pack my bags and have Sankar drive me to the airport and wait, regardless of how long it took, for the next flight out to Canada.

Instead I sheepishly responded, "I see," and backed out of the kitchen. I retreated again to the sanctuary of the bedroom.

8

As far as I know, time did not slow or stop that first day of Sydney's wake. Nonetheless, I constantly felt as if one minute might stretch on forever, even as, in that same minute, an hour's worth of events seemed to happen. By the time I left the kitchen, Sydney's room had already been cleaned, the bed remade not just with clean bedding, but with a new set of sheets fresh out of their packaging. I closed the door and sat at my desk. I pressed my hands to my ears against the sound of noise coming from the kitchen, multiplied now by the roar of the vacuum cleaner in the passageway that runs between the bedrooms.

I thought again about sitting on that park bench in the Queen's Park Savannah when Sydney had said to me, I was about to cross into a future that out of necessity would obliterate much of my past. I wanted to walk to the health centre that winter morning, he explained, because it would give me time to reflect on my past. I wanted to confirm what pieces of that past I wished to take with me into my new life.

I remember how Sydney smiled—was it a begrudging smile or a wistful one?—as he added, Of course the past is never erased, and is even always present. And as he spoke I saw how I myself could have been, that very day, the author of those same words.

Was it clutching at straws for me to believe that Sydney had been alluding to the idea, however veiled, that I was a part of his not-so-erasable past? Yearning and peevishness are a messy mix: I now realize that I heard less what he said, and more what I thought he ought to have said—that he wished *not* to erase aspects of the past.

He interrupted himself often, but he always returned to this essential story. And I had heard the story so often that I could picture the scene as if I had been there with him. If he were still here, I believe I could recite the details alongside him. That first day of the wake I imagined his words. I heard his voice saying: During bouts of wakeful anxiety the night before, I heard the growl, groan and scrape of snowploughs. I had passed the night watching their yellow safety lights dart up the far wall of my bedroom and slide across the ceiling in a one-two-rest, one-two-rest pattern. But despite their efforts, I knew, when I stepped outside that morning, that the sidewalks, with the snow, rain, freeze sequence that had been that season's predictable model, were bound to be slippery—as they were. Surely, he said, it would have been reasonable for me to break my resolve under the circumstances, to have tried flagging down a taxi.

I could almost see the darkness at seven in the morning as Sydney had so often described it, and although I have never been to the apartment he described, I feel as if I know it. I certainly have walked past the area, and know exactly how much time it would have taken to walk from the apartment to his appointment at the clinic.

Once again, I imagined his voice. I stood there between the lobby and entrance doors, he would tell me, and observed large snowflakes, flimsy and light, floating down on the other side of the door. Street lamps remained lit. The one nearest the door of the building in which I lived carried on a single-note buzzing, and its light had an irregular tremor that gave a pink glow to the dustlike flakes. The buzzing was louder than usual that morning. I supposed the bulb would blow soon. I remember all of this because it was as if everything in my environment was aware of what I was about to do, and was marking the auspiciousness of the day for me. There was a rosy aura to the darkness of the sky behind that lamp. How still the street was, with its evenly spaced rows of ginkgo trees on either side. I can see it all, as if this had all happened just weeks ago: the ginkgos bare of greenery, new snowfall delineating their branches, that pink glow above, and lower, mid-height to the row houses opposite, a yellowish tinge from the tungsten lighting over the doors of the row houses to the left and right of the red-brick tenement in which I lived. How clean and pretty the neighbourhood was in that moment, swathed in the snow's whiteness and in the pastel shades of light that, even as I watched, was dissipating. Day consumed night like a magician swallowing a string of pastel-colour silk kerchiefs.

The blushing light down Bergamot was replaced soon enough by a low and heavy sky that cast a pall of grey over everything. Cornwall Street, the main thoroughfare, had already been ploughed. The bank of pushed-aside snow that formed a barrier between the sidewalk and the road was crowned by a new layer of snow and sludge mixed with broken slabs of packed ice that had been formed in the night by the machines I had heard. I was hungry. I had been given an orange sheet of paper with information and directions: no food or drink except for water after midnight, and no water after 3 a.m. I was trying not to think of food, not to notice my light-headedness, the need, as one who was pre-diabetic in those days, to eat not long after awakening. I was wondering if I would be able to walk for half an hour in that horrid weather and not faint before arriving. But you know, Jonathan, that is something I could never quite get used to when I was in Canada. That pervasive sense of alone-ness: you could live in a building with seventy units and not make friends with a single person in it. I also found that, in Canada, even among friends, independence was practised and appreciated. Even among lovers, even among family members. The question I always ask as I think of that day is not how could any human live in such a climate, or why; but rather, how could one have lived in a city for a period of almost twenty years, yet have not one soul she could ask to accompany her on a mission such as mine?

As I remembered Sydney's voice telling me this, I saw that, over time, I had become used to the switches in Sydney's pronouns when he talked in this ironic manner about himself. Moreover, I had myself learned to be quick and creative in concocting sentence structures—often, I thought now, humorously complex structures—so as to avoid using pronouns when I spoke of his past as Sid.

In the end, continued Sydney, I felt unusually brave that day, a soldier alone in the trenches. It is satisfying to realize that even when one is alone, one is not denied the highs and lows of life. When I lived in Toronto and used to return for visits to my parents here in Trinidad, to this place where I was born and grew up, I would lie in my bed in my parents' house and listen to the coconut branches in the wind as they scraped the roof. To my ears this sound was wind chimes. In the evening I would sit on the patio and watch parrots and parakeets, their black bodies against the golden sky, and I would feel as if they were on the ends of strings I held in my hand. The rice plains, cane fields, swamplands, mangroves, mountain ranges, the sea that like an eager child scatters jewels about your feet, and then like a mischievous child runs away again, were oxygen coursing through the blood in my veins. I would know on those visits that nowhere else on earth could be my home, and I would feel a love well up in me like a tsunami. But even as the wave swelled I knew I dared not let it overcome me.

That morning of my walk to the clinic in Toronto, I wore a forest-green knapsack from Mountain Equipment Co-op. In it were letters from a very dear friend, some loose clothing recommended for my stay at the post-op facility, toiletries, my wallet and an envelope in which was a rather large sum of money in bills. I tugged every so often on the knapsack's belt around my waist to make sure it was secure. I wouldn't have wanted to be relieved of that cash! I bent my head against the cold wind and held the front of the coat's hood down. I had to reach under my glasses and wipe away cold- and wind-induced tears again and again. One eye would always tear up more than the other in a wind, and that morning it wouldn't stop. I pressed a finger against the closed eyelid towards the inner corner of my eye, as if doing so would force out all the remaining moisture, but no sooner had I done so than tears cascaded again. I had pulled the front of the wool scarf that was wound about my neck up over my nose, and took in the warmth it momentarily trapped from my breath. It didn't take long for condensed breath to bead on the scarf, dampening it. All of this, every detail, that is, seemed critical, and I wanted to experience it all, even the sensation of wet wool threads that clung to my lips and found their way onto my tongue.

I bent into the wind that swept up and down the street and walked briskly toward Eldon Street. From there it was a straight walk in a westerly direction to the health centre.

There was less wind on the east–west streets, but only marginally less. My brain would still have frozen, I was certain, had my head not been covered. And yet, there was a girl—I recognized her from the neighbourhood and knew that some days she looked no older than ten years, and other days like an old woman who had already experienced the gamut of life's harshest blows—not only wearing no hat, but sporting a white hooded denim jacket, cropped at the waist. A collar of blond faux-fur hung at her back around the hood. The zipper of the jacket was pulled up until it reached not a fraction higher than the apex of her meagre breasts. The white tights she wore rode low to offer a view of her exposed belly button, emphasizing her skimpy legs. And so, even as I was on my way to alter myself, my female body, I wondered who, or what, had ever convinced these young girls that such thinness, such fragility, such exposure in that kind of cold, was in the least attractive? The girl wore running shoes and smoked, striking a pose to catch the eye of every driver who passed. She glanced at me, turned away, and then looked at me again, and this time I could see her wondering. She must have made a decision, because she primped her pose, distributed her weight on one leg and swung her hip at me. Then she transferred her weight to the other leg and swung again. She puckered her lips at me. I couldn't suppress my delight in her mistake, nor could I contain the smile that followed. At that she stomped her foot and gestured with a fist, slowly unfurling her middle finger, pointing it to the sky. Without waiting a second longer she turned her precious time to the driver of a passing car, and I was reminded that before I had left Trinidad and come to Canada, people who recognized me as the offspring of Amresh and Sita Mahale would say when I smiled that I looked exactly like my mother, and when I was serious that I was the image of my father. I would have to ask the doctor, I thought wryly, about fixing that smile.

And so Sydney carried on, recalling the minutest details of this walk. He had at the time noticed, and, so long after remembered, even slight changes in the daylight en route to the Irene Samuel. He spoke of the nuances of scents in the cold air from the just-opened automotive shops, and from the row of North African and Pakistani grocery shops he passed. He recalled the sound of snow crunching, sludge peeling off car tires as the vehicles went by, police sirens wailing in the distance, a car alarm hailing from yet another direction, children on their way to school calling out and chatting. He spoke, once, of a particular household he'd passed on that route, recalling detail after detail even as I felt that he was trying to snatch the words back the moment they left his mouth. This household that was, to quote him, a boil on the fragile skin of the small enclave of respectability in the neighbourhood just east of the health centre and west of the Don Valley. The bank of ploughed snow, he told me, had cut off the near sidewalk and forced Sid to cross the street to use the far one. She therefore had to pass immediately in front of the house and its occupants. One of two motorized wheelchairs that belonged there was on its side, blanketed with the snow, beside the wheelchair-access ramp. The small yard in front of the house was crammed with furniture, all covered with an undulating duvet of the last night's snowfall. As Sid approached the house she played a game with herself, recalling and identifying the shapes beneath the snow blanket. Metal chairs, a lawn mower, a picnic table on top of which were a child's tricycle and a broken pram, recycling and garbage bins and a long metal box, the kind that the city used in parks to store small equipment. Sid remembered that there was usually a propane barbecue tied with a thick iron chain to the fence that separated this house from the one next to it. She noticed that it was gone and conjectured that the occupants of the house had traded it in to pay their rent, or for booze or drugs. Even in deep winter the two women who lived there would each get into a motorized wheelchair, he told me, and barrel down Cornwall and Eldon streets, against the flow of traffic, berating each other all the while for all to hear.

Just as Sid was directly in front of the house, its front door opened slightly. Her heart leapt, Sydney said, and the fright of being confronted by one of the occupants almost caused her to slip. But then the door simply closed again, without anyone appearing. She hurried on, but couldn't help recalling one Halloween when she was returning after midnight to her apartment and had passed that house. A party had spilled into the street, and a man had launched a rocket firecracker, aiming it across the street. A whizzing whistle rang high into the night and then a bang reverberated, followed by a procession of electric red and blue starlights, a trillion flashes stripping across the street and onto the lawns of the houses on the far side. Sid had held her breath and waited. The two women had screamed at the firecracker launcher, who was howling with pleasure. Sydney addressed me, saying: And I hope you excuse me, Jonathan, but this is exactly what they said, "You fucking asshole. You crazy or what? Cut it out."

I had never known Sydney—nor Sid, for that matter— to use expletives, and I admit that I was perversely pleased. Granted, he was simply reporting what he had heard, but he and I were both made shy by this. I remember laughing aloud, for he looked like a child, though one who was pleased to have been caught. On vandalized walls here on this island, the *F* word is often sprawled in paint, as it is in almost every English-speaking country, but here it is usually spelled *f-o-c-k*, and I can still hear Sydney pronounce it, that one word lower in volume than the others, the *f* soft and feathered, followed by a hollowness, as if an *h* trailed the *f*, the vowel being neither an *o* nor a *u*, and again followed by that *h* sound, and then the *cking* as usual: *fhu/ ohcking*. His handling of that one word, with apology but with some delight in its illicitness, gave him the air of a stereotypical affected and effeminate gay man. But as amused as I was, I was also reminded of my mother's long-ago accusations—made directly to Sid—that Sid felt she was too good, too classy to cuss. My mother would say this when she was attempting to come down off her own high horse, and to bring Sid down with her.

After the moment of levity for both of us, Sydney became serious again, telling me that after that first firecracker, another whizzed into the air. The sound of the man's delight followed it again, Sydney said, and the same women screamed again—but this time before he repeated the woman's words he apologized. And here I will swear, Jonathan, he said, but to clean up what they said dulls the dazzle of that neighbourhood: "Cut it out right now, you crazy son of a bitch, or I'll come out there and cut your balls off!" Sid had stood frozen, trying to seem calm, as if these events were quite natural, and one only had to be patient and wait one's turn to continue on down the sidewalk. But she hadn't looked over at the women and the man as she didn't want to be dragged into any conspiracy or camaraderie. I feared being knifed, he said, or bashed, as a consequence of some innocent engagement, and having to explain to my family, by which I mean Gita and Jaan, from an emergency hospital bed what on earth I was doing living in a neighbourhood in which that sort of thing could have transpired.

There was no one around who might have heard us, yet Sydney lowered his voice and added: My parents—who had passed away by this time—had never been able to understand why in Canada I'd lived in such different circumstances from those in which they had brought me up. You, Jonathan, he told me in that same low voice, had no idea, of course, that I was living over there in that wretched neighbourhood, but your mother did. She knew where I was. After living with her in the big old rambling Victorian house on Pellatt Green I felt like a failure for having to make such a move. I think of India, and even now—so far away, so long ago—I imagine that she must have dismissed me as being no different in the end from anyone else in that infamous area of Bergamot Avenue. Sydney paused, then said wistfully, I don't believe your mother ever really quite understood who or what I was.

Sydney's concerns about my mother's opinion of her brought to my mind an image of India at home in that house in the Annex, just south of the subway station at Dupont and Spadina streets. I saw India's back as she faced her desk in front of the window in the attic-floor study. And then another image: there she was, leaning against one of the kitchen counters staring up at the ceiling, unaware of my presence, writing in her head a chapter or fleshing out the plot of one of her books. I had never thought of the house on Pellatt Green as being any particular size, large or small, until I went off to look for a place of my own only to find that what I could afford without assistance from my mother or dipping into my portion of the inheritance left to us by her parents was a semi-detached house in Little Italy a third the size of 191 Pellatt Green. In contrast to the disappointment Sid imagined his family of origin felt about him living in a rented apartment in a disadvantaged area of the city, what my mother felt was pride; she thought it charming and immensely brave of me to take up the challenge of a "smart little hovel," as she called it, in what she thought of as a semi-residential neighbourhood, where, on weekends during the summer, a section of nearby College Street would be closed to traffic, and people from "just about anywhere," as she put it, would flock in the thousands to gorge on pizzas and calzones and panzarotti and gyros and gelato, and on every corner listen to older immigrants croon in foreign languages to awfully loud accordion music.

Of course, India is always the novelist; she exaggerates to a fault, which says more about her than about her subject. But I happened to know that Sydney's uneasiness about India's opinions of Sid were actually well founded. India might think my house—the house of her son—charming, but she had been critical of Sid's choices after leaving our home in the Annex.

I had always wondered what my mother and Sid had first seen in each other, what it was that had brought them together. Once, I had asked this of India. She and Sid had met, India told me, while sitting next to each other at the bar in the Elgin Room at the Yorkville Hotel—which was a hotel only in name; really it was an artist-run building of galleries and artists' studios. Each was taking a break from an event. India was reading at the launch of an anthology in which her work appeared, and Sid was attending a marathon video screening. As India recalled it, they turned to face each other and began to chat. On learning that India was a novelist, Sid had pulled out a rather smart black rollerball pen from the pocket of her jeans and asked India to recommend one of her novels. India took the pen from Sid, and while Sid ordered refills on their drinks, India wrote on a bar napkin the title of her most recent book. Beneath that, she wrote her phone number and underlined it twice. She folded the napkin and handed it to Sid. She said that there was instant attraction between them—and why not? They were both good-looking people. She remembered the pen, she said, the silkiness of its finish and its weight, and was immediately curious about this South Asian woman who had the taste and means to own such an item. She thought Sid well spoken, and into her mind, out of nowhere, popped the phrase *third-world aristocracy*. She was amused by this thought, and instantly hooked.

India's story about that encounter began benignly, but, as was wont to happen with my mother, turned into a complaint about Sid: Sid could never quite get used to the fact that she had left behind her family's posh life—such as it might have been in the Caribbean—when she immigrated to Canada. And worse, instead of employing the privileges of that background, which ought to have entitled her to say *to fucking hell with what others think of me*, she worried that people didn't see her for who she felt she was. Before the visit to see Sid's parents in Trinidad, India said she had assumed that Sid's life in our house in Canada was far more comfortable than it could have been over there. Well, of course, my mother said, I saw in Trinidad that those people—third-world aristocrats, they imagined themselves to be—put on a bloody good show: they were not in the least discreet about their love of all things fine and morbidly expensive. It was in Sid's bones for sure, India said, the sense that she had a right to it all. Then she thought about what she was saying and added, It's a particular kind of taste, of course, typical of people in those kinds of colonized countries. They're like magpies, able to home right in on the brightest and most beautiful things. India made the word *things* quiver. But poor Sid, she continued, Sid could not get used to what immigration does to people like her and me, people who, when we leave our families behind, also leave behind lives of luxury, of being served. Sid would not see that money was the least trustworthy aspect of class, that anyone could make money, and that those who came from it, those who'd had it in the family for eons, could still lose it. Sid, Sid, Sid. Poor Sid. She had no resilience, no tenacity. She could not in good humour take what this country offers to people like her.

India suddenly clapped her hands and laughed as she said, "But, dear Joji, what have I just remembered most vividly about Sid at the Elgin Bar? The bloody pen! A hundred years later and I can still feel the weight of the damn thing! She did have good taste; and she was, in those first flirtatious days, a wonderful lover—I'll give her that! But, but, but. Once the flirtation was over we became different people, and I believe we both must have been disappointed. I believe you were our glue."

Sometime after meeting Sid, my mother decided to get herself pregnant through artificial insemination. After India became pregnant, Sid was at my mother's side, and God knows, my mother confesses, she was grateful for the company, the help, the concern, flowers, chocolates, boxes of Chinese takeout, garlic naans smothered with mango chutney. Sid was generous and something resembling a relationship evolved. They didn't fall in love, India said, but rather into a relationship. In the fourth month of my mother's pregnancy, Sid moved into the house in the Annex.

When I was born, the attending nurse wrapped a towel about me and handed me to Sid. Sid brought me to my mother, who said she would wait to hold me until I had been cleaned up. I know this because India told me. Sid's willingness to take care of me allowed India to immediately throw herself back into her writing. When her book was published three years later, it was a finalist for three major prizes. She became busy with one event after another, with interviews, with touring the width of the country, and with travel abroad, and Sid and I became a team.

Knowing a little more now about Trinidadian families, especially those of Indian origin, I once asked Sydney if his parents had let him—well, importantly in this regard, *her* at that time—leave Trinidad and emigrate so far away without any opposition. His answer gave me another glimpse into what was going on with Sid before he and my mother met. Dad and Mum were angry, he said. There was a great deal of crying in the house in those days, he said. There was a lot of shouting between them and me. Dad assured me that if I left I would have to make it on my own, and for years he did not back down.

I was far away from the comforts I knew in Trinidad,

and I had no skills, Sydney said, other than those of a painter. I didn't tell Mum that I was struggling, but she knew in the way that parents always know what you're not telling them. She sent me money without me asking for it, and without Dad's knowledge. I was grateful, of course, but she thought she was sending it for the little extras. The truth is that I hadn't wanted to do anything but paint. If you'd asked me if I wanted to be an artist, I would have said, No, I want to paint—for being an artist seemed to entail a kind of empty posturing, and living a particular kind of lifestyle, and I used to make a distinction between that and actually making the art, between that and doing the work. I assumed that all I had to do was work hard and well and honestly to make paintings and get them shown, and they would surely be sold, and I would be a success. My strategy was to work hard, painting day and night for a month, then for two months take on temporary work where there was the potential to earn good money in a short space of time.

Answering an advertisement on the notice board at the community centre where I used the gym, I found a job where I went out into the suburbs, from door to door, and sold the residents a government-subsidized program to increase the insulation in their homes. There was also a period when I sold vacuum cleaners in the same manner, and another time I sold books of coupons for discounted restaurant meals. I made enough money to paint unpressured for a full month. Then, when I had a body of work to show, I approached galleries. But I was told in vague terms that their mandate was to show work that was "more Canadian." So then I delivered handmade cards into the mailboxes of houses in targeted areas of the city, advertising the sale of my paintings, which I displayed in my apartment. I aimed, on those open-house days, to make sales that would cover my apartment's rent and utilities, and the replenishment of art supplies.

At this, Sydney stopped talking. I felt he had more to say, yet his lips pursed and he nodded as if to say, *And that was that.*

I had to ask, "And then what did you do?"

He answered with resignation and relief at once: Then I met your mother. From the moment we began talking in the bar at the Elgin, I was quite taken by her. We became friends quickly. One day, she informed me that she had, finally, after several attempts, become pregnant. Before you were born I moved into 191 Pellatt Green with the understanding that I would use the shed as a painting studio. When you were born, India was busy with the book she was writing, and you were like my own child. We were a family. A woman was hired to come in weekly to clean and do the laundry, and I painted and took care of you, Jonathan. I painted without a worry about whether the work was good or not, whether it was too Canadian or too something else. It was the first time I had worked without a worry. The work was good, of course; I wouldn't have bothered otherwise. It took awhile— years, really—before I got a show, Sydney said. And to my utter surprise and delight—at least at first—it was reviewed. The review was long, too. But as I read it I realized that the reviewer didn't know how to think about the work. She praised the quality of the painting, citing technical proficiency and an understanding of the art history. She focused on my Trinidadian background, and this added a little colour to her review. When she began, however, to compare my work to that of a Haitian painter, my heart sank. Her conclusion was that the work's value came from its folksy, naive and crude qualities. I was devastated.

I did not tell Sydney then that I remembered that show. I was eight, and from the vantage point of the present I can say that I may well have detected already the friction between my two mothers, and for this reason I saw and remembered little things that are now meaningful as I try to piece together Sydney's life and understand my own. But I interjected quickly to say that I had lately come across a number of Sid's canvases, which were still stored in the basement at Pellatt Green. And, I said shyly, it was clear to me that Sid had been a very good painter. This was more than true, but what I could not find a way to say was how moved I'd been to see the paintings, for they seemed to offer a vibrant and vital window into his mind—the mind of an immigrant of colour in Toronto—in the 1980s.

Sydney's face lit up at my words of praise. How strange to see him blush. For a moment I could not speak, for I saw my beloved Sid in him just then.

It comes to me now that Sydney and I were sitting on the veranda as we talked that day, being indulged by his staff with food and drink. Rosita brought us hot little homemade treats as Sydney and I enjoyed the midday light and Lancelot topped up our glasses with orange juice. I asked Sydney if it had meant anything to his parents that in the early days, when he was still quite a new immigrant to Canada, he'd had exhibitions of his paintings. No, he said, this did not impress them. What mattered to them was the fact that he went to live with my mother. It mattered, he said, that I had gone to live in a woman's house, that I had gone to be with her. It mattered then that I continued to pursue my art and was still not working at any sort of paying job. They accused me of living off this woman—your mother—and they were very upset about the nature of the relationship. They told me that what I was doing was dangerous, but they couldn't or wouldn't explain what they meant by this. Try as they might, my parents also could not understand why Gita, younger than I, had done so well—she had become a lawyer, married a man who was also a lawyer, and with him had a son—and I, according to them, so poorly.

Sydney said that his parents asked him again and again why, in a land of so much opportunity, he couldn't succeed. His parents knew many Trinidadians—among them whites, blacks, Chinese, Syrians and Indian Trinidadians—who had immigrated and married, who had children and jobs, and in no time owned their own homes, at least one car, and took holidays. They could only imagine that Sid hadn't made a proper go of it because she'd had too easy a life with them, and now expected to have such a life elsewhere without working for it.

I listened carefully to Sydney, but a phrase I had first heard in our house when I was a child—*Oh, Sid, you're too sensitive*—crept into mind. I heard these words in my mother's voice and I fear that in that moment I felt the same impatience as she once had. But now I wonder: was it truly impatience with what India would have called "whining" or was it that I couldn't bear to hear of the hardships Sid had faced?

I implored my parents to see that I needed more courage than most, he said, in order to surmount the difficulties inherent in being not simply an immigrant, but an immigrant who was also an unmarried woman, a woman of colour, a woman without family around her, a woman who did not look the way women were expected to look, who did not walk and talk and act like them—a woman by whom the majority of men were discomfited. The full significance of Sydney's words—and the fact that he had referred to himself as a woman more than once—hit me. Sydney said that he hadn't had enough courage, and that shamed him, even though his parents themselves had never been in a position where they had needed this kind of courage and stamina, and so they were unable to imagine what he—as Sid—had been telling them. He said, The fact is, Jonathan, it had not occurred to my parents, who themselves had hailed from comfortable circumstances, that Gita or I would need many skills to survive on our own. Our parents, for instance, never taught us about money. They had never imagined we would need to know how to acquire it or handle it on our own. And it is true that even as a young adult at home in Trinidad I had not understood that one worked for and earned money. Gita and I were encouraged to assume that we would never work for anyone. And so, in my parents' opinion I was being needlessly contrary, and if only I would stop acting this way, I would do well. Eventually my father would have had enough and would slam down the receiver, and then my mother would call back and confide that she knew of men who were gay yet remained in Trinidad, who married and had families. They simply put a stop to all that nonsense.

As Sydney related all this India's phrase returned to me, and played repeatedly: *Oh Sid you're so sensitive oh Sid you're so sensitive oh Sid.* Sydney carried on none the wiser.

By this time I had finished my drink and in the melted ice-water was suspended its remnants, a sludge of yellow cloudiness that looked like the uncooked white of an egg. Rosita had not come out to check on us, carrying more of her treats, for quite a while. She and Lancelot were usually aware of these kinds of things and responded without having to be called. Where are they? I wondered. At the same time I saw with mingled amusement and shame—a direct consequence of Sydney's words—that I had fallen rather too easily into enjoying the comforts of a life with help who anticipated and fulfilled one's needs before one knew those needs existed. I had not grown up with servants in our house in Toronto, but in her youth in England, before her immigration to Canada, my mother's family had house staff that included maids, cooks, servers, groundspeople and a driver. I had to laugh at myself now, seeing how easily I had taken to life in Sydney's house. I decided that I would simply wait for Rosita or Lance to come and refill our glasses. They would, sooner or later, I was sure. I relaxed and tried to focus on Sydney, who was still carrying on about the hardships of his early life in Toronto.

My mother would cry and ask, he was saying, why couldn't I just do what was right, like those gay men she had known about: get married and have a family, for her sake at least. To which I would respond with a question of my own: was it fair to the wives that these men who preferred to be with other men, these men who were always looking at other men, and perhaps even secretly meeting with them, had married them? And she would say, "Well, that is true, I suppose." A moment of pensiveness, Sydney said, would pass before Mrs. Mahale would say, "But . . ." and evoke loyalty to parents, to family, to society and finally to God. But what about those wives? I would ask again. And we'd go around and around, neither of us able to inform or convince the other. Of course, there was a great deal that I could not share with my parents—the ordinary details of my life, for instance the dilemmas I faced shopping for clothing that suited my idea of myself. How I would have liked to have my mother's or my sister's help in sartorial dilemmas rather than feeling their discomfort that I didn't wear delicate necklaces or pearls or open-toed sandals with heels. And more urgently, I could not share with my parents or my sister the times when I was as high as a kite in love, or those occasions when I had a broken heart and thought that my world had come to an end.

This was not the first time that I had wanted to stop Sydney when he spoke like this, and say, *But, Sydney, I am your family and I never pushed you away.* Awash in the defensiveness that was so big a part of me in those days, I had ceased again to listen to him, indulging instead in an image of red dust whirling over waves in the mid Atlantic Ocean. I had recently read that at certain times of the year people on Caribbean Islands would find that a strange red dust had settled over their lawns, on their cars and porches, and in the louvres of the windows in their houses. The dust had been analyzed and found to be North African soil that had been blown all the way from the drought-ridden Sahel region and from dried-out Lake Chad. The dust must have risen in windstorms, I imagined, high into the air. Red clouds must have formed. They would have fastened themselves to currents of air that rolled off the land, and on meeting the Atlantic they no doubt rose even higher and swirled and swirled their way, over ten thousand kilometres or so of ocean, towards the Caribbean. I imagined the clouds arriving in these balmier climes and delivering their red cargo of sand, carrying unsuspecting bugs and worms. Reefs, I remember learning, were being destroyed as a consequence. I became immediately distressed that I had never in my life snorkelled. And in an instant I was energized by a new resolve: I would find out where the best snorkelling was off this island and see the reefs before they were no more. I would speak with Sankar that very day and ask him about snorkelling holes. Isn't that what they would be called? Snorkelling holes?

Invigorated, I became alert enough to hear that Sydney had resumed the story of his walk. He was saying now that in the summertime, the noisy, firecracker-wielding people who lived in the dreadful house across the road stayed up for most of the night terrorizing one another and anyone in the vicinity. It was not until about five o'clock in the morning that they quieted down, he added, but they were never completely silent; even in the winter, the terror they had wielded hung about their house like a thick fog. He tugged at his knapsack shoulder strap, he said, just to be sure that it was still snug.

Several cabs passed, Sydney said, although the sludge on the road held back their progress down the street. The sidewalk was icy and unevenly cleared. I had to wonder, he said, if walking was not insane. And I wondered, too, how I could feel so much trepidation, such impending loss, and be, at the same time, brimming with anticipation. I watched as a man dressed in cold-weather gear, hunched over a bicycle equipped with fat tires, laboured through thick brown slush, the water slapping alongside him, a dark skunk-line running up the back of his trousers.

Sydney paused long enough, I remember, for my attention to be distracted by the sounds of dishes and cutlery being handled, and cupboards being opened and closed in the kitchen, and hammering in the distance. This would be a good time, it seemed, to stand, to excuse myself and go in search of an activity outside the house. But Sydney had not finished his story. Staring into a faraway place and time, oblivious to what was happening around him, he added: I have to say that I was quite impressed; that man, the bicyclist, hadn't been deterred by the snow and cold or conditions of the road. You see, he hadn't given in and taken public transit, or flagged down a cab; he was clearly determined to get wherever he was going on his own steam, regardless of the weather. Is a man like that brave, or is he foolish?

Sydney turned and looked at me—for the first time in almost half an hour—and I realized that he was addressing me. But I had no words; I had understood that this was not a conversation and had not prepared myself to speak.

He saw my expression and said, Oh, Jonathan, you should stop me when I carry on like this. You look like you could use a nap. Why don't you go in? Go take a little rest from this old storyteller. Put on the fan. I'll stay here. It's cool out here. Just ask Rosita to bring me a slice of sweetbread and a cup of coffee, please.

And so I hurriedly excused myself, assuring Sydney that I wanted to hear the rest of his story but that I had indeed become quite sleepy, as if I'd been bitten by a sleep-inducing bug. He said, Yes, of course, of course—and I felt oddly accused, but of what I didn't know.

As I was going to my room, Sankar, who was in the kitchen, stopped me. It is going to be a nice afternoon, he said, as if he knew my mind. He suggested that the two of us—he and I—take a trip to the Caroni Swamp to see the scarlet ibis flying in at sundown to roost on the mangrove islands. We would have to leave immediately to beat the traffic and get to the site by four o'clock, which was when the boats for hire took off down the canals into the wide, caiman-infested lagoons.

A cup of coffee and a crab-back later, and I was like a boy ready to go off on an adventure to see swamp lizards that were, as Sid had once, a long time ago, promised, "this big."

At the Swamp, our pirogue anchored in the cover of overhanging trees. Over the course of half an hour, as the sun went down, thousands of brilliant scarlet ibises glided in, alighting on the tops of the blackened mangrove trees. Our return through the narrow channels took place in the dark. Owls swooped and hooted, followed by a flutter too close, a rush of wind above our heads: bats. A pair of brilliant dots of light skimmed the black water as it passed our pirogue—the eyes of a caiman.

I recalled all this as I sat at the desk in my room that first day of the wake and imagined, with some wistfulness, that it was now unlikely I would make another such trip to the Caroni Swamp. I remembered how, upon returning from our excursion, I had revelled in my brief escape, my freedom from talk. I knew that when Sankar and I returned, Sydney's story would continue. And it did, not just when we came back from the Swamp, but over the course of years and several visits to the island. However, I do think back now on those times when my mind would drift—when as he spoke on, I would plot escapades and too-quickly jump at chances to leave the house—and I feel remorse and regret in equal measure.

And now, months later, having listened to the essential parts of that same story, particularly the kernels Sydney had guarded until the last hours of his life, and having finally heard and understood what he'd been wanting to tell me, I cannot but wonder why the writer in me—if not the man— had not from the beginning seen and been curious about the threads, had not spotted the unravelling of a larger story.

This grand omission rattles my idea of myself as a writer. And if one of the essential marks of being human is the ability to feel compassion, what kind of a man was I who instead of being able to listen to Sydney's words and hear and feel beyond their meaning, instead of being able to hold his life's story in my heart and mind, instead of being the witness he clearly trusted I could be, spent so much of my time hoping and waiting for the smallest mention of my name?

Yes, I eventually stayed and listened to every word he spoke. But that was at the end. And it was then, when it was much too late, that I heard and understood the whole story.

If only I could do it all over again.

PART THREE

9

At first, I ignored the knocking at my door. But when I realized that the door was being pushed slowly open, I shouted
out that I was inside. Lancelot replied, reminding me that
people would soon arrive.

I had not showered yet, and hastily roused myself to
get ready. When the tepid water hit my face, I cried until
I was doubled over with the pain of it. I did not turn off
the shower, but leaned into the tiled wall, pressing my face
and belly against it, and long after there were no tears left
I remained there, my body spent, frightened as if I were a
three-year-old who had been left in cold dark silence.

"You're too sensitive," I chided myself. "You're much too
sensitive." It was of course India I'd heard use those words,
and they came to me once again in her voice. I must have
been eight when I heard and truly understood their effect.
My two mothers had gone to a party, and I'd stayed home
with Tanya, my babysitter. When Sid and India returned,

India brushed past Tanya and me. She kicked off her black red-tipped high-heel shoes and went briskly upstairs, and from this I knew that she and Sid had been quarrelling. When Sid ruffled the hair on my head and asked if I'd been good, I knew that it was she who was on the defensive.

The bedroom door upstairs closed with some considerable force. Tanya gathered up her belongings and left. I followed Sid into the kitchen. Preoccupied with whatever was transpiring between her and India, she made no attempt to send me up to bed. When the door to the bedroom re-opened some time later and I heard my mother approach the top of the staircase, I left Sid in the kitchen and went quietly to my play corner behind the sofa in the living room. India, thin and tall as she was, could stomp heavily down the stairs, and this she did. I plucked a colouring book and crayons from my toy chest and busied myself. Save for India saying as she passed me, "You should be in bed by now," and asking Sid in the kitchen, "Why is he still up?" neither paid me further notice; but I was more aware of them than of the book and crayons before me.

India threw the first hook: "It's always you. You, you, you. Always about you being a foreigner. You're more aware of it than anyone else is, for God's sake. What is wrong with you?" I hadn't needed to look at Sid to know what she was doing. I imagined her, legs parted and firmly planted, arms folded across her chest. She left the kitchen and came into the living room. With exaggerated calm, and displaying tedium at having to explain herself again, she intoned that

the evening had been yet another example of the fact that
no matter how long she lived in Canada she would always
be a foreigner among my mother's friends. My mother
strode past me and threw herself into a corner of the plush
green sofa behind which I was crouched. I guessed that
she had stretched her legs across the length of it. Adopting
her signature unwavering and ultra-rational manner, India
countered that she, like Sid, was a foreigner in this country,
but she didn't harp about it in public the way Sid did. Sid,
clearly incensed by this accusation, reminded my mother
that while she—India, that is—might be an immigrant, her
skin was white, and she had come not from Poland, Greece,
Russia, Spain or the Ukraine, but from Great Britain. And
the British, regardless of background, were to white Anglo
Canadians always more authentic, more grand, than they.

At the time, it had not been of any consequence to
me that my two mothers had different skin colours. India
was among the first single women in the city to choose to
be artificially inseminated, and while it was rather obvious
from the way I'd turned out that the sperm donor must have
been white, it wasn't until well after Sid left that I realized
that Sid and I were of different races.

Sid continued: India might be an immigrant, but she
couldn't possibly know the prejudice felt by most immigrants. That cut-glass English accent of hers put her above
even her white Canadian friends, who, easily seduced, compared themselves to her and concluded that she was the real
thing. But, Sid snapped, she was not seduced by any of it.

Gradually I pieced together what had precipitated this fight: at the party everyone had been served wine by the host in tall crystal glasses. Except for Sid. She had been offered her wine in a stocky glass of such poor quality that the thick lip had a bubble on it. India snapped that Sid was petty and went looking for such things, to which Sid responded that one didn't have to go looking, and India should become more aware. India countered that if things were as Sid had said, then surely it was simply the luck of the draw—the host must have run out of the better glasses, and whoever was served last had just happened to get that one. To which Sid barked, So why was I served last? People only seemed to pay her attention at these parties, Sid said sharply, in a voice that had by this time escalated in pitch and volume, to ask after India's progress—the great writer's latest writing project—or after Jonathan. She was always being put in the deplorable role of handmaiden to the creative genius. And, worst of all, her relationship with Jonathan went unacknowledged: she was seen as a nanny to the creative genius's son.

I remember feeling proud that people would ask about me at the parties, and was confused, too, because it seemed to me that these people were sensible to ask Sid rather than my mother. Sid, I thought, could tell them stories about me. India couldn't.

India interrupted Sid's rant. "This is so unnecessary, Sid. It's so boring. You're overreacting. You take offence much too easily." A little later she said, "You're so goddamn serious. Has it ever occurred to you that you might not put people at ease? No one wants to be made to feel as if they're forever on the verge of saying something wrong or inappropriate." India had a tendency to roll her eyes when she was exasperated, and in my imagination, from behind the sofa, I saw her do this when she cut Sid down with the most effective of all her put-downs: "You're simply too sensitive." I heard these words and saw how they crushed Sid and brought the conversation to its end.

I witnessed the effect again when the elation of being called out in a review—the very review he had only days ago spoken of to me—turned to despair. Sid took umbrage with the reviewer's classification of her work as *folksy* and *naive*. India insisted the adjectives were not an indication that the reviewer could only appreciate the work by evoking Sid's third-world heritage, but rather were compliments.

Sid's frustration with the reviewer was slight compared to how India's lack of empathy and understanding affected her. She brooded for several days, sure that the review marked the end of a career barely begun as a serious "Canadian" artist. When India could take Sid's frustration no longer, she reminded her that immigrants and minorities had unprecedented advantages, access to funding and opportunities to publish and exhibit their work. Sid should just get over herself and be grateful.

Sid's defeated response was "You will never understand, will you? But what's worse is that you don't even try to defend me."

I now know that whenever India tries to be conciliatory, she delivers a small lecture that is a mix of pep talk and reproach. This she did then: "Sid, *you* know who you are and where you've come from. If only you carried yourself with the confidence of that knowledge. It shouldn't matter that people here are unable to read who you are. That's ignorance, and you're smart enough to rise above it. But you insist on seeing in every situation an opportunity for discourse. Racism. Immigration. Classism. Sexuality. Gayness. Homophobia. Perhaps these are all things that affect you, even when you're with well-meaning friends, but you won't change anyone or anything by being so easily offended and defensive. Can't you just enjoy yourself and others, and let others enjoy you? You've got a lot to offer. Just get on with living, Sid, and good God, just be grateful for the call-out." She ended her exhortation with "You're so easily offended. *You're simply too sensitive.*"

When the three of us lived together as a family in Toronto, Sid brought up the idea numerous times that we should all visit Trinidad so that we could be introduced to her parents, who were alive then, and her younger sister, Gita. India was not excited by the prospect of a visit to a tropical country that lacked the reputation of a grand tourist destination save for during its carnival season. I, on the other hand, was eager. Sid promised starfish and jellyfish, and even lizards that took up residence *almost* like pets inside the houses: lizards *this* big, she told me, her eyes popping wide, chopping her left arm at the crook of her elbow, *this* big, and sometimes they fall off the wall and land right in your hair. Fully imagining the plop of the house lizard, its weight and wriggle, I remember doubling over, shaking my head and my air-filled cheeks. I swiped at my hair with both hands. After much persuasion, India relented and we did go to Trinidad. But India's mix of apathy and passivity when we were finally in Sid's family's house embarrassed me, and I remember wishing, even at such a young age, that I could distance myself from her, while wanting also to make excuses for her.

It was shortly after that visit and our return to Toronto that Sid left my mother and me, and departed from my life.

———

I turned off the shower, towelled myself dry, and sat naked on the edge of my bed. I did not want any part of this funeral business. I was abysmally incompetent in the face of loss and death. Sydney's world had been made small by the changes he'd made to himself—to his body—and consequently, my own Trinidadian world was narrow. I knew only Sydney and his house staff and members of their families. A wake was bound to bring strangers—at least they would be strangers to me. I did not want to be the subject of their scrutiny. I did not want my grief on display. I sank onto the bed, ruminating on how *I* had come to be in this situation. It wasn't just the physical situation that confounded me but something larger, and I eventually leapt from thoughts of my own fate to wondering again what had made Sid do to herself, to her body, the kinds of things that were affecting me today—affecting how I felt, that is, about my place in this house, on this day, among people I did not know. I see now that Sydney had been trying to explain it to me through his various stories, but I wondered then how, as a child who was so close to her, so adoring of her, I had not seen or intuited the changes that would come. Children, after all, see more than they are given credit for. What had I seen, but not paid attention to?

For instance, I recalled a time when I was fourteen: India had been dating a man I had not taken to, and I asked her what it had been like between Sid and her. This was not so bold a question as one might imagine, for I was well aware then—and exploited the fact—that it pleased my mother to see herself as a liberated parent who was able to engage in frank and adult conversations with her child. If my memory is to be trusted, the very first comment she made began with a drawn-out, ponderous "We-ell," quickly followed by, "Sid was short. Two inches shorter than I." And I remember my embarrassment and disgust, for I was at that age where everything that I experienced was imbued with thoughts about sex.

My mother carried on. "When we placed our hands palm to palm, my hands were bigger than hers, my fingers longer. But in that small brown body was an electric power and confidence that captivated me." In my mind she rolled her eyes as she added, "But that electricity dimmed within

months." After I was born, India said, she got back to the
novel she had been working on, and Sid stayed on, fawning
over me as if Sid were the one who'd given birth. "It irri-
tated the hell out of me," she said, laughing. "But at least I
got to finish my novel—and good thing, too, for it was one
of the best." Even as a teenager I was aware of the import
of her words, their severity, the refusal to understand. She
continued, "When I was finished with the book, when I
looked up from it, there was this person in the house with
you and me, this person who was no longer confident in
public, this person who had somehow become dissatisfied
with her appearance, with the fact that her hips and breasts
were, as she put it, *so visible that they betrayed her*. There was
suddenly a lot of nonsense about how her outward appearance had nothing to do with how she felt inside. She began
dressing differently, wearing obviously masculine clothing,
and, well, I suppose I just lost interest. Some of the very
things she did at the beginning, which I'd found charming
then, began to irritate and, quite frankly, to embarrass me."

Like what? I had asked.

"She greeted our men-friends not with an embrace,
but rather with such a firm handshake that there would
be comments about it. She'd step ahead of me at a door,
for instance, open it and stand aside to allow me through
first. She didn't smoke, but was always ready to light my
cigarette. You know, in private these things are tolerable,
desirable even, but when she did them in public, whether
with me or with other women, I was embarrassed. Not

embarrassed to be seen with her, but embarrassed for her. That is, of course, worse."

I do remember how Sid was before she left us. I can't say that I thought of her manner as being the result of or related to anything in particular. Sid was simply Sid. And I had looked up to her.

Sid and my mother remained in touch—although not amicably—for a while after their breakup. Sydney told me that "she" knew my mother was dating. Sid knew that my mother went out immediately after their breakup with a woman—a white woman—who was taller than India, and who had passed in public effortlessly as a man. She didn't elaborate, but by now I understood the significance of this.

Sydney once told me that it was when she was in Canada with her gay and lesbian friends, before meeting India, that she'd had a sense of what most closely resembled "family." The short-cut of shared experiences and vocabulary meant that they knew how and when to be there for one another.

But when Sid got together with India, she gradually distanced herself from these people. My mother expected Sid, her live-in lover, to be, as she said, "discreet" about their relationship.

The doorbell rang at 6 p.m. on the dot, and for an hour I was obliged to sit on the veranda with Sydney's tailor, who introduced himself to me by saying that his sister was like Sydney. He called Sydney by his last name. "When Mahale needed a suit," this man said, "he came to see me because I am famous as a tailor." His sister had wanted to wear tailored suits from the time she was a teenager. No one took her on, but she was his favourite sister and he had wanted her to be happy. So he went all over Trinidad looking for someone to sew a suit for her, and of course, there was not a seamstress or tailor who would outfit her in this way. So he taught himself to sew a man's suit for a woman so that you couldn't tell from her clothes whether she was Jack or Jackie, Bobby or Barbie, Tommy or Tammy.

Mrs. Allen, the guava cheese lady, arrived just as the tailor was leaving. She brought a tray of guava cheeses, because, as she said, people will come, and at a time like this a few sweet things can make a person feel just a little better. Mrs. Allen also, thankfully, did not stay long. When she left, I sat on the veranda and waited. But no one else came that evening, and soon Carmen and Rosita wrapped the rotis in tea towels and packed them away in Tupperware containers.

After Carmen left and Rosita and Lancelot had gone to their rooms, I once again felt horribly alone. I needed someone with whom I was close; I needed Catherine. Yes, I decided, I would telephone her. And regardless of tradition, I made myself a drink first.

I measured a robust jigger of Scotch into one of the thin-walled heavy-bottomed tumblers that Sydney used to use, tossed in two cubes of ice and filled the glass with coconut water. I splashed Angostura bitters on top and shook the glass, rattling the ice cubes to mix it all up. I had made myself a fine drink. I polished it off in one go and fixed another.

Usually when I called Catherine, I would lean against the counter where the phone was. This time, though, I was compelled to heave my ass onto the counter, sit on top of it, and speak to her as I perched there. I would not have considered doing this before. Before. *Before* Sydney's death. *After* Sydney's death. Or should that be *his passing, his going away?* In any case, the house was now mine, and I could damn well do in it as I pleased. I put down the glass gently, although I was tempted to bring it hard onto the tile countertop, smashing it, cracking the tiles and summoning Rosita and Lancelot from their rooms. The glass was mine. The tiles that might have broken were mine. The trouble to have them repaired would be mine too. But I was too adept at standing outside of myself, watching, commenting, analyzing, to execute an authentic tantrum. Rosita and Lancelot would have come running out of their rooms, and I would have had to admit to an episode of indulgence or grief-induced insanity.

I could garner social points back home by owning a house in the Caribbean, couldn't I? I reasoned. But did owning the house, and knowing how a Scotch and coconut water cocktail was made, and watching a very special man die in a hospital here, make me Trinidadian? Did saying *I know Trinidad* take on new and heightened meaning now? In that moment of grief, I saw the bequest of the house as shameless bribery: *Here, Jonathan, have this house instead of me, who, you might notice, you've never really had. Take this, and in exchange for it forgive me for my absence, for my self-absorption, for destroying the vessel that held images of all that you were as a child. I will give you this house, but I can't give you myself. Ever.* Pressure mounted behind my eyes, my jaw tightened and the top of my head felt as if it would explode, scattering my brain on my new ceiling. Looking up, I realized I hadn't paid attention to the fan on the ceiling before. The wide wood blades were furry with old dust. I could now order Lancelot to clean them, I mused. I could tell Lancelot to clean this house from top to bottom, to get down on his knees and scrub this place from one end to the other. To scrub the shame from all my useless longings and expectations that, for nine years, had built up, and dried up, here. I imagined launching my glass across the room, putting my fists through every cupboard door in the kitchen. This inanimate thing, this house, mocked me with Sydney's betrayal of the closeness he and I once, long ago, had shared.

The room spun, and my head felt light. I lifted the glass to my mouth and emptied it. Sweat rolled down the sides of my face and neck. What was I supposed to do with Sydney's damned stories and the other bequests implied in them? I had three more days before Gita and Jaan arrived. And then there would be the funeral. Catherine was right. I had been unfairly put-upon.

I mixed another drink. Two jiggers went into that third round. One sip and I knew that I was not going to get from Catherine what I needed—the fortitude to endure this time. I called my mother instead. She told me that I was drunk and quietly said goodbye.

I retreated to my room exhausted, but I could not rest. I was tempted to turn again to Sydney's notebooks, to the letters and the childhood notes from Zain. But I knew the stories they contained intimately. And every single time I read an entry from one of Sydney's notebooks, I had the sense that he was doing more than keeping a record of his life and of his thoughts. I sensed he imagined a reader—me. If anything confirmed this for me it was the last entry he'd made, written just before he stashed away the three little books in his safety box at the bank. That one, I believe, must surely have been written *to* me. I could almost recite it by heart:

> *Surely it is a failure of our human design that it takes not an hour, not a day, but much, much longer to relay what flashes through the mind with the speed of a hummingbird's wing.*

Yes, a failure of design. It surely was.

Zain's words came to me as well, and I imagined her particular Trinidadian accent. I knew parts of her letters by heart now. I would find nothing new in untying the bundle of cards and letters she'd written. In any case, I did not want to read Sydney's words or Zain's words this time. Perhaps what I wanted was the feel of the notebooks and of that bundle in my hands. I took out the package and held it. But this, too, was not what I wanted. I put the lot back on the desk and looked at it askance, and the sense grew in me that it was now *my* turn to speak. After a while, I was ready: *I* wanted now to gather up the words, to cull the stories, to understand for myself what I had been told during those nine years of visits here. I now wanted to lay it all back down in my own words. In my own words, but faithfully. As I had heard the stories. As I had read them. As I wished it all to be.

On my desk was a notepad. I opened it to a clean page. I took a sip of my drink, savoured it. I was hesitant, for I sensed that once I began, I would embark on a commitment that would consume me for as long as it took to fulfill it.

I picked up the rollerball pen.

The words came faster than I could write. In no time there were paragraphs and then there were pages.

Night in the tropics falls with no regard. Like a cleaver, it descends in an instant. We hadn't intended to stray, but the sudden blanketing darkness intrigued us. I wondered aloud how much darker it could possibly get in the valley. "Let's see," you said and turned onto the narrow little-used Golf Course Road. Half a mile or so up the quiet road, you rolled to an unsure halt in our lane, put the gear in park and pulled up the brake handle. The air conditioning was on, the windows rolled up. You left the engine idling. I looked back. There was no light, not from camps in the mountains or from squatters' dwellings. There were no snaking headlights in the distance to indicate the presence of another vehicle. All that was visible in this forest darkness was caught in the car's high beams: on either side shrubbery, which encroached on the asphalt, and a few metres of the narrow road ahead.

You switched off the engine, and I rolled down my window. The quiet was deafening. Then you switched off the lights, and the darkness seemed impenetrable. We could have been at the end of the universe, Zain, but we were not, and although I thought of you and me as a force to contend with, I worried about the possibility of unseen bandits. There was no sound of cars, no drone of planes, no machinery and, thankfully, no human noises. Then forest sounds emerged, all at once, sustained, endless, pulsing. What should have been cacophonous discord was pleasant. Cicadas. Frogs. Birds hooting. Monkeys howling. A far-reaching hollow tock—the bellbird's tock. If a quick single clip of sound could be mournful, there it was. Wind in the trees. Little things jumping in the bushes. A short distance away, something caused a commotion in the trees.

"Did you hear that?" I whispered.

I heard the keys in the ignition tinkle and knew that you were about to switch on the engine. Whatever it was that was causing the commotion, however, seemed to be falling from a height. In mid-fall it caught, or perhaps it caught itself, and in my imagination its sounds translated to wings that flapped frantically against branches and then an easier flapping as the thing, some big bird, an owl perhaps, righted itself and made away.

I thought about all the cautioning—don't stop your car in lonely areas, especially at night. Keep your doors locked and windows turned up. "Let's not go just yet," I suggested anyway. My voice cracked as I tried to whisper. "A long time ago," I told you, "cacao thieves used to collect fireflies in Mason jars fitted with lids made of wire netting. In the darkest hours of the night when they crept through the land looking to cut ripe pods off the trees, these were their lanterns."

I had rested my hand on the side of my seat. You gripped my fingers—a little coarsely, so I thought nothing of it.

I squeezed your fingers slightly.

"Tell me something," you said. "Why did you move off so quickly, back there at the beach, when I touched your arm?"

When I didn't answer, you assumed I didn't know what you were talking about, so you explained. "I mean when we were watching the sky, just after the sun had set."

"I know," I said. "I know exactly when you're talking about."

I knew because your touch still clung to me; I felt the pounding, still, of fear and panic against my chest.

"So? Tell me why."

I could not see the details of your face, but I could tell that you were looking directly at me.

"Because of the way I look," I said. "I don't look like most women. I think other people see that." It was like using plastic chopsticks to pick slippery words out of a soup. You did not respond. Then I heard the rustle of your body as you came closer. What are you doing, Zain? I wondered. My skin began to burn as if I had a fever. I felt suddenly frightened, as if my world were about to be turned upside down, or even right side up. My thoughts became muddled, and words came out of my mouth without my willing them to do so, and I could feel myself shake as if I had caught a chill. "I mean, they have no idea that we're like sisters. Like sisters, Zain. Aren't we?"

In the darkness you found my lips easily. I remember the smell of your skin, the sun trapped in it, your breath so close to my mouth, the scent of your cologne sharpened by whatever it was that was happening in the car.

"Sid," you said, and for a long time that was all. Then you said, "I wish," and again, nothing more.

This made me unable to think, and I became mute. Your breath on my cheek was like a flame and a breeze at once. I waited, and your unspoken wish hung in the air like a tiny filament of light. It was a small eternity.

I was exhausted and yet my mind brimmed. I knew the day ahead would demand a great deal of me, and that a night's rest would serve me well. But even after I relieved myself and headed to my bed, I again felt the dizzying pull of reinterpreting all I had heard and read. I went back to the desk.

Zain, just before you and Angus drove me home, you came into the guest room carrying an envelope stuffed with the U.S. dollars you'd been saving. You pressed yourself against me, put your hands flat and gentle on my breasts—and you whispered, "They're beautiful, but I know you keep dreaming of what it could be like to live in the world the way you want to."

I had told you—and you remembered—how I felt that my breasts betrayed me. I had told you that if someone, seeing my short hair and the way I dressed, was unable to tell quickly if I was male or female, they would decide who and what I was by looking at my breasts. I had also told you about the gender transformations that were done in Canada. At first you recoiled. I was embarrassed to have revealed so much to you. But some time later you confided that you'd had breast enhancement surgery, and I was surprised; I hadn't realized how much about you I didn't know. Enhancement and reduction were different sides of the same coin, you said. But you went further. "Cut the damn things off, if you want," you said. You put your hands to my breasts, this time so easily. "They won't grow back," you said. "But I bet it will be as if you have been reborn. You just might blossom yet, Sid. And what shall we call you, then? Why don't we choose something that sounds like Siddhani. Let's just squish the name. It'll sound like 'Sydney.' What do you think?" You were laughing, but I was aghast, stunned and moved all at once. It doesn't matter what you do with the money, you said, but from now on I want to call you Sydney. Okay?

When I think about how I lost you, Zain, and about how I lost the boy, my son, Jonathan, and even about how I lost his mother, India—yes, I left her, but that's a technicality; when I think of Eric—and I think of that bastard every day; when I think of Angus, of the art reviews I got and the ones I should have got, of the shows and the galleries I should have been in, and of how my paintings were always contextualized by the colour of my skin or by my immigrant status in Canada; when I imagine holding a woman, imagine how she would feel in my presence; whenever I think of any of this, I hear you saying, *Cut the damn things off.*

It isn't a directive I hear, Zain, but deep understanding.

Still I continued, emboldened.

It's been seven months now since Mum's death. I had thought that, given the length of time since then, I could broach with Gita the subject of the change I'm going to make. I am unable to be in touch with Jonathan, and this is, perhaps, a good thing for him. So Gita is the only one who matters now. But when I told her my plan she asked if I had gone crazy. She told me I needed professional help, I needed to see a psychiatrist. She told me that if I did such a thing to myself she would have nothing to do with me. She would not entertain any explanation. She asked how I could even consider doing this to her. Although it was my body that I wanted to tamper with, we carry, she said, the same family name. She said that if I went ahead with it she would consider me dead, and never allow her son to have anything to do with me. She screamed that I was a freak, that I had no respect for my dead parents, for family, for society, or for God.

I'd phoned her convinced that this was what I wanted to do, but I have now lost my nerve. I'm trying to remember why I am having this surgery and wonder if I should start the testosterone injections. Why do I want this?

It cannot be just because of the disappointment I saw cross India's face when, in the men's department of a clothing store, the line of the jacket she wanted me to try on was not right.

It cannot be because I will cut a more dapper figure if I go through the change, for regardless of the angularity the doctor says I will eventually develop, the coarser skin, the moustache and goatee that I will grow on my face, the hair that will thin and recede on my head, the voice that will forever split and crackle and the muscles that will grow— regardless of all of this I will be able to do not a thing about the width of my hips and my thighs, about my height, or the colour of my skin.

It cannot be because India wanted Jonathan, as she often told me, to grow up with a strong role model of his own gender. (It truly cannot be this, for her boyfriends Graham, Bill, Charles, James, et cetera, prove my point entirely.)

It cannot be because I believe I know how my best friend died and yet I cower from doing anything about it out of fear that the very fact of my being, and of her friendship with someone like me, will bring judgements against us—against her— and taint the possibility of a serious investigation and justice.

It cannot be because my perfect other will allow me to love her in ways that she relishes and sinks into, yet, at the end of the day, she will not choose me.

It cannot be because in your presence, Zain, I feel the limb that has grown between my legs and that wants, almost of its own accord, to rub your skin, to touch your parted lips and your face and hair, to coax you farther apart and slide in with abandon . . . No, it cannot be this, because, in the end, I will, let's be real here, never achieve such an able-bodied appendage.

So why, then, am I doing this thing to my body, to myself, to the people who love me? It cannot be, and yet it is—for all of these reasons.

And for none of them.

My head throbbed in concert with the knocking on the door. Lancelot pushed the door open and said that the pundit would be here any minute.

I glanced at the desk, and yes, I could see that there were words on the pad. Words in my handwriting. I got up out of bed and flipped the pages, and saw that I had indeed worked through the night. I remembered, then: it was not until the room had been aglow in orange light and I could see that the sun was on the eastern horizon that I had rested the pen on the notepad and crawled between the sheets.

10

On the way to the veranda I passed Rosita. She did not look at me. I knew I had disappointed her. She must have known that I had broken with tradition and had "a" drink the evening before. It was going to be a horrid, busy day, and my head as heavy as a sand-filled soccer ball.

Pundit had cataracts and couldn't drive, so he was driven by his daughter. I invited the two of them to sit on the veranda, but he directed me inside the house to sit at the dining table, he at one head of it, she and I on either side. I wondered if he possessed supernatural powers and could detect the forbidden alcohol in me. My head pounded.

Rosita brought us each a glass of orange juice. She wouldn't look at me.

Pundit told me that his sisters and brothers all lived in Toronto. He had gone once to stay with one sister. It was during the month of September, some years ago. He had visited the CN Tower and gone to Niagara Falls. It was

pretty, and very clean, but he'd found it too cold. He asked
if I was married. Even though I answered that I was not, he
asked if I had any children.

His daughter's short haircut surprised me. I suppose
I had expected that as the daughter of a Hindu priest she
would have long hair. I imagined that at this table, too, she
would be silent. Indeed, I was surprised that, on account of
the particular business at hand, she was sitting with us at
the table in the first place. She had—and again I found this
unexpected—lively eyes. They were lined thickly with the
kind of mascara that Indian women in paintings wear. She
looked directly at her father as he spoke, and when he asked
me a question she looked directly at me.

Pundit asked what I did for a living, and when I
answered that I was a writer he said that it followed then
that I must surely understand about the great events of life:
birth, that is, and death. He placed his hands together as
if to pray, but it was merely a gesture that accompanied
his pensiveness. He said that the dramas of love, jealousy,
revenge, success and failure, desire, hunger—hunger for
material things, riches or sexual fulfillment, or, say, even for
food, even for enlightenment and purity—are minor events.
They are theatre. They are dramas. The gods loved theatre
and drama. Didn't someone once call us the playthings of
the gods? he asked.

His daughter was watching me. Her face was relaxed,
yet I felt a pressure to be profoundly reflective. "You've just
described the motives in all the great stories ever told," I

said. The words might as well have been written by someone else and presented to me on a piece of paper to be read
aloud. The daughter glanced down at her lap, stifling a
smile. Sweat broke on my neck.

Sydney is on a journey. Pundit continued, as if this
naturally followed our train of conversation. Death is a temporary cessation of physical activity so that the soul can step
back, rejuvenate itself, take a look at its progress, reassess
its policies, before returning again to life on this earth so
that it can learn to free itself of earthly desires. Liberation
from this cycle is the goal of all earthly beings, he said. Not
so? he asked, and his daughter glanced up, the smile well
restrained, but in her eyes I detected a mischievous invitation for another brilliant response from me. I feared a trap
had been laid for me to display the arrogance of laity, of
writers, of foreigners to this country, of young men, of white
men, of westerners. Rather than voice an opinion, I nodded
to suggest that I was listening with an open heart and mind
to the wisdom of a priest.

He closed his eyes and said, When a person dies, his
soul and a small amount of consciousness leave his body
through a hole in his head, and they go to reside in another
world before returning to this one to continue on its cycle,
which it is attempting throughout to break. I couldn't help
but wonder now if he was pulling my leg, and, if not, if he
really believed this. I looked at his daughter, who I thought
had been hinting to me her amusement, but she had become
sombre, her eyes downcast and her hands loosely clasped on

the table's edge. She even nodded, perhaps in agreement. Perhaps she, too, actually believed this. If this was not some sort of hocus-pocus that Sydney had forced me into, then I must take it, I thought, as tradition and ritual, and simply play along for the sake of simplicity. For Sydney's sake.

Pundit said that Sydney had told him all about me. A heat rushed up my body into my face. I wanted to ask what exactly it was that Sydney had told him, but the presence of his daughter stopped me. What exactly does he know of Sydney? I wondered. Sydney told me about you, and about your mother, he clarified, as if he had read my mind. He considered you to be his son. He added, Love is all that matters, and love can come in a variety of ways. Regardless, it is love. Had he said the latter because he saw my discomfort, or because he was assuaging his own? There was no hint that he knew that Sydney was once Siddhani. I wanted to know, and at the same time didn't want to know, if he was aware of the nature of my mother's relationship with Sydney, and if he knew the circumstances of my birth. I feared that he could read my mind. But the pundit carried on with the business at hand.

Because I am Sydney's closest male family member, he said, I must carry out all the major functions of the funeral. "You are the *karta*," he said, "the chief mourner. It is Hindu custom that an open casket is used, as there are rites and rituals that are performed directly on the body, right to the end." I asked if the service was to be conducted at a funeral home or at a church. Pundit smiled wryly, and said,

"He"—meaning Sydney—"didn't bring you up as a Hindu, eh? Everything will happen at the house," he announced. Which house? I asked. His daughter looked up at me, her bemusement replaced now by what seemed to me to be puzzlement, or perhaps concern. Right here, he said. Everything will happen right here. Sydney had to be dressed in white, and I was to get Sydney's clothing and take it to the funeral home, he said. He asked if I was prepared to do my part in the ceremony—to look after the body, that is. Unable to hide my indignation and incredulity, I asked if I was supposed to dress Sydney. His daughter jumped in. The funeral home will do that, she said, and they will bring the casket with "the body" in it to the house. It was from then on, until "the body" was cremated, that I, the *karta*, was to perform the rites as instructed by her father. She was direct, her voice firmer than I had anticipated. Her hair was blue black, like a crow's wing.

Pundit looked at me then, and asked if I was prepared to light the fire, and after the cremation, to be responsible for the disposal of the remains, for these were my primary responsibilities in my relationship to this person who had been a parent to me. I had a vague understanding, mostly from movies, of this. I imagined myself in a dark grey suit, a white shirt, a black tie with grey stripes and gleaming black shoes. I was standing in a room by myself, paying my last respects, telling Sydney, who was in a furnace somewhere on the other side of a wall, of my love and appreciation for him, my hand palming the button I must eventually press. I imagined being presented a box later, all of Sydney in a package the size and weight of a clay brick. I recalled hearing once that the weight of an adult human's ashes was astounding. A tide of nausea rose inside me. To my embarrassment, my eyes filled with tears. Pundit's daughter looked down into her lap. In an involuntarily and embarrassingly softened voice I told Pundit that, sure, I was prepared to fulfill whatever was expected of me. His voice was softer now too, and he spoke slowly, as if in a hospital room speaking to a dying man. A shopping list of items that would be needed in the ceremony had been prepared for me, he said. Rice, ghee, marigolds, sandalwood, sesame oil, a *lotah*—a brass vase, his daughter translated—and water jugs. Don't worry, he assured me, Rosita would understand. She knew what to do, and where to get everything. He himself would bring other necessary things, such as the twigs and leaves of a peepal tree. A *bedi* would be needed too, he said, and his daughter again interpreted: a shallow wood box. It would be used in the ceremony at the house, she added and reminded her father that there was one in the trunk of the car. She stood up to go to the car and I stood too and asked if I could help. She would manage, Pundit answered, it wasn't heavy. The *bedi*, he explained, was to be filled to the brim with dirt, which was then to be patted flat, smoothed completely, and the surface decorated. He carried on describing how it was to be decorated, but I found my mind wandering, wondering if his daughter was truly able to manage carrying the altar, the *bedi*, by herself. I was brought back when I heard Pundit say, "We must have a photograph of Sydney to be placed on the *bedi*, next to the vase. You must find a good colour photograph of him and put it in a frame." He gestured with his hands as he added, "Not too small, but not big-big." His daughter returned with the box. We both stood. She put the box on the table.

I would be required by custom to wear a white *kurta* and white pants, Pundit continued. He followed this with the assurance that I did not need to worry about the details of where to get such a suit; he himself would go to the *puja* store that very day, and an assortment of styles and sizes would be prepared for me, and he would have them delivered to the house here. You're about a medium or so, no? he said. Before I could answer, his daughter replied for me, Yes, you will take a medium. He and his daughter conferred in some sort of shorthand, and he told me that Anta would return that very evening with the clothing. Anta, whose hair was black and shiny like a crow's wing. There are no crows in Trinidad, I recall thinking then. There are *anis*. I corrected my thought: Anta's hair is as black as the wings of an *ani*. Meanwhile Pundit carried on: after the ceremony, the son usually shaves his head.

I raised my eyebrows, and was already passing my hand through my thick red-brown hair before I could censure myself. Father and daughter looked pensively at me, both smiling now. Anta told her father, "He doesn't have to shave it, he can just have it cut short."

"Don't worry," Pundit reassured me again. He would guide me through it all.

At these words, I felt relief. It was as if a massive storm cloud had been hovering over my head, but now a slip of the dreadful grey had thinned a little, and behind it was a hint of blue. It seemed that everything would be looked after. Very little—only the larger gestures, the symbolic—would be required of me.

In Sydney's armoire there were, to my surprise, two dresses, and a skirt on hangers. There was a dark blue linen suit. There were several pairs of pants and several shirts with collars. Men's shirts. Shirts themselves had no bias, no prejudice, I thought as I ran my palm over the clothing. They could one day be men's shirts, and on another day women's shirts. There were simply people's shirts. A person's shirt. A slimmer drawer contained several pairs of socks to one side, a few pairs of boxer shorts neatly folded and, to the other side, a stack of panties opened flat. At the sight of them I covered my mouth so as not to be heard, but I couldn't stop crying. The panties were plain, the kind I and my friends might have derisively assumed older women, matrons really, would wear. Questions I had dared not ask when Sydney was alive were suddenly answered.

Just before I left the house to go into the town to find an appropriate white suit for Sydney and take it to the funeral home, the tailor arrived. He had, of his own accord, decided to make Sydney's suit and had stayed up all night working on it.

The funeral director took the suit from me and asked if I wanted to see the body. He responded to my surprise and unguarded disdain by informing me that I, if not someone else, would have to "check it" just before the funeral. When I looked at him in confusion he explained that someone had to come to the funeral home early on the morning of the funeral to make sure that the makeup looked good. Remember, he said, this is an open-coffin ceremony. I found the voice to ask what he meant, exactly, by "makeup." It is an open coffin, he repeated, so they would make up the face. Don't worry, he added, his funeral home had the best reputation for doing open coffins. Still I insisted—what makeup would the mortician be using? Don't worry, he told me: there would be no fashion lipstick or eye makeup; Mr. Mahale had left full written instructions. He asked me to return before then, as soon as possible, and bring Sydney's toiletries, the shampoo and soap he liked using, his hairbrush and a handkerchief—for the mortician preferred to use on the bodies what the people had themselves used in life. I wondered about the handkerchief but did not bother to ask what it would be used for.

In the car back to the house I reclined my seat and closed my eyes. Sankar assumed that I wanted to sleep and he turned off the radio that seemed always to be playing. What I wanted was for everything to stop. Not just the sound of the radio or the moving car, but everything. I wanted to disappear into the calm and quiet blackness. But not a minute after I managed a shallow state of relaxation, words and phrases that Sydney had spoken came to me, in his voice, as if from a far-off corner in a padded room: *The question that keeps arising as I think of that day when I walked to the gender centre is . . .* And the voice faded. But the words pulsed in my mind.

I bolted upright, fixed my seat, and from the pocket of my shirt I pulled out pen and paper.

The question that keeps arising as I think of that day when I walked to the gender centre is not why any human would choose to live in such a climate when there was ample space in the warm tropi-cal band around the earth for all the people of the world to live without need for heating and shovel-ling of sidewalks and seasonal clothing and car tire changes. No, what I wanted to know was why one would live in a city of so many people, for such a long time—almost thirty years—and not know a soul to ask for accompaniment and support on such a mission.

Back at my desk, I transposed into my notebook what I'd written in the car, and continued.

In Canada after my life with India and Jonathan, I was unable to accept and settle down with any of my lovers—for there were other lovers, but none with whom I could form a life.

I wanted to be with a woman who knew very ordinary and unimportant things such as the difference in look and taste and usage between coconut water from a coconut that has just been prodded off the tree with a long bamboo pole, and cut open right in front of you with a cutlass, and one that has been husked and imported in its hard, dry, brown shell. I wanted to be with a woman who knew that the white meat lining that shell was once soft like a baby's spit, and fragrant like the air over a coral reef. I wanted to spend my life with someone who knew when a mango or a banana or a plantain was picked too young, and forced, no matter how picture-brilliant and rosy it looked on the outside, to ripen.

I wanted to be with a woman who would know, should the knowledge ever become necessary, what a *karta* is and does, what a *bedi* is, and when I needed her to act on my behalf. And I wanted her to be ready to act.

When I looked up from my words, I could hear that Carmen was once again in the kitchen. Despite the shameful showing the previous night, she had returned, and she and all the house staff insisted we prepare again for a houseful.

Soon it was late afternoon and the house was suddenly quiet. When I roused myself and investigated, I found that the kitchen was empty. Two large basins sat on the counter, and they were covered with a tea cloth. In them were the *pholouries* and *sahinas* Rosita and Carmen had made. The two of them had retreated to their rooms for the usual afternoon rest, and, I supposed, to prepare themselves for the people they imagined would show up. I could hear the faint sounds of the radio coming from Lancelot's room.

I wandered through the quiet house and my thoughts turned to Canada. Catherine would have just arrived home. Perhaps she was heading to the gym, or to the grocery. I felt a pang: I owed her some kind of contact. It was time that I called.

I said nothing to Catherine about the pundit's visit, about the visit to the funeral home or about the details, as I understood them, of the funeral ceremony. I did not mention that the pundit had a daughter, Anta, a woman with blue-black hair. I did not tell her that the pundit's daughter would return that evening to bring me special clothing that I was to wear at the funeral. I babbled on about the food Rosita cooked even as there was no one to eat it. I told her that it was customary that meat was not eaten in the house of the deceased until after the funeral. She said, "Oh dear, what are you going to do, then?" and I hoped she didn't catch the faint glimmer of disdain that crept into my voice without me fully intending it, as I replied that one could do without meat if one had to. To soften my response I added quickly that this was easy to accomplish because Rosita made things like *sahinas* and *pholouries*, and that for dinner she had already prepared melongene and pumpkin, and that she had cooked tomato *choka* and roti for my breakfast.

I knew Catherine did not know what any of these dishes were and could feel the distance between us when she didn't bother to inquire. It was as if I had embarked on a mission to confirm her ignorance of my life down here. I heard myself say that if I missed anything it was the crabs, and I began to tell her about the crabs that were caught in the swamps and sold roadside in neatly tied-up bundles. Their backs are smaller than my fist, I told her, as if she were begging me for details. The facts of the funeral and of my role in it were like a human presence sitting in a chair watching me as I talked, but I mentioned none of this.

Catherine finally spoke: Were they soft-shell crabs? Were they eaten deep-fried? By way of answering I told her of my first experience with the small crabs, but underneath the regaling was some sort of accusation. I felt it, but from where it came and why I was doing this, I didn't know. Rosita curries them, I answered. I said that after my first time eating the crabs like this, Rosita suggested that on a moonlit night I go with her and her family to a beach village on the Atlantic side of the island, where her brothers would take me crab catching.

My voice as I said this to Catherine was flatter than I intended it to be.

Catherine interrupted. "At night? With people you didn't know?"

I was silent and she asked again, "Well, was it safe?"

It was true that I had some time before mentioned how unsafe Trinidad was said to be. I had told her about the

murders during bungled robberies, about the spate of kid-
nappings. But I wished now I hadn't, for she used the opportunity to show grave concern for my safety even though I
was telling her about an outing that took place about three
years ago, before she and I knew each other, and about which
I'd clearly lived to tell. Before I could stop myself I said just
that: "I'm still around, aren't I?"

Catherine said nothing, but in my words how could
she have not heard the suggestion that one day I might not
be around, and my absence would likely not be because I had
fallen prey to an unsafe situation? In any case, I carried on
against her silence, it had been a large group of us. We had
gone down, two cars crammed full. We'd arrived towards
evening. We swam, and ate—Rosita's family had brought
a large iron pot of chicken pelau, and there was a cole slaw
salad, and plantains. And there was mango chow. At this,
Catherine pensively muttered, *Hmm*. I feared that she might
follow that utterance with some inane question, so I quickly
added, "Mango pickled in a spiced brine," and left it at that.
We arrived at the beach, I said, the twelve of us, with three
bottles of rum punch, and there wasn't a drop left in any of
the bottles by the time we left.

At this last mention of our debauchery she said not
a word, and I had the sense that I had won something,
although I was not sure what. The tide was low by nightfall,
I continued, the moon like a searchlight trained on us, and
rather suddenly, just as Rosita and her family had said would
happen, the sand came alive. It vibrated, and I saw that

crabs were pouring down—like an unruly army—from the land at our backs, and were moving swiftly, in their sideways canter, towards the water's edge. We ran behind the largest ones—the crabs would freeze their movement, crouch tight to the sand, their knotty beads of eyes flicking outwards like stunted calcified antennae, their pincers that people here—I saw the word "here" as I spoke it, garlanded with a string of white lights, for I was on the telephone in that very *here*, and Catherine was over *there*—their pincers, which people *here* call *gundies*, waving, but in vain, for they can't actually reach behind to defend themselves from us with these *gundies*.

As I told all of this to Catherine I was reminded of the sea that night and without warning my eyes filled with tears. It had shimmered like liquid mercury, and a salty sea breeze had picked up. I remembered the commotion of the foamy waves crashing and rushing up the shore, and the coconut tree branches rustling wildly, and the sound of the twelve of us laughing and screaming and shouting gentle abuses to one another. But I did not tell any of this to Catherine. I might have described it all, but she would only have thought she understood. How could I have imparted the odour of the wet churned-up shore that was quickly being overtaken by the sea, of the fresh crabs and their strange manner of advancing sideways, of the sweat of eight excited young men with the sweetness of alcohol and pelau on their breaths? I carried on, careful not to let my voice betray the emotions that welled in me alongside the memory. You ran them down, I said to her, and just between your thumb and index finger you grabbed the backs of the little buggers from behind, and of course if you hadn't done it just right you ended up with a crab dangling off one of your fingers by the *gundy*, and you dared not scream as it closed its toothy vise because you'd already become the brunt of everyone's teasing, and they teased mercilessly, which meant that they considered you one of them.

Catherine said not a word. Are you there? I asked.

Yeah, yeah, she answered, her voice noticeably, oddly, distant.

We caught about forty crabs, I concluded. But we both knew that my story had not been about crab hunting.

After a pause, she asked when Gita and Jaan were expected to arrive. I knew exactly who she meant, yet I responded with a question: Do you mean Sydney's sister and her husband?

Catherine answered with another question: When are you coming home?

"I don't know," I said.

It was time for her to end the call, she said; it was late. After another uncomfortably long pause, I told her I missed her. The silence that followed exploded messily when I uttered, I love you.

Catherine did not reply. And I suddenly felt like a child, wanting to run behind her, to tell her that I was sorry.

II

Rosita was shaking my shoulder. I had been dreaming that I was a pirogue on open water. There was no one captaining me. The sky behind the weightless ball of silver moon was like marbled tissue paper. I was surrounded by three hundred and sixty degrees of ocean stretching clear to a distant encircling horizon. There was nothing else but me on the surface of the water. There were no waves, and not a breeze. I palpitated evenly in the undulating, shimmering sea. Salt water lightly lashed my skin, and I heard a mumble of foreign languages lapping at my sides. I didn't understand their words, but I knew their meaning and felt an urgency to remember the wisdom imparted in them.

It was not, to my surprise, nighttime, but evening. A violent red light streamed in through the window. Rosita had brought me a glass of lime juice on ice. Three people had arrived, she told me, and the pundit's daughter had returned.

The pundit's daughter—"Anta, her name is Anta," I

informed Rosita as I sat up too fast—was outside waiting
to see me! My head was like a weight on a string. I tried to
remember the wisdom that I had heard in the water's foreign
language, but it had already retreated into its other realm.
There was no time for a shower. I had to dress quickly.

Rosita hesitated at the door, and it dawned on me
that there was something different about her manner. She
seemed less confident than usual. I asked if there was something she wanted to say.

Yes, she said. She wanted to know if, after the funeral,
she would still be employed at the house.

I hadn't anticipated that the staff would be wondering about this. "Yes, of course," I answered. "You will all be
kept on."

In the time it had taken me to rinse my face, brush my teeth
and pull on a shirt and trousers, several more people had
arrived, more than there were chairs on the veranda. They
milled about expectantly. A rather tall woman of Indian
descent in a long and shiny black dress, a mantilla of black
lace clipping the back of her head and falling about her
shoulders, stepped ahead and proclaimed, "You are the boy
from Toronto."

That this woman knew of me was for a second flat-
tering, but then no longer, for I was alarmed by her voice.
She, in her theatrical black ankle-length dress, had what can
only be described as a man's voice, not a deep or husky voice,

but a *male* voice. I immediately saw that several people on the veranda were, to put it delicately, not entirely what they appeared to be. There were a number who at a first glance appeared to be women. But by the time the glance had been completed I saw that they were men who had dressed themselves so that they would be taken for women. There were, too, some who expected, it seemed, to be taken for men but who were clearly women. Two women with heavily kohl-lined eyes came towards me and greeted me as if we were acquaintances, but I was unable to reciprocate even a feigned familiarity. Lancelot and Rosita were in the periphery of my vision. They were busy serving drinks and food. I did not look at them directly, but I could tell that they were going about this gathering rather easily. I had not yet seen Anta, but knowing that she was there, that she was probably watching all of these people and me, was enough to cause my face to burn. Trying to come to terms with Sydney's many changes inside the privacy of the house was one thing, but I felt as if these people were being disrespectful by their public unmasking of him. They were exposing me, too, as being closely connected to such a person.

"I'm so sorry for your loss. He was a very special man, a hero to all of us." The words came from a deep voice. I turned to see someone who expected to be taken for a woman. She blocked the breeze from the Gulf, and the flowery scent she wore permeated the air. Her compassion, the bowed head, the lowered deep voice, the clasped hands at her chest, were as theatrical as the application of lipstick

and eyeliner, as exaggerated as her large hoop earrings, and yet I felt the genuineness in what she said. I was, however, not comforted. I looked for Anta. She was nowhere to be seen, and the only relief I had at that moment was in the thought that she had already left.

I became preoccupied with the thought that these people must once *not* have been what they now appeared to be. How long ago was this *once?* I wondered. As recently as an hour before, when they'd dressed as they had, especially to come here? As long ago as since they cut off, or had reconfigured, or built up, some part of their bodies? Did they think this was a circus for all to come as they pleased? Was this an occasion for mockery? In my view, Sydney was not a man. There was no getting away from the fact that he had altered his body. But to maintain the facade displayed by his clothing, the facial hair, the balding, the thickened muscles of his arms and back and legs, the oddly thickened torso, he had to take injections once a month. These altered his appearance, but they did not make him a man. Yes, I now used the masculine pronouns for Sydney—*him, his, he.* These concessions, I argued in my head, were in a sense forced on me. One could almost say that I had used them against my will, at least at first, and then they'd become habit, for regardless of the new pronoun, I never failed to see Sid in Sydney. I saw Sid first. In Sydney's voice I heard Sid. In Sydney's memories and motives I recognized Sid's. And in his heart I recognized Sid.

All I had learned about women and about men, including what I had learned as a child parented by two women,

seemed now to be a lie. A wave of nausea crashed through me. I felt myself falling, and the tungsten lighting on the veranda dimmed.

I was being carried like a baby, cradled in the arms of the tall woman. I breathed in as deeply as I could, for the scent of her cologne entered my lungs and assured me that I was awake, alive. She set me down on my bed. Rosita bent over me. The tall woman began to undo the buttons on my shirt, her voice deeper now, yet cooing, "Everything is okay, son. Everything is okay. This must be all so strange for you. It's hot in here." It was as if I were a cloud, unanchored and floating in an unbearable heat, yet as long as I was able to breathe in her cologne I was safe. The woman somehow knew this, for she stayed close. Her voice was now oddly familiar. She sat on the edge of the bed, one of her arms over me. She asked if there was a fan, then instructed someone to go and get it, and I remembered all at once where I had heard that voice. She was one of the two men who had been Sydney's only visitors at the hospital; she was the one with the kohl-lined eyes and the painted pinkie.

Rosita left the room. The woman's hand was close to mine. I moved the tips of my fingers so that they brushed against her. She responded by taking my hand in hers. It was a large hand. It was not the hand of a woman. I tightened mine around it.

What is your name? I asked.

"Kareen," she answered.

I knew that name, too, from Sydney's will. Kareen Akal Sharma. I saw Lancelot at the bedroom door, keeping the crowd from entering the room. Then, as if executing some intuitive choreography, the woman rose and stepped away to allow me to sit up. Anta had entered the room and perched lightly on the bed's edge.

I rose and swung my feet off the bed. I leaned forward, rested my elbows on my knees and put my head in my hands, for I was still light-headed. Soon an electric fan was brought in, placed on the dresser and switched on. People moved out of the room and the door closed, and I was left alone with Anta. She sat next to me, and I turned to face her. Her eyes were a drink of cool water. She lowered me to the bed, my head resting in the cup of one of her hands.

She brought her face to mine and we kissed as if this, our first kiss, might be the last.

———

Later, I sat on the veranda and thought about all that had happened that evening. The sliding door had been pushed in, only one of its two high-security locks engaged. One veranda light had been left on. The drinking glasses had been cleared away and the chairs pulled back into their usual places. Yellow tungsten light pooled softly in the middle of the veranda, but beyond that circle the garden was in blackness. Cicadas whistled and frogs, near enough by, grunted raucously. Against their din, even the sea could not be heard. Flames from the rigs in the Gulf here and there pulsed upward. A cool breeze whipped about me, salty and smelling of the sea.

In Anta's presence a short while ago I had found myself thinking of Zain. Lying next to Anta on the bed, I had wanted to tell her about Sid and me, about Sid and Zain. I hadn't done so, but I suspected that one day soon I would. She wouldn't stay the night, naturally, but when we kissed against the door of her car I felt as if I had already, long ago and numerous times, made love to her.

I thought about Rosita and Lancelot and the tall woman, Kareen Akal Sharma, and how when they'd left the room and closed the door, they had done so knowing full well that Anta was in there with me. The conservatism that supposedly pervaded Trinidad seemed to have momentarily dissipated. It had indeed been a strange night. I had come face to face with women and men who presented themselves in ways that did not match their voices and their bodies— and yet, at the end of the night I was left with no sense that lies had been told. No secrets had been imposed on anyone. Everything was out in the open. And this house had clearly been, to these people, a safe place. This, one of the nights of Sydney's wake, had in an odd way been one of the best I had ever spent in Trinidad.

I found myself wondering if Zain had been anything like Anta. As strange as it might seem, I felt an impossible desire now to know who Zain really was.

I went inside and undressed and planted myself at my desk. I retrieved my own notebook and began again—this time taking Zain's voice, hesitantly at first, but then in comfortable stride.

Dear Sid,

I haven't heard from you in months now. Angus and I just celebrated our second anniversary.

Life is changing for me. It seems as if I will do some business courses now. Not "it seems." I'm doing one as it is. So, I guess I will be going into the business with Angus. He thinks studying medicine will take so long that we will be putting off having a family, and that our relationship will also be put on hold. He says that when he graduates he wants to have a wife, not to be living with a student still. I don't really mind, after all. Medicine, business, it's all just work, and in the end I want my life not to be about the work itself, but about contributing to society and building a family, and you can do that no matter what your job is.

Are you still liking doing art? Do you still think you will be an artist? I sort of envy you. But you might have to teach to make a living. Unless you marry a very rich man. Have you met one yet? Is that the new friend you mentioned ever so briefly in your last letter? I want to ask you so many questions, but what's the use if I don't get replies in a timely fashion?

Well, just to tell you: I am very interested in what is happening with you, and I really miss hearing from you. As time goes by, I realize that you are the truest friend I ever had.

Take care of yourself, whatever you are doing, and know that you have a friend here, if ever you need one. Yours always,

Zain

I wasn't entirely satisfied with that passage, so I worked on another, trying again to capture Zain—her voice and cadences as they'd been in the letters I'd read.

Sid, just a short note—my busyness has multiplied tenfold, naturally. The feeling, after the baby has left your body, of her still being, not an appendage, but almost an organ—a real physical part of you, that is—hasn't gone. I am suspecting that this will not happen EVER. And I feel like a queen of sorts because of it. Mum comes over every day, and even Dad is treating Angus with much more respect now. And Angus—do you know that for three months now, every week, ever since Aliya was born, he has sent me flowers? I am actually waiting for the flowers on Thursdays, and when they come, even though I am expecting them, it is such a wonderful surprise! I think it's a surprise because I can't imagine it will go on forever, and I am wondering when it'll come to an end. You know me, forever cynical. Or is it realistic? He is working hard as usual, and the business has really taken off. He comes home every day smelling like heaven—*jeera*, and *ilaichi*, and *achar masala*. Do you know we are in talks with a company in India that wants us to make up a range of spice mixes for them? It's very odd how these things work. We will be sending a curry mix to India! But it's a very big account, and we will no doubt have to make changes here to accommodate such a client. I am hoping there is a trip to India in this soon. We are in the process of buying some land in the Central Range, to cultivate with *jeera*, *bhandania* and *chadon beni*. So, of course, the mix we will make for the Indian account will be a Trinidad blend, which is exotic in India.

So, I feel like a queen, and if giving birth is what it takes I think I can do it a few more times. I'm already thinking about playmates for this sweet little child. She needs a brother to take care of her, and she needs a sister to confide in—not siblings to look after—so it'll have to be sooner than later. I have totally become used to this family life—this mothering life, this wife thing. I think it is the most natural thing on earth. Are you getting ready for it? It would be great if we could have kids that are around the same age. Wouldn't it?

———

Anta telephoned the next morning during breakfast, and I had to take the call in the kitchen, where there was no privacy. However much I had marvelled last night at the atmosphere of openness and truth-telling, I was unable to carry that higher state of mind, that ennobled life-condition, into the new day, and I felt unusually self-conscious knowing that Carmen, Lancelot and Rosita—who had answered the phone—were all in earshot. They would surely be able to tell from the sound of my voice that I had cherished the feel of Anta's steady hand beneath my head, the smell of her skin, the taste of her mouth.

But I needn't have worried. As if nothing had passed between us, Anta said that she called to make sure that the *kurta* and pants fitted. I had not yet tried on the suit, and she reminded me, although I needed no such prodding, that the funeral was the following morning. I ended the call easily, knowing that I would speak with her again after trying on the clothing.

Two flower arrangements soon arrived. No one knew the names on the cards that accompanied them. Rosita hovered about the dining room as I finished eating, and I imagined she wanted to reassure me about my falling apart last night. She followed me when I went out onto the veranda. Before I could turn to her, she began to deliver a lecture: "Those people. They all go to Baphomet where Mr. Sydney used to have to go to. He was the oldest one, and the first to do it. Those people were his friends. They were his family. People might be uncomfortable with how they are, but *they* were his family too."

I felt the heat of blood rising in my face.

"Just some months ago," she continued, "they wanted to pay him a tribute, and they say they was going to name a fund at the clinic, *Sydney Mahale Priority Fund*. Why Mr. Sydney go and tell Miss Gita, I don't know. I suppose it was because he was so proud. But she did vex-vex, too-bad-too-bad, for when she hear the family name was going to be used like that she say, No! Not over she dead body. So, just like that he back down. He didn't even bother to fight she. He just go back to them and he tell them, quiet so, thanks, but no thanks, not to do it."

I should perhaps have been gentler in my response, for Rosita had not been privy to my process throughout the evening before of opening my eyes and mind; she had only seen my intense discomfort. In any case, had she so accepted Sydney—she who washed his clothing, and she and Lancelot who bathed him and changed his clothes, and administered his medications and injections when he himself no longer could, and surely knew who and what he was then, and what he had been in the past—had she so accepted him that she hadn't seen my struggle to do so? Moreover, I was startled by the presumption of the kind of relationship between her and me that would allow her to speak with me, or rather *to* me, in such a manner. "I appreciate you clarifying that," I said, perhaps too tersely, and headed towards the garden wall that overlooked the Gulf. As I walked, I wondered if she had ever had cause to speak with Sydney in such a manner. Perhaps it ought to be permitted at times?

I returned to the house and in a softer manner asked her if she had everything she needed for the day. Her manner was gentler too, when she replied that she had everything, and added that Carmen's daughter would be joining to help with the cooking and cleaning. I saw no reason for this, save for the delight of fuss and chaos the occasion of a death here offered, but of course, I made no objection.

The shirt and the pants were of a startling white colour, their fabric as light and soft as that used to swaddle a new-born baby. I tried them on—the first time I had ever worn anything Indian, even though *kurtas* were not unfamiliar to me. I thought of Sydney. Of Sid. I heard Rosita's words, spoken numerous times since his death, that he was right here, watching over and seeing everything. I had dismissed these words as merely typical of Rosita's ways of thinking, but here I was, imagining that he was indeed watching, that he saw I was preparing to carry out my duties at his funeral.

When I telephoned Anta to report that the *kurta* fitted me, she asked what the day had in store for me. I told her that I had to return to the funeral home to approve of Sydney's appearance. It would be a stressful morning, she commiserated; would I be interested in doing something that offered a respite, if only briefly, from all that was going on? I accepted her offer to meet at a café in Port of Spain. She would take me from there on a short relaxing hike up to a nearby waterfall. As I put down the phone I could not tell which was greater: my desire to see her, or my nervous-ness over returning to the funeral home and the prospect of seeing Sydney again.

Just before entering the cold room where Sydney lay, I mused how, in Canada, I had never heard of anyone doing this kind of thing. I wondered if seeing the body of the deceased was a more natural way of being, a healthier attitude towards the dead and death, or part of a backward way of life.

As it turned out, Sydney in death looked remarkably as he had in life. If it were not for the frills in the interior of the coffin, how its cushioned walls hugged his body tightly, and how straight he was arranged, I would have thought he was lying in a strange bed, merely asleep.

The mortician allowed me some minutes with Sydney, and the question I had arrived with was answered in part when I gave in to a surprising and urgent desire to touch Sydney's face. Although I had expected it to be cold, I was startled. The surface of the skin seemed soft until I let my hand rest too heavily, and I felt beneath it a sobering hard-ness. He looked so much like himself, but the one expres-sion on his face, while certainly his, was all that there was. I was in the room alone with him for no more than three minutes, but it was long enough for me to believe that his soul had, as Pundit had told me, flown away and this was what had been left behind. Still, I rested my hand lightly on the cheek of the face of that body, and felt regret that I had not been physically closer to Sydney in the last years of his life. I felt, too, humbled by this opportunity here in Trinidad to take care of him one last time.

Back at the house, as I packed a bag with my swimming trunks and a towel, I naturally thought of Catherine. I felt some guilt—not because I was about to head off to meet Anta, but for having held on to Catherine. I knew in my bones that our relationship had, for both of us, ended. The guilt was so strong that I gave in and phoned her. Thankfully, she did not answer her land line or her cellphone. I did not leave messages on either.

Anta was an only child, she told me as we went around the Queen's Park Savannah. She was the daughter *and* the son her mother had wanted, and she was the daughter and the son her father had wanted too. This wasn't my first time around the Savannah, but Anta drove slowly and pointed out the colonial buildings that were now used as government offices, and the island's two most prestigious boys' secondary schools, Saint Mary's College and Queen's Royal College, the former looking like a monastery, the latter like a grandiose German Renaissance facsimile. In some ways, it *was* the first time I was seeing them.

Her time was clearly her own and I wondered aloud if she had a job or profession. She explained that she had an undergraduate degree in music, and on afternoons she gave private lessons on the harmonium and the sitar. She sang, too, and played these instruments at her father's temple.

Her family, I learned, was an odd mix of Indian and Hindu tradition and modernism. Her father, she told me, used to provoke discussion with her and goad her on to disagree with him, taking one side of an argument one day and quite the opposite the next. He no longer did this, for now they knew each other so well that they anticipated too quickly what argument each had waiting. When she did something that displeased him and her mother, she was made to choose her own punishment, one that was appropriate, neither lenient nor exaggerated, and she was made to defend the choice of punishment rather than to dwell directly on her infractions.

Pundit used the excuse nowadays of his cataracts for asking her to drive him about, but he had begun to teach her to drive when she was ten years old and had to sit on cushions so that she could see above the steering wheel. She remembered, she told me, at age fourteen driving him one night to a neighbour's house. The place was not too far away, but it was illegal and dangerous for her to drive all the same. Her father had taken her with him everywhere he went when she was a child, much to many people's dismay, but those people came, in time, to regard her with the respect they would have given her brother, had she one. If those people had daughters he would preach directly to the daughters, sometimes to the amusement, but more regularly to the chagrin, of the girls' relatives, pointing out his own Anta, saying that if she could do all of these things herself—if she could study and come in the first three in her class, if she could build and decorate a *bedi*, if she could rub her father's and mother's legs with sesame oil, if she could go to the shop for her mother and tell any wayward young men who had words for her along the way what was good for them without swearing or disrespecting herself, if she could climb a mango tree and bring down the chicken from it—if she could do all of this and still be the daughter any parent could want, including a pundit, then they, too, should be able to do these things. Nowadays, she gave her mother a rest by doing the driving that, on account of the cataracts, her father could no longer do, and she read the newspapers and magazines to him. There was little time for a social life, she told me, but she liked it that way.

And boyfriends? I asked.

There is no one special, she said. There were always, of course, inquiries from families who were interested in her as a wife for their son. She could have been born with leopard spots on her face, she said, and there would be interest in her, because she was the daughter of a pundit.

And you haven't accepted anyone? I persisted. We were both grinning like teenagers now.

"My heart had not been moved yet," she said, more seriously, and it was as if her breath had suddenly been caught.

"Your heart?" I asked, adding, What does the heart have to do with a pundit's daughter?

My parents, she answered, believe in love.

Later that afternoon, blissfully tired from swimming, I did not want to write. This time, I went to Sydney's room and got the knapsack out of his cupboard. And once more, for a last time, wanting to confirm Zain's voice in my mind, I read a handful of her letters.

Dear Sid,

I was very surprised to get a response from you at all, and so quickly. Everyone is well, thanks. I can't imagine leaving Aliya for another year or so, and even then it would be difficult, except that sometimes I think she thinks my mother is actually her mother, which I don't really mind. I love how close she and Mum are with each other. Anyway, I will one of these days surely visit you.

Congratulations on the exhibition. Can you send photos of your paintings? I'll have to buy one of them before you get so famous that they'd be out of my reach. We are building a new factory on the land in Central. We're also acquiring a lot of new machinery. So it's really busy here.

I see you took offence to me saying that it was natural to be a mother and a wife. Can I say that it is natural for me? And that I am totally fine—I make no judgement—if it isn't something you want to do? I am a little surprised at how verbose you were about it. From this I realize that the subject means a great deal to you. So you got me thinking, in truth, about the idea of what is natural and normal. I can think about it with a touch more clarity than I can write about it, but what I want to say is that I can see how these things—the value given to being a mother and a wife—might be cultural. (And it sure is a value in a lot of cultures. But maybe cultures change with time. And with the times.) But you and I are from the *same* culture, and since I trust your judgements about what you need for your own happiness, all I can come up with is that somehow our cultures might be a little different. We're from the same country and same race—so maybe you being Hindu and me Muslim has something to do with it? But every Hindu girl/woman I know shares the same idea as mine about being a wife and a mother, so either I know only the ones who think like me, and not the ones—besides you—who don't, or this difference might have something to do with how liberal your family is compared to mine. Or maybe it is just that you *are* different. You are unique, and there is nothing unnatural about your idea—it is just different, and you are just different. In any case, it was always your differences that made you so interesting. And I wouldn't want you to be anything else, or anything you didn't want to be, or are not. I don't need to understand you, I realize; but come to think of it, I want to understand you. I just need you to be more like me so I can do that.

I hope you're following me, as this is all very important to me. The one thing I don't need to understand is my connection to/love for you. It's just a fact.

Love always, and all ways,

Z

Sid, I'm sending this to you with much love. Aliya is six months old in this picture. She has Angus's chin and my eyes. Mum spends a lot of time over here these days so that I can study (one more course to go and I am finished). It's good to have Mum here with us—we're eating well, for a change. You know I can't cook roti to save my life. We usually buy it from Ali's but Mum's is so much better. And cheaper! I can't believe I just wrote that. It's not like we have worries about money at all. I'm not boasting, you understand; I just want to tell you all that is happening to me. Anyway, the other side of Mum's presence here is that we're all putting on a lot of weight. Aliya is such a good baby. She doesn't cry—except when she is hungry or wet. Otherwise she smiles a lot, and makes the sweetest attempts to have conversation with us—and I find myself talking back in imitation, in baby talk. I never thought I'd do that, but she gets so excited, and looks really satisfied when I speak back to her like that. I wish you could see her before she grows up.

Z

Dear Sid,

I have been writing you in my head all day, and I still can't find the right words. I don't know if I ever will. I only know that the words I have are the wrong ones. I know this instinctively, but I don't have others, no matter how hard I try, to talk with you about what you told me in your last letter.

First of all, I want you to know that ours is a 'til-death-do-us-part connection, just as I always knew it would be, even if you didn't. So I think we just have to try to figure out how to talk to each other about this. I have to tell you that I am very very happy that you told me. It explains so much to me. I never understood why you didn't have a boyfriend. And I always knew you were—I want to say strange, but I don't mean it in a negative way. I suppose I could say different. It can't be easy for you. This makes me wish I were close by, so that I could be there for you, and so that you could know how much you mean to me.

It is hard, if not sad, to think I have known you all these years, and thought of you as my best friend, only to realize that I didn't really know who you were. On the one hand I wasn't really surprised when I read your letter, but on the other hand I was *very* surprised. Both at the same time. I guess my surprise was more that you had been this way while I knew you, and I was oblivious to it. You must have been going through agony and I didn't know about it. I can understand that this was not an easy thing to tell me, but still, I am your best friend, and I can't help but feel as if you weren't truthful to me. Can I assume that I meant so much to you, that you didn't want to lose me? I'll accept that! But did you also think so little of me? That I am so small-minded? I don't understand what it all means, and I want you to tell me. You'll have to have patience with me. But I think this is only fair—payback for all the patience I have had with you.

I have questions to ask you. How long have you known this about yourself, and how did you know? And do you mind if I tell Angus? I talk to him about everything—but I don't have to tell him this if you'd rather I didn't.

One thing I wonder is if you knew about yourself since we were in high school—and if you did, how hard it must have been for you, having to make sure no one found out. I can't help but think of Jenny Ginsun. Do you remember her? We used to say that she was—well, I don't want to repeat those things. I feel so badly about how everyone used to bad talk Jenny, and I also remember you saying to me that people should just be allowed to be the way they are, and that we shouldn't harass her so much because we don't know anything about her life at home, or how our lives would turn out.

Do you remember saying these things? Did you actually know about her then, and did you know about yourself too? How you must have felt. I do know that she never really bothered me or, rather, I couldn't really be bothered with her—because she never actually bothered anyone, did she. But I never tried to stop others from bad talking her, even if I myself didn't. I feel so terrible about so many things right now, and wish you were here so that we could talk. It's difficult to say everything in a letter, especially when you have to wait for a reply—and may never get one! I love you, Sid.

Take care of yourself, and be happy. You deserve to be. There is so much I admire about you.

Your best friend forever,

Z

Before putting Sydney's notebooks aside, too, I succumbed to the hunger for one last morsel of knowledge about this man who meant so much to me. I cupped one of the dairies in one hand by its spine, allowing the little book to fall open where it would, knowing that the act was like that of a believer who turns at random to a spiritual text in the confidence that the chance reading will speak directly to his need.

Zain, if you can hear me now, you will realize I am still waiting to hear how you could have gone first.

Your death is not something I had ever imagined, and so many years later it is still unimaginable. Do you know what I did before returning to Trinidad for your funeral? I went down to my storage locker to look for the two photographs, the only ones I have, of you. My locker was so crammed with stuff, Zain, I could hardly move through it. But that was good because, as it turned out, it was useful to see this snapshot of my life, starting with the wall of boxes and piled up furniture that greeted me. I had stored away everything I didn't use on a daily basis to make room in my little apartment for my canvases, which I would spread out and paint on, on the floor. But now it was oddly calming, reassuring, to see this collection of clothes, kitchenware, tools and books.

I pulled out one of the boxes of books and opened it. On top was a manual on how to care for antiques. I was struck by the realization that I had bought this book imagining that in Canada I would live in a home full of priceless antiques and, like my mother, have to care for them. I pulled out a blond maple-wood coffee table, the surface of which, with a wood-burning pen in my first year at art school, I had etched with a mass of banana leaves and anthurium lilies. It had moved from India's basement to this locker. On a shelf in the locker were sculptures in clay, wood, and metal. There were, naturally, the rolls of canvases, work I'd done during the years I lived with India and Jonathan. There was camping gear I'd bought and used once, a fishing rod and vest that still had the sale tag hanging from it, a rack of dumbbells for weight training. You'd think I was a real jock. There was a filing cabinet crammed with papers—I couldn't remember now why I'd kept them. I surveyed the collection, feeling that I didn't know the person to whom these things belonged.

I thought of all that money you, Zain, had given me one week before. You, the only person who had ever accepted me as I was, were gone now, and very possibly because I could not stand up for myself, and could not protect you. There in my locker, your death gave me sudden clarity. I had intended to deposit the money, but the envelope was still on my dresser. I knew that with it you'd given me the means to rectify what had put you in jeopardy, even if it was too late. I knew, unequivocally, what I would do with the money. I would go to your funeral, and on my return I would begin to think about the lengthy process—which you in so many ways had set in motion—of altering my body.

I opened box after box until I came across the bundle of letters and notes that you wrote me when we were in high school. I have read them so many times since then that I know them by heart.

Sid,

Don't pass any more notes through Singh-Johnstone.
I don't know what's wrong with her today. She might
tell on us. We didn't get our marks back in Chemistry
yet. I can't wait. I bet I beat her ass again. She has
brains but no sense of humour and no community
spirit. Did you get any of your mid-term marks yet?
What am I supposed to do for Assembly? I don't
want to talk about being a Muslim, don't want to talk
about God. I could hand out the recipe for seiwine,
have everyone recite it along with me. Sid, Look at
Augusta's shoes. What do you think of them? Where
on earth does she shop? She can't dress to save her
life. I hope she doesn't keep us in late today. Dear
Sid, Just close your eyes for one minute and think of
the countless number of people besides you in this
world. It's frightening—you in the midst of them all,
a non-entity. And then it's warm, hot actually, as a
blanketing cloud of brotherhood creeps over us.
Love, Zain

You used that word—"love"—sparingly, but whenever you did I tortured myself, parsing what you
might truly have meant by it.

Finally, there at the back of the cold locker, were
the boxes of photographs. In one of them were
photos I'd taken when I had first arrived in Canada.
I could see in them that my eyes, which had only

known one landscape before, had suddenly been bombarded by incomprehensible views, the unrecognizable shapes and colours of a far northern landscape. The photographs showed how, as I attempted to understand my surroundings, I would isolate some detail in the landscape, as if it were a trinket I could catch and examine. In a number of photos I had trained my camera on a coniferous tree from which icicles hung, the branches weighed down in glassy sweeping arcs.

Eventually, I found the two images I had come for. When you gave them to me you'd coyly refused to tell me who the photographer was. I still don't know. I don't need the photos in front of me now to recall them. I remember them by heart, just as I remember the notes you'd written. One of them was taken in your back yard. You are holding the hands of your two children just as one is about to jump into a little round concrete pool. Your long, shiny black hair is parted on one side, and pulled back. You seldom wore shorts because you thought your knees were "knobby"—your words—but in this photo you're wearing red running shorts. And you have on a loose, pale yellow tank top that falls to your waist. Your hands are outstretched—Peter clutches one, pulling you to his side, and Aliya clings to the other, pulling you towards her. Aliya reaches you at your hips, and she wears only her baggy kid's panty.

Peter's free hand is in the air as he readies himself to jump into the pool. The three of you are perched on the edge of the concrete, which is painted the exact yellow of your tank top. Your toes, the nails painted the same red as your shorts, grip the lip of the pool and the three of you look as if you're about to tip into it. The children are gazing into the pool, Aliya with a grin so wide you can hear her laughter, Peter serious, his face contorted with the concentration of an old man. Your head is slightly dipped, to keep the sun out of your eyes, perhaps, but you're looking up at the camera. I know your smile. It's as if you're saying "yes" and "don't" at once.

Who took that photo, Zain? I never saw you look at Angus like that. Did you, once? If so, when did you stop? Was that a look shared only with him, or was the photographer someone other than Angus? The wading pool is set in a lawn. There are no flowers or shrubs, just the pool, and behind it a chain-link fence. Beyond the fence, it's all sky, pale indigo darkening the edges of the photo, with a faint smudge of loose white cloud at the top centre. Given the distance between the three of you and the photographer I shouldn't have been able pick out the fine hairs, like the wisps on a newborn baby's forehead, that ringed your hairline, hairs that were always a little damp, but I could see them, Zain, feel the wet of them on the tips of my fingers that had time and again pushed them back. But it was your smile, the intense look at the camera, and by extension at the photographer, that made me tuck that photo away. Zain, when you gave that photo to me so many years ago, I felt as if I were being treated—as well as being subjected—to the gaze of that photographer. Were you trying to tell me something, Zain? Or were you trying to dare me too? I never showed that photo to anyone. It was a photo of my best friend holding the hands of her two children who adored her, but I wouldn't show it to anyone. I hid it away in a box in my basement. That day before I returned for your funeral, though, I took it from the locker room up to my apartment.

The second photo had been cropped by hand into a ragged shape approximating a square, creating a bust portrait. I remember you handing this one to me. I had looked at it for a second, shy and a little confused, and glanced up to see you grinning mischievously. "I am wearing a maillot. You don't see it, but I am," you explained.

In the photo you are standing under an outdoor shower, the large lime-green leaves of a traveller's palm fanning out to create the photo's background. The showerhead can't be seen, but it was opened full on you, your head directly in its spray. It is a full frontal shot and you are staring at the photographer, your eyes soft, your lipstick-reddened lips shining and slightly parted so that glistening water seems to fall between them, and then off your lower lip. Your right arm is raised, bent at the elbow, your limbs so long that the point of your elbow is well above your head. Your hand is obscured at the back of your head, out of sight, resting on your neck. Your exposed underarm is shaved, pale, smooth as the palm of your hand. Your black hair in this photo is pulled back, but looks as if it has been freshly groomed, with deep grooves that could only have been caused by the teeth of a large comb. Because of all this, and because the water spraying out of the shower tap hasn't disturbed your hair, and the mascara and the kohl that thickly outline your large bright eyes haven't run, the photo seems staged. The water from the shower hits your hair and each drop, or rather each dash, each smart dash, shatters like fireworks. The dashes of water reflect the green of the traveller's palm behind you, and the blue slash of light with a pin-point of red. Water runs down your arm and your face, and drips off your eye lashes, your nose, lip, and jaw line. A shiny bead hangs off your elbow, with another in formation, in quick pursuit. I was uncomfortable when I first saw the photograph, Zain, but I managed a trembling smile and said, "That's a great photo, nice shoulders."

I still wonder, so many years later, who was the photographer, Zain?

The upturned fanned-out lines of the palm branch and the downwards spray of water, the deep grooves in your hair, that raised arm, the paleness of your underarm and, above all, the hand-cropping of the photograph are dizzying. Why is it cropped? What didn't you want me to see? I was glad to have that photograph. I wanted to keep it to myself, to protect it, so that no one else might be stirred by the same questions.

After reading that section, I was compelled to turn to the following well-thumbed passage:

Zain, you were like a child wanting to be held. But you were not a child. You were a woman. Regardless of what I look like, of the body parts I have or don't have, or of the crime that there isn't another word, beyond *male* and *female*, to describe someone like me, I am not what you were. At least, that's how I feel about myself and my place in the world. And even if it was true that you felt nothing as you lay at my side like that, your head on my shoulder, facing mine, my lips not an inch from your forehead, your breath like a feather moving back and forth on my neck, I can't say I felt nothing. Far from it. You wouldn't have dreamed of lying like that with a man unless you were in an intimate relationship.

I didn't have to say it: you knew I loved you, and

you probably even knew how, exactly, I loved you. Was it fair or right that you could lie so close to me and not expect me to fall and fall and fall for you? Was it right or fair to either of us that I indulged in such covert intimacies with you? At least I never let it come between us. Or did it in the end pry us apart?

Who killed you, Zain? Was it Eric, or was it, in some way, me? Are we—that word *we* making collaborators of the bastard and me—both guilty?

Oh, Sydney. This grief, this idea you have carried for so long that you were responsible for Zain's death—how I wish I had known of it. I regret that you and I never discussed it, that I was never given the chance to allay your fears, tell you that you were guilty of nothing.

But whose fault is this? Should I not be the one who carries the burden of guilt—for bearing prejudices you knew you had to be wary of? Oh, Sydney, the silences you had to keep, the unspoken words that tortured you. Your body lies cold in a funeral parlour, but wherever your spirit lives now, hear my words: it is not you who is guilty.

Never before had I considered the concept of heaven. But on the day of Sydney's funeral—another for which I had no precedent—my mind was wide open.

I was Sydney's custodian—not of his body as it lay in his casket, but of the part of him that was not perishable. I wanted the impossible: to correct the misconceptions that had swirled around him when he lived, and to organize how he was to be remembered. To this end I prepared and practised my eulogy until I knew it by heart. Sydney's two friends from the Baphomet group would speak first and then I would deliver a eulogy that would reveal what a compassionate and understanding parent Sid had been to me. I wanted to say how he and I had been apart from each other for many years but were reunited nine years ago and how in those nine years he had bared himself to me, and I had learned about his courage, his humanity and his unfathomable ability to love. I wanted to say that he was a hero to me, and an example to us all.

As I waited for the ceremony to begin I felt in moments like an angel, benevolent and fierce; in others like a child, unknowing and in awe; and in still others as if I were a divining rod that sought truth, like a fierce and fearless demon. And sometimes I saw my utter powerlessness, and I felt raw and ignorant. In those moments, I was unsure of everything.

The time arrived, and I stood on the veranda next to the open casket and Sydney's body, garlanded and sweet-smelling. Before us sat a small gathering of about thirty people, including Gita and Jaan, who had arrived the night before. I looked at Sydney and then at the gathering. And I opened my mouth to speak, but no sound came out.

I cleared my throat and tried again.

I had no sense of how much time passed before a voice I did not recognize came out of my mouth. It said simply that Sydney had been the best parent anyone could hope to have.

The lineup of cars headed for the parking area of the cremation grounds advanced no more than a single car-length before stopping for several minutes, then moving again. This was the pattern and the pace for about a quarter of a mile on the road that ran parallel to the Caroni River.

We lost sight of Pundit's car, and of Gita and Jaan's, but I saw a hearse about five vehicles ahead of us and assumed it was "ours." If Gita did not come to the cremation, I thought, I would be furious—and yet, I also did not want her anywhere near Sydney during those last minutes when his body was still visible to all. I turned to see if I might be able to spot her car behind us, and saw that Rosita had her hand on Lancelot's on the seat between them. Lancelot had not spoken a word throughout the journey.

In the distance, three discrete plumes of grey smoke whirled heavenward. That I was to be the one to press the button that incinerated Sydney's body still weighed on me. I was ignorant of the details of things to come, but after the small fiasco of not being able to speak earlier, I resolved to do whatever was required of me.

Sydney's last hours in the hospital—after his only two visitors had left and he began to speak to me again about his life—came back to me then. I recalled how I had taken the relative vigour in his voice to mean that his condition was improving.

He had been telling me of arriving in the office at the Irene Samuel on that morning of the blizzard. But he did not begin with leaving his apartment or speak of the journey in the snow, as he usually did. Instead, that last time he had told me of his final minutes of consciousness as Siddhani Mahale.

He began his story at the point where Siddhani was in the surgery ward, and was handed a dark blue gown and ushered to the changing cubicle by a perfectly kind woman. The woman's kindness had meant everything to Siddhani. She was aware, as she prepared to go under the knife, that she was all alone, and that when it was over, when she came out on the other end as a different being—as she had imagined she would—she would be all alone then too. She had stood motionless in the cubicle for several minutes, in a sort of confusion. What if she had found love here in Canada? she asked herself. What if she'd had an income, and a home with her own front and back yard, a garden with lilac trees and blueberry bushes in back, and peonies and roses and a mulberry standard in front—a place of her own, that is, one that had made her secure and comfortable? What if India and she and I had remained together as a family, a happy family? What if she'd had success as an artist and her work had been in important exhibitions, and her paintings were bought, collected and written about? What if in Trinidad she had seen that the mould in which women were cast could be broken, and yet women not themselves be broken? What if she had been told from a young age that it was all right for a woman to love another woman?

She removed all of her clothing and stood naked in front of the full-length mirror. On the verge of losing her breasts, it was as if she was seeing them for the very first time. Indeed, she could not remember ever having really looked at them before. Well, she had, but only when they were covered up with clothing—and then, to her, they presented an unsightly bulge that made her feel as if she were twice an imposter: once because she did not feel like someone who should have such appendages attached to her own body—they gave her no pleasure and she had no interest in them becoming anyone's objects of desire; and twice because even when she took pains to disguise them—wrapping

bandages about her torso, wearing sports bras that flattened
her chest, donning clothing made of heavy fabric—whenever she caught a glimpse of her reflection what she saw
first were her slight eyebrows, her full lips, her small hands
and feet, her hips and thighs. In effect, she saw a woman
with flattened breasts. She could not lop off her hands and
exchange them for bigger hands. Nor her feet. Nor her hips
and thighs.

Standing naked in the cubicle she had looked at her
breasts, and she'd imagined them to be not her own, but the
breasts of a lover. Had they been on someone else she would,
she saw, have found them interesting. No, not simply interesting. She would have found them beautiful. She would
have thought they were desirable. She'd want to touch them.
She had never had a lover who was of her own race—or,
for that matter, who was not white—and so she was pulled
towards this new sensation in several ways. She turned one
way and regarded her breasts, then turned another way. Her
breasts were pale, creamy. They had not the slightest blem-
ish. *Unused* was the word that had come to her mind. They
were unused. They were new. They were virgin breasts. The
nipples, she said, and then corrected herself: *her* nipples
had reminded her of a nectarine seed. She put her hands
beneath her breasts, and imagining them again to be those
of a lover, she cupped and lifted them so that she could feel
their weight. They sat in her hands like small cakes that,
had they been on her lover, she would have set her mouth
to. She lifted them and ran her thumbs over the nipples,

her nipples, and it was the first time that she had felt such a sensation. She would not cry, she told herself. Naked, she sat on the bench in the cubicle, her heart sinking, her courage waning. She looked at her breasts and admitted that it was odd to remove a couple of large, healthy chunks of herself, parts that were alive, parts that had not been compromising her physical health and were, she suddenly saw, beautiful. In a few hours these two parts of her body would be gone. She saw them in her imagination, set carefully down by baby-blue latex-covered hands, into a pale blue bucket that sat on the floor. They were cut off from their blood supply, and had begun immediately to wither and die, to rot. She thought of her first big love, India Lewis-Adey, of when she and India had first met and there was that crazy, delightful thrill between them. And then she recalled India telling her that she had to leave. And, finally, she thought of me, the child she had brought up and had loved.

Siddhani knew, Sydney told me, that she could have changed her mind about the surgery. There would have been a fee to pay, naturally, but she hadn't had to scrimp and save for the money. She thought of Zain pressing the bills into her hand. She had a choice, and this was her last chance to make it. And then she was overcome at the sudden memory of sounds outside the guestroom door as Zain had lain in her arms—sounds of footsteps quickly taking the stairs.

She remembered lying on the narrow table, imagining her reconstructed chest, picturing herself walking up Parliament Street—why Parliament Street she couldn't really say, but there she was walking on it—in an ironed blistering-white dress shirt and blue jeans. She had all along refused to take injections of hormones to affect a greater change in her appearance, but just as the doctor lifted the syringe into the air and told her to count backwards from ten she resolved to start the hormone therapy as soon as she was able to. Instead of counting from ten, she imagined herself in that white dress shirt—no need to bind her breasts—and those jeans, and even though she knew better, she saw herself taller too. She was already more lithe, she was already feeling new confidence. And she went under smiling.

The *kurta* and pants I wore bore no pockets, so I carried with me a small cloth shoulder bag in which I had placed my wallet with my ID and Sid's three notebooks. I had brought them along, intending to place them in the coffin before it was closed and taken away. The bag lay on the seat of the car beside me. From the bag I removed the last of the notebooks and turned to Sydney's final entry. I knew it well, but I scanned it, my eyes lingering on the lines: *And yet, ten years later, when we broke apart, I hadn't stopped loving her.* Farther on, I read, and held on to the words: *I could not bear to say goodbye to Jonathan and so I did not.* And towards the end of the entry, I read the words I had wished, on every reading, that I'd had the chance to respond to: *How do I explain it so that he doesn't think I ran away, gave up, failed?*

I tore out the pages of that entry and folded them so that, tucked into my wallet, they fitted neatly and safely. I put the notebook back into the bag and drew the bag close to my body. I kept one hand on it, feeling the shape, the weight, the size of the diaries it held.

We were beneath the flight path to the airport now. Intermittent planes passed low. I imagined myself in one of them, sitting as I had been on the flight here just over a week before. I imagined myself looking down, exactly as I had done then, tracing the brown bamboo-lined river as it wound through cane fields and rice paddies. On the plane then, I had known that Sydney was ill, terminally ill even, but I had no clue as to what this meant or what awaited me. Sitting in the car, I imagined that on one of those planes coming in to land was a man, a man like myself who, unknown to him, was arriving to face all that I had experienced these past days. If I possessed powers that allowed me to rise up from the car and sit alongside him in the plane, I would do so, I thought. But knowing what I knew now, what would I say to him? I would put my hand on his, as Rosita was doing now with Lancelot, and tell him that he was about to find out that nothing he had learned before was going to be of any use to him in the days to come. I would tell him that whether he was aware of it or not, he had so far gone through life with the assuredness that—as a young man, as a young white man from a first-world country, as a young white man from the great city of Toronto— he was capable of anything. There was no reason for him to

imagine that he was not in control of his own life. I would
point out to him that he likely felt he knew what there was
to know about everything that had anything to do with
his life and with the future that awaited him. I would tell
him that he was, however, about to find out that he was
incapable of understanding certain things that might have
seemed obvious before. He was about to find, for instance,
that he was incapable of stopping the forward movement
of time, and of reversing it. The young man on the plane
would no doubt remove his hand from mine and look at me
as if I were mad. He would say, "But who doesn't know that
it is impossible to stop time or reverse it, or advance it by
even a fraction of a second more? Only a fool, that's who."
I would answer that it was one thing to intellectually know
the impossibility, but quite another to face the reality and
the unfairness of it, and still more difficult to accept it. You
cannot know what it means to be alone and to be powerless
until you experience this, I would warn him. And I would
say that I had learned that time was deaf. It was unfeeling.
It had no regard for anything but itself.

My thoughts were interrupted by Sankar saying he was
afraid that the car would overheat. The windows were turned
down and we four, Lancelot and Rosita in the back, and I in
the front with Sankar, were assaulted by an immediate and
unrelenting tsunami of heat and dust, made all the worse by
the sickening silence as hundreds of cars inched along.

When finally we arrived at the cordoned-off area that
served as the cremation-grounds parking lot, it was crammed

with vehicles. I was sweating profusely. An attendant directed us into the lot towards another attendant who sent us farther along to yet another attendant, and so we went until one of them ushered us into a spot. Sankar was displeased with himself. He muttered that he should have dropped me off and then returned to park. Before I could assure him that I was pleased we would all walk to the site together, Rosita spoke up with the very same sentiment. For the first time that long day, I smiled.

———

Now, two months later, I do not recall how I came to be standing behind the hearse as the coffin slid from it. Try as I might, even when prompted by Rosita and Lancelot, I do not remember the walk from the car to the site. But suddenly there was Anta, her hand on my back, saying that I must hurry, that everyone was waiting for me, that they couldn't begin without me.

We had left behind the dry ground of the parking lot and we were in an area that had been planted with shade trees and flowering shrubs. An attempt had been made to keep lawn grass on either side of the paved path upon which we now stood, but constant foot traffic that spilled off the path left only patches of the crabgrass intact. We were on a large mound that sloped gently to the wide river, where brown water flowed fast. I stood at Pundit's side; Anta, Rosita, Lancelot and Sankar were behind us. The back door of the hearse was open and the pallbearers, Kareen Akal Sharma among them, were ready. On the sturdy lower limbs of the samaan trees I noticed groups of young men standing upright as if they were on solid ground. The accentless voice of an ageless man, sounding as if he knew everything there was to know, looped intermittently and empathetically through a public address system whose speakers were positioned in the heart of samaan trees throughout the site: "No one knows your suffering. No one knows your pain." The three plumes of smoke I had seen on the drive in, were, I could see now, from three burning pyres at various stages of disintegration. Positioned nearest to us was a tall, ready pyre. On seeing the open construction of bamboo poles and wood planks, and realizing that it awaited my Sid, my mouth went dry, and my chest tightened. There was no crematorium; there was no button to press. Clumps of white flags raised on tall bamboo posts were planted at the edges of the cremation area. They fluttered in the muggy breeze. The handkerchief that covered Sydney's face was removed, but from where I was I could not yet see him. We were at a standstill as the pallbearers were given their instructions; some discussion ensued. I kept in my mind that Pundit had promised to guide me in everything.

People lined the narrow paved path and milled throughout the site. I knew so few people in this country that I would not have recognized any who might have been there for Sydney, but still, desperately looking for someone I might know, I peered at them. All were dark-skinned, sombre

Indians. They were not of our group. Still they crowded near, watching us, expressionless. I imagined that behind the passivity there must have been curiosity about why I, a white man, would be performing the final rites for an Indian man. The white shirts of the men shimmered in the blazing sunlight, and the navy and the black of their trousers and of the dresses of the women soaked up the air. Sydney's casket was finally slid from the hearse and rested on the ground for the first rites of this part of his journey. I was gripped by the sight of his face, around his head a halo of wilting marigolds. It was but a matter of minutes before I would never see that face again.

I was handed a brass platter on which were several items. I was instructed to take from it, with my bare hands, a large pinch of rice, and to throw it into a small fire that burned in another brass plate held by someone else. The fire sizzled and sputtered. I do not remember who handed me any of the items, or who was guiding me. I was told to take a peepal leaf from the platter and to use it to scoop up some of the ghee, and then to place the leaf in the fire, and to do the same with a pinch of sandal wood chips. The flames grew tall, their tips turned black, and aromatic black smoke curled upwards. I was handed the plate of fire and instructed to pass it counter-clockwise around Sydney's face. Pundit offered prayers, first in Hindi, which I couldn't understand, and then in English I wasn't able to hear. I offered my own. Precisely because Sydney was now in another realm and therefore different rules might apply, I behaved as if it were possible to communicate with him telepathically. I blocked out as best as I could all sound and all that was in my periphery and I stared at his forehead and bore into it my thought: *No one knew me so well as you, Sid. And you told no one else but me your stories. It has taken me a while to see that this was your way of telling me what I needed to hear from you. Thank you, my dearest Sid.* My hair, skin and clothing were quickly doused in the smoky sandalwood aroma of the ghee-fuelled fire. The voice coming from the speakers in the trees sympathized: "No one knows your suffering. No one knows your pain." The casket was picked up by the pallbearers, and together we all walked on.

From some short distance away came religious Hindu music, a man's mournful singing voice accompanying the sombre tones of the harmonium. It was only now that I realized that tassa drums off to one side were being beaten, and with wild abandon, the speed and fury a chaotic contrast to the man with the harmonium. There was a crowd of women in bold red saris moving through the grounds like a flock of swallows, and when they swarmed and pooled and then fluttered again, bells tinkled about them. They seemed to be laughing, or rather twittering like birds, and I thought they were out of place here. I could not help but see them as I carried the plate with the fire behind the pallbearers. Anta sidled up beside me and whispered that these women and the tassa drummers were part of a sect that had originated in South India and who believed that death was the ultimate freedom for humans, a happy occasion, the only true cause for celebration in life. I was calmed by this—not so much by her enlightening me, or by the beliefs of that group but by Anta's perception, for she had been behind me and must have understood that I would be confused.

The scent of women's cheap colognes mingled with that of over-heated bodies, unfortunately scented deodorants and burning ghee, camphor and sandalwood. The pallbearers lowered Sydney's casket to the ground again. I was relieved of the plate of fire, and the platter with the ghee, peepal leaves and rice was held out for me again. I knew what to do this time, and did not wait for instruction. When this part of the ritual was complete I took the brass plate with the fire and stooped to circle Sydney's head with it. Pundit again uttered words of prayer, and I again told Sydney that I saw that I was in the stories that he'd told me, that I had figured in his life all along, and that I wanted him to know that I did not think, as he'd said in his last entry in the notebook, that he "ran away, gave up" or "failed." On the contrary: precisely because of the choices he had made, he was my hero, and I loved him no matter what. Beads of water now covered Sydney's skin. They might have looked like nothing more than perspiration, except that they were large beads and running down the side of his face. The pallbearers hoisted the coffin and the entourage moved on again.

The voice in the trees droned on: "No one knows your suffering. No one knows your pain."

Ten paces along, Sydney was lowered for the third time and the ritual was performed again. We continued on, then rather suddenly came to a stop. When the casket was put on the ground, we were encircled by a crowd. We had arrived at the side of the platform on which was the waiting pyre. I looked for Gita, in vain. Earlier, I had not wanted her to be here, but now how I wished she were. Rosita held a large unbleached cotton bag, which she opened, revealing a quantity amount of rice, a container of sugar cubes, a tin of ghee and bundles of sandalwood kindling. Swiftly, Sid's body, Sydney's body, already covered in a hundred sun-coloured and wilted marigolds, was strewn with more flowers, handfuls of rice, small blocks of camphor and the kindling. I stood watching, at a complete loss about what I was to do next. Someone was parting Sydney's lips, and someone else was emptying cans of ghee over his entire body. His hands had been rested on his belly and I noticed that his thumbs were tied together. When I looked back at his face, cubes of sugar, rice grains and camphor were neatly arranged between his lips, which glistened with a smear of ghee and sesame oil. Everything seemed to move in slow motion, and the sky darkened as if a cloud had dropped in front of the sun. I stumbled. Anta gripped me firmly by my arm. "Steady, Jonathan. Steady," she whispered. Out of the blur of brown faces Jaan's came into focus. I expected Gita to be with him, but I could not see her. Someone took my hand and shook it. It was Wilson, the son of Mrs. Allen, the guava cheese lady. He offered his condolences and said that his mother was very-very sorry that she couldn't come for Mr. Sydney's funeral. She had swollen legs, you see, and it was too painful to stand for long periods of time. He must have thought I didn't know who he was talking about because he added, "My mother, Mrs. Allen. Guava cheese. She used to bring guava cheese." He used, I noticed, the habitual past tense.

I recognized two faces now, neighbours whose names I didn't know from the Scenery Hills neighbourhood. I felt observed and a little too exposed for comfort. I wanted my hand in Anta's, could almost feel hers around mine, but I had come to this island enough times to know that it would at this time be an impropriety. Lancelot stooped at the foot of the casket, the plaid wool blanket in his hand. He took his time arranging it on the lower portion of Sydney's body, smoothing it on Sydney's legs, tucking it against his sides. Although it was I who had presented Sydney with this blanket, and it was the one he had used ever since—despite the heat of this place—it would not have occurred to me to send him off with it. My heart swelled with gratitude for Lancelot.

Now the casket had been picked up, and everything was happening too suddenly and swiftly. I followed the pallbearers to the pyre. A voice in my head kept saying, "No, no, wait a minute," but I had no plan for what I would do if the ceremony were to come to a stop for that eternal minute I longed for. A hand was placed on my shoulder, and in the short moment that it took for me to look back and see that it was Jaan's—his hand heavy, as if pulling me back—and to ask where Gita was—to which he shook his head to indicate that she had not come—Sydney's casket was already inside the centre of the tall pyre, and I was being pushed forward now by Jaan to stand at Pundit's side. I could just see the top of Sid's head, the tip of her nose. I was given a clay jug of water and told to walk around the pyre counter-clockwise while I sprinkled the pyre with the water. When I reached the foot of the pyre, directly away from where I had begun, I noticed that at another platform some distance ahead another body had just been placed on its pyre and three young boys, perhaps no older than eleven years of age, were running—they seemed to be racing each other—around the pyre brandishing fires on long poles. I returned to the head of the pyre, and five or six people shouted directions, but I could not hear or understand what I was being told to do. Jaan came to me and put his hands around the clay jug and gave instructions: I must walk around the pyre two more times, and at the end I must dash the jar to the ground to break it. I did as I was told, and when I returned Pundit took from one of the cremation ground's workers a long pole, at the end of which a fire blazed. He handed it to me and said that I was to walk around the pyre again counter-clockwise, touching the flame to the wood beneath the casket.

This shocked me, and I hesitated. Pundit ushered me on gently with the tips of his fingers on my back. I did as I was told, a lump growing in my throat. The wood caught as if it had been doused in something flammable. On arriving back at the head of the pyre, at Sid's head, Pundit said to me, "Now, go around again, twice more, and this time you must touch your parent's right shoulders with the flame, and then his chest, and his legs." I backed away a pace or two. "Come," he said, "you have to do it."

"No. I can't. That I won't do," I said, my voice low, growling and unfamiliar to me.

"You have to." He faced me, looking directly into my eyes. Tears—not of fear, but of anger—began to roll down my face, and again Jaan appeared. He turned me to face the pyre, where the fire on the lower part had begun to spread, and said, "This is what the son must do. Do it for Sid. No one else but you should do this. You know this is what she wanted."

The heat intensified. I reached into the cloth bag that hung across my body and took out Sydney's three notebooks. I clutched them and pressed them to my lips, then flung them one by one into the fire. They were consumed instantly, with no fanfare. I stepped back.

It was the second time in a few days when time itself seemed to stand still, to flip backwards, to race ahead unpredictably. People had already moved under a marquee that had been constructed by the funeral home for Sydney's friends and family. I was alone at the side of the fire.

I did not notice when the tent emptied, for I remained with Sydney's burning body. I had to step back again and again as the fire roared more and more ravenously; sweat trickled along my scalp under my hair, and ran down my face and neck and back. The palms of my hands were damp, yet to my surprise in such heat, they felt cold. My *kurta* and the thin cotton pants clung, as wet as if a bucket of water had been emptied over me.

The fire raged for some four hours. When it was less than half of what it had been at its height, I walked to the tent, where—the crowd long gone now—Rosita, Lancelot and Sankar sat keeping their watch.

I thought of my mother—of India, that is—and of Catherine. The two of them, and Canada, seemed a lifetime away and unrelated to all that I had just experienced.

I was told that Pundit had left shortly after Sydney's skull was heard to break. He had accepted a ride with Jaan. At my show of confusion—for I knew that Anta had driven her father here—Rosita jutted her chin towards a grassy area not far away. Anta was sitting on a concrete bench in the shade of a tree, facing the river.

As I walked towards her, I thought of what I might do now that the funeral was over, now that Sydney was gone. Canada was far away from my thoughts; Rosita and Lancelot had become like family to me. We were one.

Anta stood when she heard my approach, then came quickly to me. Her hair glistened, and I thought I saw highlights of blue, like the wing of an *ani* in sunlight. She touched my face with her hands. "You have to bathe before I can kiss you. It isn't just that it makes good sense. It's part of the rituals," she said apologetically. But her voice was soft, and she had touched me all over with it.

We stood quietly. The fast-flowing water, densely brown as it was, was calming. Into my mind, unsolicited, came the view from Sydney's house of the grey, low land mass of Trinidad's southwestern tip. Out of nowhere, a

ACKNOWLEDGEMENTS

The following people were kind enough to read a draft of this novel at one stage or another in its evolution: Karen Alliston, Dionne Brand, Faye Guenther, Janice Kulyk Keefer, Carlyn Moulton, and my brother-in-law Shekhar Mahabir. Their insights and comments were invaluable and greatly appreciated. Richard Fung certainly belongs in this list, but I must also thank him for allowing me to poach the wonderful and evocative story told to him by his mother, and later related to me, about cacao thieves moving through the Fung's forested estate at night with lanterns powered by the light of fireflies.

I single out Smaro Kambourelli to thank her for reading drafts of the manuscript. Her continued interest and encouragement are invaluable to me, and move me greatly.

Sue Hierlihy sent me in the right direction for the answer to a question concerning a detail, nevertheless important. My brother Ramesh Mootoo, Zaphura Linda Chan, and my dear friend Brenda Middagh provided support and encouragement at crucial moments. To them I am indebted.

To Dr. Mark Fortier and The University of Guelph's Writer-in-Residence Program; Dr. Paula Morgan and Dr. Funso Aiyejina and The University of the West Indies, Trinidad, Writer-in-Residence Program; The Ontario Arts Council Works in Progress grant program; and The K.M. Hunter Foundation's Artist Award for Literature—thank you all for recognizing my work and giving me time, space and financial support to write this novel.

Thank you to Ellen Levine and Trident Media Group for taking care of business, and Kristin Cochrane and Doubleday Canada for taking on this book. It is my fortune to have once again worked with publisher and editor Lynn Henry. My admiration and appreciation for her have deepened with this book.

Despite the physical distances that separate us, my family of origin—my father, Romesh, my two sisters, Vahli and Indrani, and two brothers, Ramesh and Kavir—continue to play a significant role in spurring me on.

Deborah Root, not least, is owed everything. To enumerate the reasons, and the ways, is to embarrass us both (in a good way), and would, in any case, run the length of a small book itself. It is not enough to say that she saw, beginning to end, every draft of this book, and was tireless and generous with her time, prescience, insightful questions and provocations, and with her belief in me and in this story. A simple thank you must do, as words themselves are, in this instance, entirely inadequate.

A NOTE ON THE TYPE

Moving Forward Sideways Like a Crab has been set in Adobe Caslon, a typeface based on the original 1734 designs of William Caslon. Caslon is generally regarded as the first British typefounder of consequence, and his designs are widely considered to be among the world's most "user-friendly" text faces.